FAERIE PROPHECY

FAE ACADEMY FOR HALFLINGS BOOK 3

BREA VIRAGH

She made it to Faerie, but staying comes with a price.

Despite being half Fae and half wolf shifter, Tavi Alderidge has finally realized her dream of making it to Faerie, far away from her dangerous fated mate. The King of Faerie declares she's destined for greatness and grants her a place at an elite academy usually reserved for full-blooded Fae. Now she not only has to work to hide her secrets, but she must also try to fit in and prove him right.

Every year the academy hosts the Summer Games, a televised event in which all students are required to participate—and which seems designed to ensure her failure. Between schoolwork, preparing for the Summer Games, and struggling with her growing feelings for Faerie's Crown Prince Michael Thornwood, Tavi has a lot on her plate.

Soon, Tavi finds herself torn between receiving help from another half-shifter—for an undisclosed price—or risk having her place in Faerie compromised. And when Prince Michael fails to keep her safe from the castle guards, she realizes that the one person she thought she could trust is powerless against his father. All while the time of the Faerie Prophecy draws closer...

Fans of Sarah J. Maas, Bella Forest, and K.F. Breene will find themselves enthralled with this dark paranormal romance full of magic and betrayal.

1

———

The portal to Faerie closed with a thunderous crack of magic and gold sparks. Leaving me facing the baffled Elder Council member who had thought he was holding a precious relic but whose hands were now empty.

My cognitive manipulation had failed. The fake Augundae Imperium, conjured out of nothing to replace the real one I'd stolen for that witch Barbara, had disintegrated under the arcane enchantment powering the portal. Did he know it was me? Did the man from the council somehow suspect? Was he looking at me suspiciously?

A group of what appeared to be more elders rushed toward us, and I had a moment of panic until they swept right past me and surrounded the man who'd just come through the portal and demanded explanation. Which he of course couldn't give.

"Tavi! Oh, my goodness. I am going bonkers right now." Melia jumped up and down and dragged me along with her, clammy palms and all. "Girl, we aren't going to be separated after all! We're doing this together. Just like we planned. Did you know Headmaster Leaves was going to make that announcement? I mean, what a surprise! I can't believe it."

I tried to smile at her as I turned away from the confused council members. I shook my head, my unruly auburn hair curling around my face and I wished I could hide behind it. I attempted to share her excitement over this life-changing news when all I really wanted to do at that moment was puke.

No one else had seemed to notice the shifters sprinkled in among the graduation crowd at the Fae Academy for Halflings. But they'd noticed me. We'd made eye contact before the portal closed, sealing me on one side and them on the other.

But not before they'd seen the fake Augundae Imperium dissolve into nothingness. And the lengths they might go to in order to possess the original had my insides churning.

Melia Haversham hadn't seen anything out of the ordinary, still gripping my hand and shaking with excitement from the last-minute announcement: the top five first-year students were getting a one-way ticket out of town.

Neither had Mike Thornwood, striding toward me and clapping me on the shoulder with a wide grin. "Tavi, it's okay. I'm here with you. I wanted it to be a surprise," he said.

He thought my hyperventilating was because I was upset at the thought of leaving him behind in the mortal realm? Jeez.

And Persephone Glaski certainly hadn't seen anything —*unfortunately* also in the top five students transferred to the Fae Academy for Halfling campus in Faerie. She would rather have pushed me back through the portal than see me progress. Not many people could claim to have a mortal enemy. I could.

But I had bigger issues to worry about, such as the wolf shifters hiding in the crowd and how they'd found me.

Grimaldi's men. I'd been so careful about keeping my location a secret and apparently failing, since they'd found me anyway. Then, as if divine intervention had occurred, I was invited into Faerie. The very place I'd not expected to enter for at least three more years, if ever.

If I didn't flunk out of the academy, that is.

Yet here I stood. The portal had disappeared, sealing us away in this new world and keeping the wolves at bay. *Literally*. I didn't have time to think about the future here or worry about what was happening back in the normal world. Hands were being clapped to draw our attention, and Melia, Mike, and I, along with the other four top students who'd also had their world rocked less than ten minutes ago, shifted toward the sound.

We stood in a mishmash of dresses and pressed slacks, waiting on further instructions. We hadn't even gotten to pack our bags or say goodbye to our classmates.

My eyes focused on the man leading our little group, and then on Mike with strands of blond hair hanging a little roguishly across his brow. A quiet desperation filled me. My heart had been set on the idea of moving to Faerie for so long, the search for a way out my only priority...and now my mind almost couldn't comprehend that it hadn't all been wishful thinking. That the reality had actually arrived instead of remaining a dream in the back of my mind.

"Come along!" Our guide from Faerie swept a bird-of-prey gaze among the students. "There's no time to waste, we must get you settled," he continued with more authoritative hand-clapping. "Graduates, form a line to your left over there with my associate. Miss Beacon will show you to processing to get you set up with paperwork. First-years, you're with me. We'll get your paperwork signed and get you on to a brief tour of the station. I'm sure everyone is excited. Let's go. Move it along. The king awaits."

For a moment I froze, swallowing back the rising fore-boding in my gut. Was no one going to address the wolf shifters or the fake exploding Imperium?

Did I really make it to Faerie?

Melia's grip on me broke under the press of bodies. Her classmates pushed her in the opposite direction. Melia and the rest of the recent grads moved to the left and the lucky few from my class were shepherded right.

I'll find you, she mouthed to me. The hand she'd held dropped to my side.

"Tavi, are you okay? You look a little green," Mike leaned close to whisper. "I thought you'd be excited."

Under normal circumstances, his being this close would send shivers through my whole body, melting me with wide spring-green eyes and gold hair that hung past his ears. Lips that every girl in both worlds had probably admired a million times over.

No one said any of this was *normal*.

"I *am* excited," I tried to assure my friend. "Really. I'm very, *very* happy to be here. It just took me by surprise, that's all. I thought you were staying behind for next year."

He shrugged. "I'd planned on returning to Faerie after graduation anyway, but my father insisted that I return now, for some reason. Which means I'll be here to guide you every step of the way."

Okay, newsflash! He'd never told me about this plan. Or why his father would want him back. And did that mean he'd already known about the top five first-years getting an invite?

"But aren't you—"

The guide pushed us forward and I choked on the rest of my question.

This whole experience was about as far from normal as anything in my life. Because not only had I made it through my first official year at the Academy, but I'd gotten my ticket to Faerie like a godmother snapping her fingers and conjuring it out of thin air.

I've done it.

Now my cruel and lecherous fated mate would never find me. The thought drew a grim smile but did nothing about the shaking.

Or at least I'd thought he wouldn't be able to find me, until I saw his minions in the graduation crowd, staring at me. Now a nagging sense of dread had me thinking differently.

I would have to make sure none of them managed to find a way to access a portal. As if I didn't have enough on my plate already.

"This way, this way."

I barely heard the guide speaking to us above the darkness in my mind and my heartbeat gathering enough speed to kill me. Glancing over my shoulder, the last sparks of the portal disintegrated into a trail of smoke and a lingering heaviness of potent magic in the atmosphere.

"Get your head out of the clouds, Alderidge, and walk," Persephone snapped. She hadn't bothered to look back at me, flipping her hair to accent the statement like a perfect blond exclamation point. "You're holding the rest of us up. Can you be *any* more selfish?"

"Sure, I'm coming." I used my most agreeable voice to answer her instead of snarling. Still, it took every bit of self-control I possessed and some I did not.

Mike kept close to me as we stepped out of a patch of green forest—a perfect match to his eyes—and toward a two-story metal and glass building in the distance reflecting the butter-yellow sun.

I wondered why we hadn't portaled *there* instead of into the woods. Soon I lost sight of Melia and the rest of her graduating class as our host shuffled us toward the building, seeing nothing more than the bounce of her brown curls in the distance before we walked through the door into a massive entry hall.

The world exploded in a rush of sound and light, and pushed the thought of the wolves entirely out of my mind.

The gilded hall was bright, the sun shining through the glass roof and illuminating food stands, market stalls, and musicians with instruments I'd never seen before. Delicious smells swirled in clouds through the air. My mouth instantly watered, heart thumping in time with the beat of the music.

And the Fae themselves...

There were dozens of fairies roaming around the upper balconies of what I guessed to be a transport station. They wore a rainbow array of clothes in all styles and shapes, some with orange butterfly wings poking out of their shirts and others with pants made entirely of pearlescent bubbles. There were elves and pixies darting through the open air, with sparkling wings and sharply pointed ears. Magic. So much magic.

Although we'd walked in at ground level, we now stood above multiple lines of moss-covered tracks with silver trains pulling in and out with an explosion of sparks. Clearly powered by magic. I could sense it like static in the air, a pressure unlike anything I'd experienced before. Less dense than gravity yet present all the same.

We certainly weren't in Massachusetts anymore.

We were about as far from the United States as we could get, yet close enough for the two worlds to overlap and access each other. I drew in a long breath and held it in my lungs. The magic seeped through my cells. Even the air tasted sweeter here. *Alive*. My blood woke and thrummed with the power, like a welcoming home.

"There you are. I missed that smile." Mike elbowed me in the side lightly before sweeping his hand out for us to keep walking. "I thought you were going to be queasy through the rest of our introduction."

I shook my head. "Not queasy, but definitely over-whelmed."

"I understand. If you aren't used to the magic, it can be a crazy adjustment."

A man in a black suit stepped up to speak to our guide before taking over and leading us deeper into the transport station. All business, no nonsense. He waved a hand and I noticed that the tops of his knuckles were covered in soft white-and-gray feathers.

I had a lot to learn about the inhabitants here.

"Okay, first-years, this way," he instructed.

I tried to ignore the vendors calling out their wares. Waiting for buyers to take the knickknacks and snacks and jewels off their hands. Various species of Fae in crazy dress meandered by us, some with skin the colors of the rainbow and others garbed in fanciful wide skirts, lace tops, and leathers. All unhurried. All focused on their own goals rather than the small group of halflings walking through. Not one of them looked toward me, or if they did I didn't notice.

Each Fae I passed seemed more beautiful than the last and I had to resist the urge to tug at my drab dress. So mortal, so human.

Except I wasn't either of those things, was I?

I spared a glance at Mike. His hair the color of the sunlight, he looked somehow *larger* since we'd stepped through the portal. Larger than life, my mind corrected, my heart doing a little flip at the set of his eyes, the point of his ears, and the breadth of his shoulders.

7

Yes, this was the Crown Prince of Faerie. Tied to the magic of the land more than any of us.

Why was he still here? I thought for sure he would have stayed behind at graduation to finish the rest of his term at the Fae Academy for Halflings. He'd fought hard to keep his place. His friends had killed for it. He'd cheated for it.

But he'd come back to Faerie. *With me.*

Why?

Each step we took toward the transport tracks was both an eternity and over in the blink of an eye. I'd been waiting a lifetime to get here, ever since my uncle, the alpha of the Alderidge wolf pack, had announced on my 18th birthday my impending marriage to Kendrick Grimaldi, brutal alpha of the Grimaldi pack. "Fated mate"—yeah right.

I could *not* imagine a less appropriate union, or a less appealing mate. The idea was what had driven me to such extreme measures as applying to the Fae Academy for Halflings in order to hopefully get into Faerie at graduation and be outside his reach.

For the smallest moment, the weight on my shoulders dissipated as we walked down a curving starlight-colored staircase toward the train platform. I soaked in the details of Faerie. The glass walls let in the soft light of the mild summer day, with waist-high grasses and flowers bending in a soft breeze outside.

"Come along," the new man barked out to us. Our first guide was gone.

Off to deal with the fake Imperium?

Oh, God.

Our new guide led the way toward the train platform, two large, dark wings protruding from his back. Now I understood the feathers on his hands. The wings were there and gone with each exhale and I wondered if it was part of his magic.

"God, the look on your face," Persephone scoffed as we boarded the train and it suddenly shot out of the station. My stomach plummeted to my shoes.

"What about it?" I asked, even as I swallowed back rising bile from the sudden acceleration.

I was glad to have Mike at my side. Because I felt *way* out of my depth. The other passengers on the train didn't look at us as we shot toward the city powered on magic. I turned toward the window rather than give Persephone any more of my attention.

Easier said than done.

"You are such a newb. You're looking around like you're on Mars instead of in Faerie. Have a little grace, at least, Tavi. Try to keep your mouth closed," Persephone teased, her eyes narrowed.

"Maybe you should shut your own mouth, Persie. You grew up in Brooklyn with your human mom. You've never been here, either."

I didn't expect the cutting remark from Mike. Nor the sharp look he sent our classmate. Still, I was glad for it, and to hear the irritation in his voice.

"Everyone," Mike said calmly to me, "who hasn't been to Faerie before is delighted when they see it at first. Especially any of the way stations on market day. Don't let her make you feel bad."

We passed through a tunnel and my ears popped rather painfully. I gripped the silver railing to keep standing, and turned to Mike, working my jaws to open the passages and alleviate the pressure.

He anticipated my question and with a smile said, "Spells and wards. To keep the undesirables away from the castle. Only those with pure intent are able to pass through, otherwise they will be frozen in place and dealt with once the train comes to a stop at the village gates. This is Eahsea,

9

the king's town. Not one of the busiest places in Faerie but we focus mostly on academics and workers for the school and castle."

I nodded as if I understood.

The train continued toward the city and I got a glimpse of sloping cobblestone streets lined with charming houses capped with copper roofs and chimneys that would surely puff smoke in the winter. Businesses of the same aesthetic were interspersed.

In the distance, the sharp spiral spires of the king's castle cut through the cloudless sky. It looked like Eahsea had been built on the side of a sloping valley, with all paths leading down to the palace.

My fingers numb and fumbling, I stumbled out of the train once it stopped. I managed all of three steps on my own before Mike drew me to a halt.

"Hold on a minute," he murmured. "We need to wait for the others. I know you're excited."

"Excited doesn't begin to cover it," I said dryly.

The train platform opened to the outside world, revealing a better view of the town. At the very bottom of the hill, the streets wound and curved around a river sparkling with deep shades of navy and turquoise. It disappeared among the buildings and pretty houses with their shining roofs. The city had been built to face the castle, a crown jewel at the base of the valley with a meadow behind and streets fanning from its front walls. The houses and shops were warm and inviting shades of brown, taupe, and brick-red, working around the foliage of the landscape instead of against it. There were vines and trees and flowers blooming in rare shades no matter where I turned my attention.

There were no monsters hiding in the darkness here. No fear, no worry.

My hands curled into fists and I couldn't hide the shaking. Had I *really* done it?

Senses abuzz, I turned to gaze at the castle, the guardian of the city. The same stone that had been used to build the town buildings also created those high, curving walls. Though I made out the large rectangular shape of the massive meadow behind the castle, beyond it the forest flowed as a living border around Eahsea itself. The edges of the river disappeared beneath the palace and reappeared in the meadow, then into the trees beyond. I wondered if somewhere beyond those shadowed mountains in the distance I'd find the ocean.

The earth felt awake to me. Sentient and aware of everything.

Persephone pushed past me, rolling her eyes. I twisted left and right to scan the land, wanting to see everything, the rolling hills and the mountains far beyond, the architecture almost leaning toward the palace. The gold roofs of the castle sparkled like fire beneath the sun, the myriad windows reflecting the light back to the village below. I took in ornate gables, gardens, patios, and tiered pavilions each with their own spectacular view.

"This way."

Our guide, who had never bothered to introduce himself to us, snapped his fingers to get our attention. Fine. I wanted to get this part of our orientation done so I could get settled.

My body refused to still, fingers twitching at my sides as a muscle tic began at my temple. Jeez, this place was *huge*. Not so much the city itself but the land, the sense of expansion. Everything was more *alive* here.

"Hey, Tavi."

When I glanced up, Mike waved his arm to get me to follow. We ventured off the platform and down a short cobblestone side street into a secondary building about two hundred feet away. This one looked straight out of a fairy tale, like some godmother's cottage.

The man ushered us into a large building and the interior was a jolting contrast to the outside, with a distinct office space vibe. I lost track of Mike almost immediately, pushed into a single cubicle with partitions keeping me from seeing my neighbor. I sat down across from a bored-looking Fae woman with alabaster skin and ebony hair pulled back into a drastic bun, her blue eyes neutral and distant.

"Name?" she asked, her pen poised over a sheet of blank paper. Her tone nasal.

My mouth went dry. Swallowing, I tried to speak without sounding like a complete idiot. "Tavi Alderidge." Apprehension ate at me, warring with a determination to prove, even to this woman I didn't know, how I belonged here.

She tapped the pen to the paper and instantly black script rose to the surface. Information about me from my school records.

"How old are you?" she asked.

Shouldn't she know my age if she had my information? Instead of looking down, the woman stared straight into my eyes, freezing something inside of me.

"I'm eighteen. My birthday isn't for a few more months," I said. Was this some kind of test to make sure I was the person on her paper?

Her smile was close-lipped and thin. "Which of your parents had Fae blood?" she continued.

"My mother."

My parents died when I was six, which was why I'd grown up under my uncle's care. We'd taken special precautions to make sure none of the other wolves in the pack knew I wasn't a full-blood wolf shifter. Just as I'd had to take precautions at the school to make sure none of them knew about my wolf side.

Shifters and Fae hated each other. It was in their nature, in their blood.

Just as being a freak was in mine.

"Your position in your class?"

The question took me aback and I shook my head, apparently taking too long to provide an answer if the impatience in her gaze was an indication.

"I am in the top five." Obviously, otherwise I wouldn't be here.

The woman chuckled to herself—had I told a joke?—and guided me through the rest of her questionnaire. I didn't have the courage to ask the meaning of a few of the questions. I didn't want to make a fuss. The last round of questions sounded as inane as the first.

Finally, the woman held out her hand for mine.

I put my palm in hers obediently, wincing at the sight of the silver needle she conjured.

"Is this really necessary?" I hissed as the metal pierced my skin.

Another blood test. But I'd just taken my potion to suppress my shifter side right before the graduation ceremony in the mortal realm.

Oh God. Would the glamour spell even *work* here?

"Necessary? Oh yes," the woman assured me. "It's to establish there were no mistakes made during the choosing process. There have been several people in the past who sought to fool their way into Faerie with powerful enchantments."

I was unmoving for a long moment before finally saying, "I see. It's a good thing the king requires these extra steps, then."

She twisted her mouth to the side, her fingers stilling on

mine, then continued. "King Tywin does his best to promote the safety of the realm from all threats. He is a diligent and strong leader."

I had a tense moment where I thought I would puke waiting for the results, as the woman dipped my blood on a strip of paper and waited for the analysis.

I'd always believed that the moment I crossed the portal to this world, I wouldn't have to worry about hiding anymore. I wouldn't have to worry about people getting a weird vibe when they saw me, or having to pretend I was like everyone else.

No, apparently, I wasn't like everyone else. I was delusional.

What if the woman saw my shifter blood and raised the alarm? I nearly died on the spot.

Seconds ticked by before she released my hand, nodding politely. "Half human, half Fae. You're eligible."

Her eyes met mine, her lips shifting back to a tight line.

"Eligible for what, exactly?" I asked.

If I expected any further answers from her, I'd be waiting a long time. She didn't seem inclined to speak. She tapped her pen on the paper twice more and magic sparked from the area. Rising out of nowhere, a rectangular shape popped into being. I craned forward and saw my face on the tag for a split second before the woman grabbed it.

"This is your Faerie ID," she told me as she gave me the tag. "Think of it like your mortal driver's license. It has all of your information."

Another tap of the pen, and this time she magicked up something even better.

"Miss Alderidge, your key to Faerie."

The woman handed off the four-inch iron key to me. But before I could take it completely, she grabbed my wrist to keep me in place.

"The rules," the woman said slowly, "are these: This key is for your use only. Do not allow anyone else to borrow it, or the consequences will be dire. The key allows you to move between the mortal realm and the Faerie realm without issue. You can, I'm sure, appreciate the seriousness of that responsibility."

At long last, she released me and I cradled the key against my chest. It was heavy and cold, the script-work on it intricate and ancient. "I'm sorry...is this *iron*?"

The woman shuffled her papers, staring down her nose at me. Whatever further discussion she'd planned on having paused and I tried not to take her widened eyes personally. "Yes. All the keys to Faerie are made of iron."

She said it like I should have known that.

"I thought iron was poison to the Fae?" I gestured to the key.

Okay, now I *really* sounded like an idiot.

The woman laughed and when she finally met my gaze, hers bored into mine in a way that shook me to the bone. "You must be *brand* new. The old iron-is-poison thing has been around for centuries, circulating like water down a drain. It started as a misdirection ages ago and simply never died out." She cocked her head. "Iron is completely safe for our kind. Trust me."

Another little chuckle rumbled in her chest before she turned away.

I tried my best to ignore the metallic tang of power in the air as I said, "Thanks for clearing things up for me." Sweat seemed to gleam on every part of my body and I wasn't sure if the heat caused it or my own embarrassment.

"One last thing before you go, Miss Alderidge."

The woman handed me a slip of yellow paper.

"What is this?"

She gave me a lazy grin. "Your certificate of citizenship. Congratulations. And welcome. You're all set."

My stomach flipped and not in a bad way. I stared at the paper for a moment longer, tears in my eyes.

I did it. I'd made it.

Kendrick Grimaldi will never find me here.

2

The one thing old Friendly Face back there hadn't given me? A map. Apparently, the Fae never got lost.

Like I've always said, I make a terrible faery.

A few moments later the man in the suit came by to collect me and the others. I kept my paper, ID card, and key close to my chest because of course I'd worn an outfit without pockets.

Once the five of us newly welcomed citizens were gathered, we walked back up toward the platform. The train arrived in seconds. Like magic.

I saw Mike cutting through the crowd, everything about him radiating grace and ease. Back in his natural habitat, I thought. The gleam of his hair offset the hues of his skin, eyes deep and green. They held amusement as they fell on me.

For a moment we said nothing, smiling at each other, with me resisting the urge to bite my lip. Then Mike jerked his chin toward my hands. "At least the administration part of things didn't take too long. Tell me now, Tavi. Now that you're holding the key in your hands." His eyes glistened. "Are you excited?"

I couldn't help but laugh, the sound ending on a snort. "You think? I can't even tell you." The magic of the land seemed to press in closer. It made me hesitant to speak to him for fear of tying my tongue.

"You made it, Tavi. You should be proud. And you did better than me! I'm never going to live it down. If I weren't part of the royal family, I wouldn't be here."

I nodded. Yes, I had done better than Mike. A dream come true. "You waited around for me?" I asked, worried I kept him from something important.

"What? Oh, no, I was talking to Mr. Stacey, from the welcoming committee," he said, nodding toward the man in the suit with the wings. "Catching up on things I'd missed in my absence. But it didn't hurt seeing me here, right?"

"No, definitely not." If anything, it made me feel much better to have a familiar friend by my side.

The doors to the train opened. We piled inside amidst other faeries, most of them in outfits the likes of which I'd never seen before. I scanned the crowd and my eyes met with one of the Fae whose skin looked like fine fish scales in tones of red and russet.

We darted toward the castle insanely fast. I kept my face pressed to the window to watch the landscape pass in a blur. Beautiful, otherworldly. There were so many things to see in the city.

"Eahsea," Mike supplied again. "The city name. It's Eahsea, just off the eastern seaboard of Faerie. You'll figure things out soon."

I smiled my gratitude.

In the few minutes that passed by between our last stop and our final destination, I saw markets and squares and houses that would have been royally out of place where I grew up. There were fabric flags hanging from porches and precious metals hammered into sills. There were covered walkways and gardens. Too much to take in at once and my brain spun around and around.

When I finally turned back to him, I saw Mike watching me with a half-smile gracing his face. I blushed. I was acting like a little kid in a candy store.

"You don't have to be embarrassed," he said at my blush.

"Are you kidding?"

He craned his neck until I had no choice but to meet his gaze. His grin had my heart wincing.

"Don't stop. It's cool to see your reactions." He took a step closer to stand next to me at the window. His presence was nearly overwhelming. I had to remind myself to breathe. "I grew up here and I didn't know any other place for the longest time, until my father had me join the Fae Academy for Halflings in the mortal realm to learn about the halflings there. Seeing how my home affects you...it's like getting to experience it myself."

I was surprised Persephone didn't have anything to say about the subject. She kept oddly silent, standing on the opposite side of the train by herself. I didn't see an ID card or key in her hands. Then again, she was the type of person who would know where to stash something to create the best first impression, whereas I always tried to ignore what other people thought of me. I brought awkwardness to a new level.

Mike continued to chat with me about what we saw until the train pulled into a small circular station. It wasn't until I stepped outside and turned in a circle that I noticed the second castle directly opposite from the one I stood near, across the valley and situated as if perched on the hillside.

A similar stone fortress, it boasted only slightly smaller spirals, perhaps two floors less than the king's.

"What is that place?" I asked Mike. I was full of inane questions.

The suited man stepped up, his gaze riveted on the second castle. "The Elite Academy, for the exceptional Fae. If you look over there, you'll see the sister school to the Fae Academy for Halflings tucked against the far edge of the town limits. That is where you all will be attending. First, you must get through a meeting with the king and the Elder Council. Then we'll get you settled and commence with our tour."

Stomach lurching, I blanched, thinking about standing face to face with Mike's father for the first time. The man from the oil portrait Melia had shown me when I first arrived at the mortal academy. He'd made an imposing figure then, captured on canvas.

I really didn't like the idea of seeing him in person.

We continued through the streets toward a stone walkway covered in moss and flowers. The street level entrance to the castle. The flowers were endless, sparkling brighter than diamonds. Yet nothing inside of me stirred at the sunlight, the glimmer of flags in the breeze, the slightly musky scent of the river canal winding beneath the castle.

Then we passed through the gates of the palace courtyard. I let my gaze travel up past the archways toward the castle beyond, the doors swung open wide in invitation. Guards in matching outfits of navy and yellow stood to either side.

My heart thumped.

Two elaborately carved doors rose up toward the second story, gilded in gold and inlaid with precious jewels. The glint from the sun nearly blinded me as the guards stepped aside to allow us to enter. The huge foyer beyond, bathed in blessed coolness, was filled with large sculptures and exotic flowers growing out of the walls themselves. The bubbling of water sounded from nearby, nearly indistinguishable from the harried voices and footsteps of castle employees and servers.

I could hardly take in everything at once. I placed a hand over the knots in my stomach. Everything I'd done led to this moment. All my preparations...to stand *here*.

A thousand things that could have gone wrong swarmed my mind, but Mike stood by my side, leaning against a carved pillar and watching my expression. Dragging me back to the present.

"Tavi, it's okay. You don't have to be scared."

I wrung my hands, unsure if the crawling sensation on my skin was excitement or dread.

"You look like you've never seen a castle before."

His idea of a joke.

"Funny. I've just never seen a castle this size," I deadpanned. "It's a little...small, don't you think?"

"Oh yes, I agree. We've been thinking about enlarging it. Maybe a couple more stories would do the trick. Make it into a real showstopper." Mike took a slow breath and followed my gaze. "There isn't enough space as it is."

Okay, that was weird. I was only joking, but Mike, it seemed, was not.

Our guide huffed, his eyes smoldering with impatience. "The king is waiting."

I didn't dare joke with Mike now. Not when my skin went cold at the thought of meeting the monarch of an entire freaking land. I flinched, wanting to hide, wanting to run away and see if I could outdistance the fingers of dread squeezing my heart.

As if meeting the King of Faerie wasn't enough, I worried that he'd be able to see right through my ruse. To penetrate my glamour and expose me for an imposter. I mean, he was *the king* after all, so didn't that mean he had extraordinary powers? I shuddered at the thought and feared my knees might give way.

Yet my legs had straightened beneath me and took me inevitably toward the throne room. Without my permission, the traitors.

Mike definitely wouldn't understand the nerves. Or... maybe he would. From what I understood, he didn't have the best relationship with his father.

Luckily, none of the guards lining the interior corridors of the castle looked twice at me. Perhaps they were used to graduates from the mortal school coming in to meet the Faerie royals and didn't care *who* we were as long as we didn't step out of line.

Mike walked a pace ahead of me with his hands in his pockets. Every now and then he offered up bits of information about pieces of armor or paintings in the castle. None of the guards met his eyes. None of them whispered when he passed or made any kind of expression or gesture to him. For all the emotion they showed, they were alone here. They reminded me of the videos I'd seen of the Buckingham Palace guards, staunch and stoic regardless of how the public teased them, trying to get them to break their rigid bearing.

But Mike grew quieter the closer we came to the throne room. We paused at the threshold of a creatively painted door, more like part of the stone itself. I took one look at the great knocker and my bones turned to rubber.

What was I doing here? This was by far the most dangerous position I'd ever been in.

The man in the suit—what had Mike called him? Mr.

Stacey?—stepped around us and knocked once before cracking the door open.

"Your Majesty?"

"Enter, please, Mr. Stacey," the king responded.

Oh boy, showtime. The room opened up around us, showing various Fae and fairies I'd never encountered before in a semicircle around a raised dais with three thrones.

Three.

Only two of them were occupied.

To the left, the throne room opened up into a wall of windows with spectacular views of the gardens surrounding the palatial estate. To the right we met nothing but stone and those thrones.

The Fae stared at us, a spectrum of human features altered by a lifetime of magic. Some of them were covered in scales of shifting colors. There were those with horns jutting out of the top of their heads, others with eyes like stars. There were fur and talons and hands and wings.

None of them seemed to like what they saw with our halfling group. All of them, however, remained silent. Waiting to see what the royals would say about our arrival.

When I dared shift my gaze from the crowd, I saw the handsome gray-haired gentleman from the painting. Today he wore a crimson-red tunic with obsidian buttons down the front, his countenance stern without a hint of softness. I saw no similarity to Mike in his face. This was a man with confidence in his own power. Who clung to it and wielded it the same way a master chef would handle a knife in a kitchen. Power crackled around him until the air was electric.

King Tywin Thornwood.

At his side, Queen Laina sat with her hands folded on her lap, delicate fingers hidden among the folds of midnight-blue velvet. She shared the same shining golden hair she'd passed to her son, the same green eyes and warm smile.

I felt her attention land on me and knew I'd probably make a fool of myself before the day ended. If I hadn't already.

The room remained silent until the only thing I heard was the beat of my pulse in my ears.

Odd how Mike still stood at my side.

The booming voice of the king ripped through me like a bolt of lightning. "Welcome, students from the Fae Academy for Halflings. We commend you on your successes."

A small round of applause followed his statement.

"My congratulations on your accomplishments. You have done well for yourselves, for your families, and for Faerie," King Tywin continued.

I didn't notice the Elder Council until one of them rounded the dais to address us himself. He wore a sapphire-blue tunic hanging down to mid-thigh, with short chestnut-colored hair curling in whorls like seashells near his ears. "The lot of you will be schooling with some of the best and brightest minds to ever come to Faerie. We understand this will be a bit of a transition for you, and we ask much when we bid you to leave your life in the mortal realm behind. You should count yourselves among the luckiest of students. Though you may be halflings, your intelligence and strength have allowed you to rise among your peers to join the ranks at our illustrious sister school."

The man gestured for two of the Fae clustered around the thrones to step forward. In their hands they held information packets, the covers lined with glittering quartz crystal.

Nothing ostentatious *there*.

"Please," the man continued, "step forward and receive

your information packets. We will assign your sleeping quarters on campus and get you set up to begin classes in two days' time. Once again, on behalf of King Tywin, Queen Laina, and the Elder Council, congratulations on your accomplishments." He glanced behind him once, offered a small and simpering smile to the monarchs, then linked his arms behind his back.

Persephone stepped forward as though she'd one day sit on one of those thrones. I had to hand it to her. She was committed to the dream. And to see her standing amongst the rest of the Fae creatures, if I hadn't known her personally I might have said she belonged there.

She walked up with the other three top students, the council members handing off the glittering folders before moving them along. The suited man escorted them back out the doors and I felt Persephone's gaze lingering on me. Wondering why I still stood there, and why I was told the moment I tried to step forward to remain in my spot.

I couldn't have moved if I tried. Mike had grabbed my hand, keeping me rooted, telling me to stay put.

The man who'd spoken after the king stared at the two of us for a long time. Clearly confused as to why we'd stayed behind. Not Mike so much, but me.

Oh boy. If I could have melted into the floor and disappeared, I would have. Well, I *did* have the power. But I'd die for it if people found out what I could do.

King Tywin raised a hand, his face unreadable for a long moment before he said, "Leave us. Now." A swish of his fingers sent a pulse of power through the room, a rippling tremor before an earthquake.

His tone left no room for argument. In a silent wave, the rest of the Fae scattered around the throne room disappeared. Only the man from the Elder Council stayed behind. His eyes remained on me for the longest time before he too disappeared on a sigh.

"You did better than I expected." This was directed at Mike.

I felt his hand tighten on mine and when I dared glance over, Mike stood with his shoulders square but shaking under his father's scrutiny. He wore his graduation garb, a tastefully tailored black suit with a crisp white shirt and no tie.

He nodded. "Thank you, Father."

"You'll return to the Elite Academy, effective immediately," the king snapped out, his voice gruff. "I expect you to continue to improve."

And done. No *hello*, no *how have you been* or *I missed you*. Not even a *job well done*.

I instantly disliked the way the king spoke to his son. There was no affection there, nor in his face. There was nothing but a chill desire for *more*. For Mike to do better. It left a bad taste in my mouth.

Mike remained quiet now; his head inclined slightly though his posture was alert. Poised for...I wasn't sure what. I focused on his mouth, on anything so I wouldn't get flustered and make a complete fool of myself.

I sensed rather than saw King Tywin turn his attention to me. Like someone had switched on a flame thrower and turned it gleefully in my direction.

"Miss Tavi Alderidge."

I didn't like the way he said my name, either, though I kept my mouth shut, nothing good to say. Not to the King of Faerie.

"Word has reached me about your standout performance. The entire school board had great things to say about you. Every teacher I spoke with gave a glowing testimonial."

I raised my gaze to him and our eyes met. King Tywin leaned forward on his throne with his left elbow to his knee. He gave me a bad feeling. Like he wasn't at all happy to have me here. Plus he seemed stern and disappointed with his son.

"Your professors say you are destined for greatness," he finished.

The word echoed among the cavernous expanse of the near-empty hall.

I *also* didn't like the way his words made me feel. Like someone had hit something inside me, creating ripples out from the point of impact. I wanted to scream all of a sudden. To drop Mike's hand and throw my key at the windows and watch them shatter. I wanted to show these people the wolf boiling beneath my skin, show them who I really was and tell them the reason why I'd had to claw my way to this land.

"Go easy," Mike whispered under his breath.

I narrowly avoided whipping around to face him. As it was, my breathing remained ragged.

The king didn't care how I felt. His face was unreadable as he continued to stare at me.

"We have something a little different in mind for *you*, Miss Alderidge. Instead of attending the sister school with your classmates, you will be joining Mike at the Faerie Elite Academy. The two academies are connected in the minds of the citizens of Eahsea. Two proud institutions of higher learning. However, the Elite Academy is by invitation only."

Mike gave my hand another squeeze. My fury vanished, leaving me hollow.

Through it all, the queen hadn't spoken. She continued to peer down at the two of us, taking my measure. Determining her feelings toward me, no doubt.

"You will be the first halfling in over two hundred years to step foot through the doors to the academy," the king said. He tapped his fingers on his chin before sighing. "You'd better prove you're worth it."

The king's smile darkened at those words, barely noticeable, as if to say my "destined for greatness" partiality would only be tolerated as long as I remained valuable to him.

I was *valuable* now. But for how long?

3

What felt like hours later, the door to my quarters closed behind me. My quarters *in the castle*.

I remembered how my throat had bobbed at the king's declaration. The first halfling in over two hundred years to attend the Elite Academy...how was it possible? I hadn't thought I'd done well enough at the Halfling Academy to warrant the invite.

I had a terrible memory, one no number of sticky notes could help me overcome. Yet here I stood, trembling, waiting to see what fresh hells would come next.

Even though I was alone, I still couldn't breathe.

The king had told the servants, who appeared seemingly out of the woodwork, to take me up to my room on the second floor. *A guest in his home*, he'd said with fake warmth. We both knew why he wanted me here. To keep an eye on me. Because he knew something about me didn't seem right.

He also knew I had eyes on his son.

The room was nice, I thought, taking another step inside, larger than I was used to no matter how wealthy my uncle and how plush our mansion when I was growing up. This room was made of magic. A recessed fireplace stood on the wall to my right, a massive four poster bed to the left. Sunlit, the room faced an herb garden at the back of the castle, large windows peering over the fields of green and the sleeping mountains in the distance. From here, atop the small rise of the cliff and two stories up, the forest was beautiful. The setting sun cast light off of shades of green I couldn't begin to describe.

The bed certainly dominated the space, soft white linens accented by touches of gold and blue, the same as the guards' uniforms. The walls were rich wood and the floor was covered in a massive plush rug.

A few pieces of furniture dotted the space, including a large oak armoire on the wall nearest me—because I had *so* much clothing—a desk beneath the windows, and two marble nightstands on either side of the bed. Even so, there was still enough space in the room for me to turn cartwheels over the rug.

I wanted to throw myself down on the bed and stay there with my eyes closed for the next *decade*.

Letting out a breath, I listened to my voice bounce off the walls. "Oh, boy."

Indeed.

I'd thought getting to Faerie was the last step in this play. The final goal. Yet here I stood at the threshold of something bigger.

Destined for greatness.

Why had the Halfling Academy staff all said the same thing to the king? I hadn't even realized they were in such close contact with the monarch, but it made sense.

I hadn't had time to ask myself a few basic questions, to at least see how I felt and try to look out for my own welfare going forward. Would I anytime soon? I didn't know.

Walking forward, I placed my new key to Faerie on top of the desk. This was my new home. A giant bedroom with a nonexistent closet in the king's castle.

In Mike's home.

Thanks to some strange turn of events, I was living in the castle, so I'd be able to travel to the Elite Academy through a portal kept within the castle walls. *With Mike.*

With Michael Thornwood, the Crown Prince of Faerie.

Finally, I did flop down on the bed, letting out a long exhale. My insides still shook. At least it would be nice to have my own room and some privacy again. I hadn't quite gotten used to the dorm-like setting of the Halfling Academy. I mean, my bottom bunk mate had been *Persephone.* See the problem?

Having my own bedroom would go a long way toward soothing my nerves.

Drawing up on a groan, I headed for the door next to the fireplace, delighted to find a small attached bathroom with white-and-black marble floors and a giant-sized clawfoot tub. Okay, yes, a soak in the bath would be a great help. Another line of windows looked out over the garden and the thick line of tall pines and oaks bordering the edge of the meadow.

I stood in the doorway, unseeing. So, I'd be going to an *elite* academy with a bunch of pure-blood Faeries...

"Great, perfect," I said out loud.

Like my life wasn't disastrous enough up until this point. What if I wasn't strong enough to stand next to them? Lord knew my memory was iffy. The power I'd tested for, cognitive manipulation, was not very useful when it came to academia. Plus I'd have to work hard to keep my transfiguration power a secret.

What if the others didn't accept me? I was a halfling, after all. They might not take kindly to my "human" blood.

And with that thought came another, more startling one. I had learned, thanks to Nurse Julie, how to make my own potions to conceal my wolf half. But would the same ingredients be available here? And if so, might their potency be vastly different?

I could foresee a lot of trial and error ahead. I must watch my step very carefully.

The one small mercy? I'd have Mike with me.

I turned on another sigh and opened the windows to let in a breeze. The room smelled a little musty, to be honest, as though it had been closed up for a while. It made sense. The palace was one of the biggest buildings I'd ever seen. The odds were good no one had touched this room in years. I supposed someone had opened it up in anticipation of my arrival.

Someone had planned for me to stay here. Of course, I was the last to know.

And I was definitely going to get lost trying to find my way around the place. That was a certainty.

When I moved back into the bedroom, my heart jumped into my throat as I saw my luggage piled on the bed. Magic I hadn't been expecting.

We'd departed the Halfling Academy with only the clothes on our backs. No time to retrieve anything. But no matter because everything had been gathered up from there and transported here as if by...well. Persephone was right. I was going to have to work hard to keep my wits about me and stop acting like all of this was new.

A hysterical laugh bubbled up. What would Uncle Will say if he could see me now? Trying to keep it together, this mess I'd made thinking it was salvation.

Maybe I should stop worrying and start enjoying myself. It wasn't every day someone like me found themselves in this position. Especially not with my history, my secrets.

I shook my head to clear it before I started unpacking. Mike would be up soon to escort me to dinner. Lord, I was going to eat with the king and his court. I'd been told to *dress for dinner*. I probably didn't have anything suitable. When I'd run away from my uncle's house to attend the academy, I'd thrown whatever I could into one suitcase. Mike had once accused me of packing bricks. It's hard to judge what you'll need when you bolt. I'd wanted to cover my tracks, to disappear without being followed, so I'd left my old cell phone and laptop behind and took only necessities.

It didn't stop me from keeping the empty picture frames, though.

They'd lined my dresser at home. Holding one of them now, I took in the room, the windows, and the garden. I set the empty frame down on the desktop. When I first bought the frames, I had given serious thought to keeping the stock images so I would always be able to look at the smiling faces of the photogenic family unit, the family I would never have. Until I realized the thought of seeing what I could never have, every day, would slowly kill me from the inside out.

My parents were dead, Fae mother and werewolf father. Doomed from the start—and dooming their only child along with them.

You want to talk about forbidden romance? When I got swept away in thoughts of Mike and me, I should start reminding myself about what happened to *them*. So, a future between the two of us...

Yeah, right.

The more I unpacked, the easier it was to unwind the knots inside of me. And the more my mind drifted.

Did my parents ever visit this village? Had they walked along those same streets I saw from the train today? Did my mother ever attend the Elite Academy? I would never know; they'd been taken from me.

I had the last of my clothes folded and put away when I received my first visitor. Through the open window I heard the flutter of wings, a clicking of talons, and a low squeaky peep.

Turning toward the fluttering, I saw a bird on the ledge. We faced each other for five seconds, ten, without either of us moving. Larger than a normal crow, the twilight sun glinted off each midnight-black feather, its deep ebony eyes meeting mine with an intelligence I wouldn't expect from a bird.

I eyed the crow suspiciously. "Hello there," I ventured. Still not moving. "What are you doing? You're not afraid of me."

The crow propped itself on the stone ledge of the open window with its beak clicking. If it wanted to, it could fly right into the room. There were no screens on these windows. We continued to watch each other. The bird looked too smart for its own good.

Slowly, I walked over to greet it. "What's the matter, little one? What are you doing here?"

It continued to click its beak at me, and when I glanced down, I noticed something clutched in one of its feet. I couldn't make out the shape between the talons.

"What do you have there?" I'd never been this close to a crow before—if this was a crow—but I definitely didn't expect those wicked black blade-like talons protruding from its feet. *Damn.*

"You know what? I might have something you'll like. And I could use a snack, too." I crossed over to my backpack and slid the zipper open, dragging a bag out from the depths. I always tried to keep some kind of snack stashed there.

Good to know my food had traveled safely across world lines.

"Do you like chips?"

Who didn't?

"Either way, here you go. Why don't you try one and see what you think, huh?" I offered the crow a plain potato chip. It didn't take long for it to reach out and snap the crisp from my fingers. Watching it eat, I pulled a chip out for myself.

Offered another one to the crow.

Then I ate one too. We continued the back and forth for a few more minutes.

"You're a pretty bird," I spoke through the potato pieces. "Thank you for coming to visit me. It's been a little intimidating in the castle. I'm new here, in case you can't tell."

I tossed a chip toward the crow and it snatched the piece up in a blink. Maybe chips weren't good for birds, but hey, we were bonding.

"Earlier today I was hugging my best friend, sad she was graduating from school and coming to Faerie without me. I only finished my second semester at the Fae Academy for Halflings in the mortal realm. I never expected to have everything turned upside down in a heartbeat."

I wasn't sure why I spoke to the bird. Something about its presence made it easy to say my thoughts out loud. Or maybe I didn't want to feel alone.

"I'm not sure how I'm going to fit in here," I confessed.

The bird eyed me.

"I mean, I'm a halfling, and I'm supposed to be starting classes not at the sister school but at the Elite Academy attended by the full-bloods. By the *prince*." Even with the bird, I couldn't bring myself to talk about my crush. Some things were sacred.

We finished the bag of chips, the crow accepting the last one, and it cawed at me. I wasn't sure if it wanted more chips or if the noise was its version of thanking me.

The sound drew a smile. "Did I just make friends with a

crow? I'm sorry, buddy, but I don't have any more chips. This is all you get for now."

It snapped its beak once more before flying off into the dazzling blue sky. But not before leaving whatever it was it had been holding on my windowsill. Okay, weird. I knew crows and ravens liked to hoard shiny things. Had it dropped a recent stolen trinket?

I grabbed the object, turning it over in my palm. My throat went hot and dry along with the rest of me.

It was a silver amulet...with a howling wolf's head engraved on the front.

4

___

The crow's gift brought with it a whole new meaning to the term *freak out*. Which was exactly what I did. I went into straight up, full-on panic mode.

Hyperventilating, I stumbled away from the desk and grabbed at the cell phone in my bag, brought with me from the Halfling Academy and outfitted, surely, to work in this realm too.

What...*why*...how did the crow *get* something like that?

I couldn't catch a thought to save my life. They fought each other in my brain and each one brought me to new heights of hysteria. My skin prickled, like being stabbed with a thousand tiny needles at the same time. A wolf pendant—

I needed to talk to my best friend. Numb fingers dialed the number I knew by heart. It felt like hours went by as I waited for Melia to pick up.

Clutching the amulet, I listened to the electronic rings until she finally answered. "Tavi? Girl, this is unreal!" Melia's voice rang out over the speaker. Clearer than she would have been standing in the room with me.

Faerie magic.

"I cannot even believe what I'm seeing. Where are you? What's going on with you? I've been waiting for you to call but I know you're probably busy, and I didn't want to bother you in the middle of settling in or whatever you're doing!"

I didn't want to quash her excitement as her words rushed out in a swell of constant sound. But as I paced the room, with the amulet biting into my palm and panic mounting, I couldn't help myself. "Meli—"

There were the sounds of shuffling in the background. Melia pushing her clothes onto the floor, surely. Wherever she was. "I'm getting settled in myself," she continued breathlessly. "I'm down at a boarding house in the village. Great view of the castle. Apparently, this is where all the recent graduates come after stepping through the portal to Faerie. We get a week free to acclimate and look for a position."

"Wait a minute...I thought you were going to stay with your family in another city?" I couldn't for the life of me remember the name. I could barely remember my *own* name right now.

"Nah, I'm going to stay here for a bit. Try to get my work in somehow. Besides I...ugh, Tavi." Melia paused for a long moment before finally saying, "I'm worried about you being here alone." She spoke carefully, as though afraid of what I would think. "The king is right on top of you."

"If only you knew the half of it," I muttered.

"I'm staying closer to you in case you need me. I mean, I'll feel better knowing we have each other to lean on, at least for the first few months while we both get our bearings. You know what I mean? I'm sure you don't need me hovering over you like a mother hen but I'll always be your mentor, here if you need me. Besides, I like knowing we are close to each other."

I let out a rush of air, relief slowly replacing the dread squirming inside me. Clearly, I *did* need Melia, even though I hated being responsible for the change in her whole plan.

"Meli, you didn't have to stay around for me. I understand if you have other places you want to go after your complimentary first week at the boarding house."

I listened to her scoff, and almost laughed at the sound. "Tavi, girl, get real. You would do the same thing for me in a heartbeat. We have been there for one another since day one. Since I was assigned to be your mentor. And what else am I going to do, right? I don't have a job yet. It will be nice to stick close, get a feel for the place, take my time with things and see you whenever we want. Keep each other out of trouble."

"It's funny you should mention trouble…"

"Oh no, what did you do now?"

I blinked. Why did she always assume it was me? "Nothing! I've been doing nothing but unpacking for the last hour. Listen to this." I dove into my retelling of the afternoon, paying close attention to what I said about the king and giving Melia every detail about the crow and the amulet. I definitely needed to keep my dislike of the monarch to myself, in case there were little ears listening.

I turned the silver piece over in my hand, only a bit larger than the size of a quarter and twice as heavy. I ran my thumb over the raised muzzle of the wolf. The amulet captured the creature in mid howl with enough detail I felt an identical desire welling up inside of me. "I think it's a little weird there are birds dropping off jewelry with wolves on them. I'm right to panic. Aren't I?"

Melia always did her very best to be the voice of reason no matter how far into the deep end of crazy I went. She had the unique ability to pull me back from the brink. "Okay, I'm going to hit you with some hard truths. Are you ready for them?"

My stomach flipped. "As ready as I'll ever be." I dropped back down on the bed with the cell pressed against my ear.

"Let's try not to make everything about you right now."

"What?" I squawked in indignation. "Come on, Meli—"

"I'm serious! It was a crow. They've been known to pick up shiny things."

"I mean, I had the same thought..."

"They're social creatures. They have a tendency to like and actually bond with people. It's not weird. You might have really made a new friend. Look at you, in with the local wildlife," she joked.

"It's a *wolf*," I repeated, stressing the last word. "It's a wolf in a place that *hates shifters*. It's *very weird*."

"Look," Melia said with a sigh, "I know this last-minute move to Faerie is super stressful for you, and a large, nay, *huge* adjustment to your plans. It's bound to have you a little keyed up. You have a ginormous secret to hide and any little thing is going to push you into major stress at this point."

"My nerves are raw." Admitting that cost me nothing. "I'm happy to be here with you but my insides are shaky."

"*Exactly*. Try to relax a little, do what you can to unwind, maybe eat a little, and we will meet later after your first week of classes is over. Sound good?" Melia soothed me like nobody else could.

And honestly, it sounded like heaven to me. I stared down at the wolf-head amulet, rubbed my thumb over the little metal symbol.

"Not good, *great*," I agreed hollowly.

If I even made it through this week. Somehow, I highly doubted my chances.

≈

Mike came to gather me for dinner at the exact time he'd said he would. One of the things I liked about him: He was punctual. He always did what he said he was going to do, which counted for a lot in my book.

A knock sounded at my door and I drew it open moments later, pushing a lock of hair behind my ear and hoping I didn't come off as too eager. Then I lost my ability to swallow.

"Hey, Tavi. You settling in?" Mike asked with a smile.

The slight sheen of his black tuxedo jacket emphasized the breadth of his shoulders. A crisp white button-up shirt beneath showed off his chest, helped by the folded white pocket square above his left pectoral and a black bowtie with the same satiny finish as the jacket. Tailored black pants ran down to polished leather shoes.

I felt like a bum in comparison. A dense bum, since I couldn't find an answer for him. Despite the dressier shoes and the good quality of the linen dress I wore—the only non-essential indulgences I'd allowed myself when escaping from my uncle—it was nothing compared to the elegance of Mike's tuxedo. Ooh boy, was I underdressed.

He stopped to take me in, his gaze traveling from the top of my curly red hair to the black heels with straps around my ankles. The yellow linen played off the tones of my hair and emphasized the shades of gray and green in my eyes.

At least I thought I'd looked fine in the mirror, before seeing Mike. Bless his heart. He did his best to compliment me.

"Wow, you look great," he said, eyeing me up and down before settling his gaze on my lips. "Seriously."

I tugged at the hem of the short dress, the pleated skirt ending just above my knees. *Wait until he sees the open back.*

"Are you kidding?" I replied. "You look like you stepped off the pages of *The Great Gatsby*. I look like I should be shopping for gifts at some factory outlet mall."

"No way. That color is flattering on you." His head cocked to the side as if challenging me to say something to refute the compliment. A strand of hair fell across his eyes.

I looked away because otherwise he'd see the hunger on my face. I wanted to eat him up.

"I might have to buy a few fancy dresses if I'm going to be living here."

Mike rolled his eyes. "Don't worry so much. Not every meal we eat at the castle is going to be fancy enough to warrant dressing up in your finest. Most will probably be casual kinds of affairs. This is a small party my parents are putting together to welcome me home. It's nothing."

Yeah, nothing for *him*. Uncle Will might be the head of the Alderidge pack, but even growing up with his wealth, I wasn't sure I'd get used to a castle.

Thinking of Uncle Will had my stomach dropping.

"Come on." Mike held out his elbow for me to take and, with the door swinging shut behind me, I let him lead me down the hall. I had to let him lead because he knew his way, whereas I'd be lost in seconds.

"Nice of them to do this for you," I murmured. Still not quite believing where I was, who I walked beside. How this day had taken such a strange and exciting turn. Damn, had graduation only been this morning? Not years ago?

"Yeah, you'd think so." Mike's voice was dry. "More likely they want to impress their friends and courtiers. You saw how my father was today. He wants all eyes on him."

We fell into step beside each other. I had to think about my words carefully. "What do you mean?"

He shot me a side glance. "Come on, Tavi. You don't need to watch what you say around me. My father can be a real bear sometimes. You would think he'd be happy to see me? He'd much rather see a bug in the garden than he would his own son."

"Maybe he has a lot on his mind."

"Or maybe you're trying to play devil's advocate," Mike joked. His smile didn't reach his eyes.

"Hey, someone has to. We can't always think the worst. Well, I can, but I shouldn't, you know."

He jostled me enough to have me looking at him. Seeing his rueful smile and the stray lock of blond hair falling over his face. Dear God, had a more handsome man ever been created?

I didn't think so.

"We both know I didn't perform up to par at the Halfling Academy. My father will never understand the way I am or the way I do things. I will forever be a set of obstacles to overcome and if I don't do things his way, then he won't see me."

Mike led me down a series of labyrinthine hallways until we reached another set of wide double doors opposite the throne room, with the strains of laughter leaking beneath.

He paused. "Brace yourself."

My stomach twisted even as the prince laughed at my reaction.

Then we were inside and the noise ratcheted up tenfold. The ballroom would have dazzled me on a good day. Decked out for the occasion, it was a place of magic. The polished silver marble beneath us reflected the starlight coming in through the glass atrium ceiling and each step we took felt like we hovered over water. Fragrant pink and yellow roses wound up along white columns supporting the ceiling, and everywhere I looked were Fae dancing in costumes.

Oh yes, I'd underestimated the dress code tonight by a long shot.

His shoulder knocked into me, a reminder to keep moving, keep walking. "It's going to be okay, Tavi."

He might have said it, or I might have imagined his voice in my head. Either way I allowed him to lead and draw the two of us smoothly through the crowd. Although my nerves were nowhere near the level they'd been a few hours ago after my crow visitor, they were still pretty tense, and being around this many magical beings didn't help. I held on to Mike for dear life.

As the crown prince's companion, I knew I would have to sit at the high table with the king and queen, and I definitely tried not to focus on the thought as he artfully cut across the ballroom floor, stopping now and then to make low polite conversation with people he knew.

There were flowers everywhere, their heady fragrance going straight to my head. Or it might have been the magic. The very essence of the land itself was a part of each breath I took, winding through me, promising to wake up aspects of my blood I'd never known existed.

And when was the last time I'd eaten anything? Oh yeah, the bag of chips the crow and I shared. No wonder my head spun up through the ceiling and the rest of me felt light.

"Over here," Mike called out to be overheard. "There will be four courses after eighteen bells."

"What?"

"Bells. Think of it like a Faerie version of military time. Twelve bells equals noon."

I followed his lead, letting Mike pull out my chair for me, and sinking down into the plush velvet cushion. Trying not to squirm when it felt like the rest of the room turned in my direction.

I survived the first round of dishes without making a complete jerk of myself. Queen Laina sat on Mike's right, with me at the left next to a courtier who hadn't bothered to learn my name or make any kind of polite conversation. Fine with me.

"So, Miss Alderidge."

The sound of my name snapped me back to the present. Especially considering it came out of the queen's mouth. I jerked, spine going straight as I turned my attention to her. "Yes, Your Majesty?"

Her spring-green eyes sparkled as she leaned forward to speak to me. Blond hair curled intricately around her crown, the old metal gleaming and the jewels larger than goose eggs. The center stone, a large sapphire, perfectly complemented the midnight-blue gown she wore draped casually around her bust to show off ivory shoulders. Wow, perfect skin.

"Michael tells me he put you through the wringer with your late-night study sessions," Queen Laina stated, and although her voice remained soft, it carried.

I swallowed hard, the magically delicious food turning to dust in my throat. He'd talked about me? To his mother? "Mike spoke to you...about m-me?" I asked her, hoping I didn't stammer too much. Trying to remain calm.

"Oh yes. He said you've been a tremendous help to him. You have our thanks."

"It wasn't a hardship," I replied with a smile. "He's a fast learner and a good friend."

"Yes, he is." Laina looked kindly at her son. "He's always had a heart of gold as well."

I remembered the phone call home Mike had made last semester, how he'd spoken to his mother in an attempt to get information for Melia and me. Moreover, I remembered how his mother had spoken to him. The obvious care and affection, the worry and the love. This was a woman who really adored and supported her son. And it was probably the only reason she made the attempt to get to know me now.

"I couldn't agree more, Your Majesty." My comment must have struck a chord because the man in question, taking a sip of water, began to choke on it.

Laina laughed, her head tipping back and nearly touching the rear of her chair. "Oh, he's told me lots of stories from school. Your name came up quite a bit."

I couldn't help the blush creeping up my neck to stain my cheeks red. "Oh." What else could I say? My insides turned hot and the rest of me floated away.

After the meal, the four-piece orchestra struck up a lively tune and the ballroom floor was cleared for dancing. I stared at the couples for a moment, watching the way partners formed instantly. The dancers shifted and twirled in synchronized movements.

Mike tapped me on the shoulder. "Do you want to dance with me?"

My heart leaped at the statement and I divided my attention between him and the dancers. "I mean, I definitely do, except I don't know any of those dances. They look a little advanced for me."

Was the prince seriously asking me to dance with him? Here, it was hard to think of him as my friend Mike, harder to separate the person I knew with the vision of him in front of all these people, *his* people. Or the idea of him sitting on the empty third throne in the opposite room.

"Don't worry. I'll lead." Mike held out his hand to me, lips pursed, hair perfectly tousled. "Come on, Tavi. Consider this a challenge, like it's your next school project you need to ace. You have to manage a dance with me."

I momentarily met his gaze, caught by another easy

laugh, and ducked my head down on a scoff. "You haven't seen me dance yet. If it really were a part of passing at the academy, then I would fail. For sure." I chuckled. "There would be no more top five." Or any other impressive stats.

Mike didn't want to take my demurral for an answer. "Nope, I'm not listening to any of your excuses." He grabbed my hand and pulled me forward, leaving me no choice but to follow him, feeling like I'd topple over on my heels at any moment.

"You never do!" I objected.

I didn't have time to catch my breath. Mike swept me around the dance floor at the next swell of the music. His right hand moved to my waist and his left hand took my right hand, holding it out to the side in a straight horizontal line.

Then I forgot about my embarrassment. I forgot about not knowing any of the steps. I forgot about anything except the feel of him being so close to me, and I indulged in the depth of a connection I'd never felt before. With the feeling came a smug delight. I'd met the prince by chance, but he'd chosen me to be his friend. To dance with him.

Maybe he'd asked me to dance out of politeness. Out of a sense of chivalry and duty because he was the prince and I had no one else here. My fantasies about his feelings nearly crashed down around me.

"Tavi, stop worrying," Mike said close to my ear. "And stop stepping on my feet because it hurts."

His statement made me smile but brought my attention to the floor, and on the very next move I crushed his toes.

Mike winced.

"I'm sorry!" But I couldn't help a giggle at his exaggerated expression.

"Try to relax." His fingers tightened on my waist. But the

closer he pulled me, the more my magic stirred to life inside of me, and the more my mind flew the coop.

Eventually we caught the rhythm. His hands guided me around the floor. It seemed cliché to say I was *dazzled* to be so close to him...yet I was. He dazzled me completely tonight, this different side of the boy I knew. The boy I had taken into my heart.

My breath caught in my chest. The nearer he moved, the more I lost myself. His fingers curled around mine, and the more the music played, the more we danced, the less I minded what the other Fae thought of me. Even the strangers who couldn't help but stare in our direction.

I didn't even mind not knowing the steps. I just followed his lead and felt as if I were floating on air.

"We dance well together, don't we?" Mike murmured for my ears only, and the warmth of him soaked beneath my skin. "Even though you don't know the steps. Our bodies find the rhythm naturally."

I closed my eyes at the heat in his voice. At the whisper of desire I recognized there, a hunger which if fed would leave both of us burning in its wake.

He pulled back and I stared up at him, my lungs aching as he smiled. A smile I wasn't sure I'd ever seen on him before. Full of fire. One I felt sure he didn't want the rest of the world to see.

"I'm very glad I met you, Mike," I said softly.

He blinked. "I feel the same way about you."

Dangerous territory, my mind warned. I needed to watch what I said, watch my next step. Mike met my gaze and whatever it was I felt, it was mirrored in his. The longing. The surprise.

I swallowed hard. I didn't think I was breathing.

"Thank you," I said, grateful the words coming out of my mouth weren't entirely ridiculous.

48

Mike leaned away and stared down at me, his shoulders relaxed and his mouth slightly upturned in a grin. As though daring me to look at him. Really look at him. He smiled and our dancing slowed until we just stood there. Holding each other and swaying to the melody. One hand slid up my back to stroke my hair, his fingers grazing my neck.

And I found myself leaning closer. I felt faint all of a sudden.

"I'm hot. I need to go outside," I whispered.

Even the air inside the ballroom sweated with the early June heat, though an occasional breeze drifted between the open doors.

Mike remained silent for a moment but his eyes were bright. "Of course." He tugged on my hand, fingers tightening as he looked down at me. "Whatever you want, Tavi."

"Whatever I want," I repeated carefully.

He led me through the dining room and when I would have dropped his hand, he didn't let go. It was enough to have me hyperventilating, walking quickly as though I could outrun every thundering beat of my heart. Or the sheer presence of him beside me.

He brought me to the patio, and the cool night breeze hit my skin in a welcome contrast to the warmth of his hand on mine. The glass doors closed behind us, cutting off the sounds of the orchestra. The music and the laughter and the loud conversation took a back seat to the hush of night. Somewhere in the distance were the peeps and squeals of crickets, frogs, probably other magical creatures I'd never guess to name.

Finally, Mike leaned on the stone balustrade beside me, his head tilted to the side to stare at me. Still holding my hand.

"What's the matter?" I asked breathlessly.

"Nothing's the matter." He tossed a too-knowing look at me. "I'm right where I'm supposed to be. How about you?"

My skin was on fire and itchy, each nerve ending feeling like the lit end of a sparkler. Especially when he shuffled closer. No one had ever looked at me the way he did.

"Mike…" I trailed off, swallowing hard.

"Yes?"

The world around me became richer. Clearer than anything I'd seen before and I knew it was because of him. The trees were clothed in a faint shimmer of moonlight and magic radiating out from the land itself, present in every vein of their leaves. Jasmine and roses filled the night air and I knew I would never be able to go back to the real world. Never be able to live without the richness of this, the feeling of it.

Magic. Everything was magic, and when I looked at Mike, he was part of it. My heart cracked.

His face was almost touching mine and I stood there mesmerized by the sight of him. The scent of him and the feel of his breath caressing my skin until my own breathing became shallow.

"This is dangerous," I finally said on a whisper.

I let him tug me closer, his palm brushing against the plane of my lower back until our bodies touched.

I tilted my head back to see his face.

"To hell with caution," he whispered.

Another breathy laugh and—he leaned in. I exploded when his lips touched down on mine. How many times had I wanted this? How many times had we come close only to be interrupted? Or to have some perceived obstacle keep us from moving those final few inches toward each other?

His mouth was warm, soft. It was a gentle kiss, one promising all the time in the world. I groaned against him and the sound seemed to unleash whatever hold he'd kept over himself.

Mike scooped me against him until I was pressed flat to his chest and deepened the kiss. I wrapped my arms around his neck to hold him closer. It was the magic I'd dreamed of and more. His tongue lashed along the seam of my lips until I opened up for him.

Oh God. I could lose myself in him. I wanted to. I plunged my fingers through his golden hair and he let out a low laugh.

He kissed me again, harder. Before, he'd been gentle, uncertain. Now he did more than dip his toe into passion. I dissolved against him, drowning in sensation. My hands went around his neck to keep him close to me, his hands playing with my hair, grabbing at my waist, as though he couldn't get enough of me, too.

His hands burned where they touched me, and I felt it all the way through the thin fabric of my dress. He pulled me to him like he couldn't get me close enough. A groan turned into a whimper and Mike swallowed the sound.

My head spiraled to the sky. The moment he tore his lips from mine, kissing and nipping his way down my neck, I knew this was a very bad idea. It was impossible. Not worth thinking about. I trembled and hoped I wasn't about to pass out. But Mike didn't pull away.

It meant one thing. *I* had to do it.

I pushed him hard before I could think better of it.

"Mike, I'm sorry—"

"Tavi?"

He said my name as though it was the first time he'd heard it. As though it was something to cherish. I shivered. Licking my tender lips, I forced myself to keep my hands at my sides, forced myself to stop touching him. The embrace broken, I could finally breathe again. Breathe and think and brace for the regret of what I was about to do.

"We..." My voice caught and I had to clear my throat before trying again. "We can't do this. I'm sorry." I left him behind, red-faced. And I ran away, the sounds of his erratic breathing and barely articulated objection echoing in my ears.

5

I didn't sleep at all, my thoughts returning again and again to Mike and the kiss. The kiss that shouldn't have happened. The way his arms felt around me, tucking me close, his presence solid and warm. It would always be one of my favorite memories. One of my favorite memories and a time I'd treasure for the rest of my life.

When the sun rose to peek through the windows, my eyes were already open and my insides were...ravenous. For him. For more.

I found myself wondering why I'd felt compelled to push him away. Why I couldn't have allowed myself to enjoy more.

The light outside shifted from navy to periwinkle, the sun peeking through clouds tinged with pink. If I'd gotten more than a grand total of two hours of sleep—a generous assumption—I might have enjoyed the sight of the sunrise in this new world, in a moment where it felt like I stood as the sole witness.

I'd made it to Faerie and I should be happy.

My mind was to blame. I couldn't stop thinking. I

couldn't get enough of the boy with the gold hair and green eyes, remember how he felt pressed to me. More, *more*...

Mike was my only friend in Faerie besides Melia. I needed to try and remember that.

If I pursued this and lost him, then I'd be all alone at the Elite Academy. I couldn't let anything happen to jeopardize our friendship or my future. Besides, I was half shifter. *He's the Crown Prince of Faerie.* A relationship between us wasn't possible no matter how badly I ached for him.

My throat bobbed and I rose, kicking my feet out from the sheets. Last night had been the happiest moment of my life. The thought brought tears pricking behind my closed eyes. I shouldn't let the need for him grow inside of me. Though it had. With every movement of his lips and his tongue, it had.

Stupid me.

I stood in front of the mirror, with black circles beneath my eyes and lines where they shouldn't have been. My face had pressed against the pillow as I tossed and turned until the creases seemed to have transferred to my skin. Oh boy, my restless night hadn't done me any favors.

Hissing out a breath, I splashed water on my face hoping it would wake me up. My lips were pink and a little swollen from kissing. I touched them gingerly, my stomach curling with heat at the memories.

I finished getting dressed in my old normal clothes from the academy. Well, the blazer had been left behind as property of the school, but I figured a white button-up and black pants wouldn't offend anyone. Honestly, I didn't know what I was required to wear. I supposed the Elite Academy would have a dress code and perhaps their own blazer. Classes started in a few hours! I definitely would have liked a little more time to settle in before diving back into schoolwork.

At the mortal academy, students had the summer off.

Here, not so much, I guessed. All I knew was that I'd gotten a missive in the middle of the night telling me to be ready at a certain time. A stamp with the initials EA authenticated the scroll. Elite Academy.

Better than an email, and certainly not something to ignore when it pops into existence next to your head on the pillow.

A knock at the door sounded and I moved to answer, my empty backpack over my shoulder. Empty because I had no fricken' clue what I'd need.

Talk about being unprepared.

Hey, at least I'd made it to Faerie. I'd accomplished the last step of my goal, and much earlier than expected, too.

Only to realize there was more to it than I'd thought.

Mike stood outside my door with a half-smile and a lidded cup in his hand. He'd exchanged his tuxedo from the night before for a pair of black slacks and a white shirt. Ah, okay, at least I had the outfit down. "Are you ready to go?" he asked.

The longer I stared at him, the more I lost some of my surety to end the kisses cold turkey. My heart flip-flopped at the sight of him. Butterflies like these didn't happen every day. Did they?

"Tavi?" He said my name to get my attention, his eyes narrowing, about a second away from snapping his fingers to get me to concentrate. "I asked if you're ready. We have to go through the portal for school."

Dammit. I was in *so* much trouble.

"I'm ready," I assured him. Rubbing at my temples and hoping he wouldn't question my unusual silence. "I think."

"Perfect. Let's go."

He led the way down the hall again. He didn't mention the kiss once. Nor did he mention how I'd run away like a frightened rabbit.

"I have no supplies," I said, more or less to fill the awkward silence.

"You aren't going to need much," he said lightly. "Or so I understand."

"I feel a little behind since I didn't get the welcome packet."

Mike chuckled. "Okay, yeah, I know it's a little nuts to jump straight from one academy to another without a break in between. I'm going to promise you no matter what happens, you'll find your footing. Welcome packet or no welcome packet. And I'll be there to help you."

"That'll be a change. *You* helping *me*."

I didn't expect him to pinch me on the arm, and I yelped at the hint of pain.

"Did you sleep well?"

Should I tell him the truth? Absolutely not. "Well enough," I hedged. "It's kind of crazy to be here. I'm not used to it yet."

"Hey, at least you have your own room this time around," Mike said. "You don't have to share with a billion other girls. And I can tell you, personally, your view is one of my favorites in the whole castle."

I knew he was trying to make me feel better and I appreciated the effort. "And *you're* back in your own bed."

He groaned. "I can't even tell you how I missed the bed. It's much better than anything at either academy. Oh, I almost forgot. Here." Mike reached around to his own backpack and pulled out a brown paper bag. "I brought you a croissant from the kitchen. Chocolate-filled. And this coffee is technically for you but I had a couple of sips on the way up. I didn't think you would mind."

I accepted the bag and the coffee cup he carried, thrilling at the thought of his lips on the cup. I didn't mind one bit. "Thanks. What a sweet thought." My stomach grumbled immediately, and although Mike heard it, he hid his chuckle underneath a cough.

"I'm sure you're hungry."

Ha, yeah, hungry enough I was actually glad we had places to be. Otherwise he could have had me right there in the hallway. I wanted his hands running over my bare skin. His mouth all over me.

"I know how nervous you get at the start of the semester," he went on. "I've seen you go through it twice now, and although you try your best to hide it, with these unusual circumstances I know you've got to be hiding a good bit from me. Are you sure nothing is bothering you?"

"I'm sure," I replied a bit distantly as I tried to ignore the way his gaze flicked to my lips. Keenly aware of every movement he made and resenting the ocean of secrets between us. "I mean, yeah, I'm nervous. There's nothing I can do except try to get through it and do my best. Right?"

He gave me a smile that instantly brightened my mood. "Right."

Mike led us down to the first floor along the same stairs we'd used yesterday. It would probably take me a few more weeks to memorize the route, honestly, no matter how many times he showed me the way.

With breakfast to go, we could get to the school and get checked in with the office before the rest of the students arrived, I figured. He continued a line of polite conversation about what I could expect today as I ate the croissant. The familiar taste was soothing.

"As far as I'm aware, they'll take it easy on us newbies, since someone from the castle council spoke to the headmaster about our joining last-minute. Of course, I don't want you to freak out too badly—"

"Sounds like a warning before a surefire meltdown, Mike," I interrupted.

I could hardly stand still. Nerves ate at me as we walked and when I took a sip of the coffee he'd brought me, I sloshed some of it on my shoes.

"Well, you should know that the Elite Academy is a year-round school."

I wanted to smack myself. I should have guessed when we were being sent to class during the summer semester. Unfortunately, I'd been too preoccupied to give it much thought. "Come again?"

He looked like a kid with his hand caught in a candy jar, except one who knew he was cute enough to get away with it. "We're going to be coming in at the tail end of the second term, not a new term after a break. We'll have a two-week break coming up at the summer solstice, and then the new term will start." He spared a glance in my direction. "You might be a little out of your element for the next two weeks. Fair warning."

I swallowed hard and suddenly didn't feel like touching the last of the croissant.

"Hey, it's okay," Mike hurried to say. "Don't sweat it. I have friends who are attending the same academy. You can stick by me and you'll be fine. I'll show you the ropes."

"I thought you were supposed to be at the mortal academy until graduation?"

"Well, things change. You're here. Now I am, too. We're gonna stick together."

Our footsteps echoed against the stone paving as we turned a corner down yet another hallway. The idea of starting in the middle of the semester really bothered me. Not to mention leaning on Mike for assurance and absorbing his friends, like friendship through osmosis. I needed to be able to find my own way, build my own life here without relying on Mike and his status as prince.

I mean, I'd made friends at the Halfling Academy just

fine, hadn't I? I promised myself I would be fine in Faerie, too. Still, I flashed Mike a reassuring smile. "Yes, we'll stick together," I repeated.

"The portal to the academy is in a room on the first floor, near the room where my father meets with the Elder Council," Mike said as we approached. "He had it put into use last year, before he sent me to the Halfling Academy instead. This way I could avoid having to cut through the village. He likes to preserve our royal image. As you've no doubt already guessed."

"You probably feel much better being home. Right? You proved to your dad you can get through school in the mortal realm. You can adapt."

Mike paused at the door and shrugged, his hand on the knob. That was it, right? Why he'd been at the Halfling Academy? I still didn't know, and thinking about it caused a strange itching sensation in my chest.

Was it something I needed to know?

"I haven't proven anything yet. I have a feeling my dad has an agenda...not only for me, but for both of us."

I shivered. I didn't like the way he spoke. "Both of us?"

He shrugged again and this time I noticed he had a hard time meeting my gaze. "It's not like my father will let me in on what he plans. I guess we can be happy we have the portal at our fingertips and keep our eyes open. And that we're together."

He was right about being together. I did take a certain comfort in having him close, a familiar presence in a wholly unfamiliar world. But when he led the way into the room, toward the glowing orb anchored by a disc of gold in the floor, I hesitated. Doubting.

"It's okay."

Mike took my wrist and drew me forward. We crossed through the portal, the weight of magic pressed against us, drawing the air from our lungs until we crossed to the other side and stepped into the school courtyard. Slowly the world righted and the sturdy castle solidified in my vision. It rose up in two stories with ivy and climbing vines decorating the exterior walls like something straight out of medieval Europe. Except this place probably predated those ancient dwellings by a thousand years.

I drew sweet air into my body, staring around at the courtyard. Students walked around in packs like wild animals, sticking to their own kind. My skin continued to tingle as Mike hustled me along.

"Come on. Let's get you to the office."

My head twisted from side to side, trying to take in everything and registering nothing. He dropped me off in front of an office door and offered me his slow smile. My heart stuttered. It was going to be hard not to follow through on this kind of desire. I wasn't sure how long I could hold out against his smile.

"You're gonna have to check in here before you do anything else," Mike told me. "Have the staff give you a rundown of what to expect and any kind of paperwork necessary for classes. Are you going to be okay?"

"Sure, I will," I hurried to assure him. Wanting to get this over with. Seeing the way he glanced over his shoulder toward the rest of the students as though he were eager to join them.

"You promise?"

I gave a half-hearted attempt at a scoff. "Don't worry about me." I was doing a damn good job worrying about myself.

"Okay, then, I'll meet you for lunch. We can work out the logistics for going back to the castle then."

I watched him walk away, chuckling under my breath.

Back to the castle. Would I ever get used to hearing him say the word *castle*?

Standing still, I waited for a moment longer, clutching my coffee cup and the brown bag with the croissant. Preparing a plan of attack.

No nerves, I told myself. *Get through today and stop worrying about this year-round school thing.*

Okay. First things first. Time to meet with the school counselor and figure out what the heck they expected me to do here. I drew in a deep breath, staring across the cobblestone courtyard at the gold placard above the door for a second. Finally, I steeled my shoulders.

The interior of the school opened up in a vast columned hallway leading toward the rear of the castle. No views there, though, since it was built into the side of the mountain itself. I turned to the left through a wide-open doorway, reading the signs as I went. It didn't take long for me to find the office and have a friendly elf—an actual elf!—point me in the direction of the school counselor.

Two doors down and plenty of time before they expected me in homeroom for the daily check in. Lucky me.

I knocked on the doorframe before calling out, "Hello?"

"It's open."

Great. Walking inside, I stared down at the Faerie equivalent of a guidance counselor, her hands folded on her desk and her smile welcoming if not a little robotic.

"You must be our new halfling from the mortal realm. The king's council told me you'd be joining us today."

During my school years back in Virginia, when I'd lived with Uncle Will, I'd gotten sent to the counselor once after a fellow wolf tried to pull my skirt down and I punched her in the face. Completely provoked, for sure, but I'd been forced to spend over an hour talking about what I'd done and why.

Here, I was sent to the office for a different reason but it still had my throat burning with apprehension.

"Yes, I'm Tavi Alderidge." I sat down in an uncomfortable chair, waiting for the Fae woman in front of me to speak.

"I know. I'm Holly Raines, nice to meet you."

Tall, with chocolate-brown skin, high cheekbones, and purple-tinted eyes, Miss Holly looked like she could have walked the runway for a beauty pageant instead of counseling Fae students. At least she seemed kind enough to the "new girl."

Miss Holly gave me a stare over her glasses, the same kind of genial but bored counselor stare I'd seen every time I wound up in one of their offices. I wondered if it was something taught to them or if the look was naturally developed over the years.

"Seems we have a lot to discuss and not a lot of time to do it in. However, I've got some papers for you." She slid the folder across her desk until it landed in front of me. "Here's your schedule for the next few weeks. You see I've given you mostly free period where you can catch up on the curriculum at your leisure. I suggest speaking to your professors for next semester to get the material from them."

I grabbed the folder and opened it, eyes scanning over the schedule.

"Also, as a visiting student staying at the palace, you will be expected to work to earn your bed and meals." Holly tapped her hands, nails clicking against the wood.

"Excuse me?" I jerked my head up to meet her eyes. "What do you mean, earn my bed and meals?"

I hadn't even wanted to stay in the castle. Now the king wanted me to work for him because he'd forced me to sleep under his roof?

"Think of it like a work-study program. Instead of paying tuition, you'll be donating your time to the palace staff."

"I have money. I can pay for my own rent and food somewhere else." Like maybe the same place Melia was staying. I'd have enough to think about with this new class load without having to work too.

Miss Holly shook her head. "No, I'm sorry, Miss Alderidge. Those were the king's orders. He specifically wants you doing work-study."

"Wait a minute, the *king* told you this?"

"Yes, he did. The note came through his counselors and straight to me. You've been assigned to the kitchens. You will report there every day after your classes are complete." Miss Holly adjusted her glasses. "It's the same kind of deal you would have had if you'd remained at the Fae Academy for Halflings, except instead of paying it forward working for your tuition, you are doing so for room and board here. Quite a cozy deal, but don't take my word for it."

My stomach dropped. How was I supposed to do well in this swanky school when I had to work every day? It wouldn't leave me any time to study. Or see Melia. Or Mike.

"Chin up," Miss Holly said with a cluck of her tongue this time. "You'll have weekends off."

Like I was supposed to be happy about that.

I forced a grin for her benefit and because I didn't want to seem ungrateful. "Sure. I like the sound of weekends off," I said meekly.

Something in my tone must have reassured her for she answered with a grin of her own. "Here's a map of the school." She handed me another piece of paper to add to my folder. "I've taken the liberty of marking the rooms where you'll have classes. You're going to need to keep this handy. We aren't as large as the palace but if you aren't sure where

63

you're headed, odds are good you'll get lost. The corridors can all look the same to a new arrival."

She showed me how to use the map, pointing out my homeroom.

"Your first stop. Good luck, Tavi Alderidge. Welcome to the Elite."

Unfortunately, I heard what she didn't say. I was going to *need* the luck. Boy, did I feel the pressure, too. It barreled down on me harder than a falling rockslide.

At least here I wasn't required to wear a uniform. Double-edged sword, however, because I'd kinda worn one today, with the black and white—looking much better on Mike than it did on me—and it wasn't going to make a very good impression with the other students. They'd think me weird.

Weirder than I already was by being a halfling in a school full of purebloods.

Like I wasn't already intimidated.

I kept the map out in front of me when I walked out of the counselor's office, checking left and right to get my bearings. Miss Holly had marked off our current location with a giant X. Based on the time, I needed to get to my homeroom for the morning check-in before heading through what she'd assured me was a light class load.

Fine with me.

I took a twisting, turning corridor up to the second floor with my nose buried in the map. Tonight, back in my room, I'd take some time to study the paper and familiarize myself. Better than risk being taunted for having the map in the first place. Unfortunately, I wasn't watching where I walked.

"Get your nose up, half-breed."

The voice sounded a split second before I ran headlong into someone coming around a corner. And I fell backward right on my ass when the other person didn't budge.

A flash of pain echoed through my tailbone and up my spine, radiating and stealing my breath. "Why don't *you* watch where you're going?" I called up to the strange boy.

He clearly didn't like what I had to say. Or the fact I'd dared offer up a sarcastic response.

The mountain I'd hit bent low to shove his face in mine. After what seemed like an eternity, the mountain spoke, and although the voice came from an abnormally handsome guy with waving brown hair and steely blue eyes, the sneer detracted from the good looks. He sniffed the air above my head before his sneer grew to disgusting proportions "Ah, you must be the half-blood. I heard the king had lost his mind and admitted someone not worthy to the ranks here," he said.

I struggled to get to my feet and pushed disheveled curls out of my face. The stranger made no move to help me. I shouldn't have expected one, considering his first words to me.

The mountain had the build of a football player and lacked any kind of social graces. He stared at me, clucking his tongue. He stood up to his full height, towering over me.

"Did you not hear me, halfling?"

"I heard nothing intelligent enough to warrant a response, no," I replied. Then forced a smile, wishing I had teeth to show. Sharp ones.

Crap, I'd dropped the map. Where was it?

I found it underneath the mountain's shoe.

"I'm sorry. It sounded like you had something to say to me." Rude and abrupt, the Fae boy leaned closer. Daring me to answer him. "Do you have something you want to say? Perhaps an apology for not watching where you walked?"

I made it a point to maintain eye contact with him. To let him know I wasn't afraid of him or whatever kind of intimidation tactics he tried.

When he got bored of the silence, the mountain sighed. "Just so you know, you'll never make it here. I don't care how well the king says you performed at your other school. The Elite Academy is simply that. *Elite*. Your kind aren't welcome. You might as well go back to the mortal realm." He turned with a sniff before saying over his shoulder, "Where you belong."

6

I was still shaking when I reached homeroom.

My interaction with the *dick* set the tone for my entire day, sadly. It took me way too long to feel normal again, and I didn't pay the attention I should have in homeroom.

I made it through the first round of classes treated like the outcast I was, and none of those classes included Mike. Each class was the same. The professors looked at me like I was a bug on the floor, snapping at me to find a seat with the others and diving into magic I couldn't begin to keep up with. The majority of students snickered behind their hands about me like I somehow couldn't hear them.

They didn't even know my name. It didn't matter.

As I'd leave the room, everyone watched me with narrowed eyes and more comments about how I didn't belong. I didn't hear the *specific* things they said but I had some pretty good guesses.

My insides wrapped around each other tighter than someone wringing water out of a towel.

Yup, this day was getting better and better, I thought, walking through the halls with my head down and my paperwork clutched against my chest. Homework already, tests coming up, and a whole two weeks before I got a break.

Besides the obvious pitfalls with the locals, the curriculum was well beyond where I'd been at the Halfling Academy. And at least there, with the exception of Persephone, people had pretended to be nice to me. No one accepted me here. Clearly.

Leaning against a row of lockers, having tried and failed to find my own, I paused. Closed my eyes for a second and drew in a breath, trying to ignore the others whispering around me.

I didn't belong at the Elite Academy. It became clearer and clearer as the day wore on. No matter what I did or what I said, it never seemed good enough. I'd been called on several times during my classes, no matter how Miss Holly assured me I'd been given free periods to adjust, and I never produced the correct answer.

Did I have a choice, going forward?

Nope, not one. I was stuck. After I'd worked so hard to get here...

Sighing, I kept the map gripped close to my side and walked with purpose like I actually knew where I was going. Better, as Uncle Will used to tell me, to fake it until you make it. I thought about my defense attorney uncle then, my father's brother who had stepped up to raise me after my parents died, who'd given me everything in the world. The man I'd betrayed by running away once he announced my future arranged marriage.

He'd be ashamed of me for even considering giving up. That is if he didn't murder me himself first, for what I'd done.

I had to keep my head up high and keep doing the best I could though a tendril of fear curled in my stomach.

I didn't know the name of the dick who'd run into me,

but there were plenty more of his kind crawling along the corridors. High Fae who thought they were better than me because of their blood.

Lunch time couldn't have come soon enough. I passed through the doors to the cafeteria after ten minutes of trying to find my way and caught sight of Mike's blond hair above the crowd. Every part of me leaped to attention. I didn't even notice the soaring cathedral ceilings of the space, nor the tables carved of stone, each packed with students.

He finally saw me and waved to get my attention. Thank goodness. I hurried over, dodging around the tables to get to him. At least here people were distracted by food; thankfully, no one seemed to notice me. Yet. Give it a few minutes and I'm sure the conversation would turn.

I recognized a few girls from my classes, one with oddly rounded blue eyes and another with hair the color of a purple lollipop. God, I hated being the new kid at school. Especially when everyone else already knew each other. They had advantages I couldn't dream about.

"Hey, Tavi," Mike called out as I sat down. "You survived! How do you feel?"

Like I've been run over by a truck. Keeping the snarky remark to myself, I mustered up a smile for him and searched for my voice. My pulse throbbed, black spots flickering across my vision. "Hi, Mike."

Tall, with high cheekbones and sunny hair, Mike was easily the best-looking man I'd ever seen in my life. Even here surrounded by other high Fae, he stood out from them as though he'd been marked. Blessed with something the rest of them didn't have.

I hadn't planned on getting this attached to him, and hated feeling like he was my lifeline here. It was too much pressure for the both of us.

Mike gestured to the seat across from him. "I grabbed

69

you some food. Thought you might be a little stressed out from navigating the halls of this great institution and you shouldn't have to deal with the lunch line. Good thing I know what you like. And absolutely no garlic anywhere."

Oh, bless him. I sat down, setting my backpack on the empty seat next to me. Yeah, no way was anyone going to sit there. "You're an angel," I sighed. Contemplating shoving the entire sandwich into my mouth. One bite.

"Are you okay? You seem a little stressed."

I scanned the lunch room then shrugged and grabbed the orange from my plate. "You think?" I began. "This place is *huge*. It's going to take me a long time to be able to navigate without my trusty map. Not to mention getting the hang of the seriously advanced magic they're teaching."

"You, ah, have a copy?" Mike gestured with his nose. "Of the map."

"What's the matter, you feeling a little rusty with your navigational skills? What happened to your confidence this morning?"

Mike peeled a piece of crust off his brown bread and tossed it at my head. It got stuck in the curls. "You don't want to know what happened to the last person who spoke to me like that," he warned, eyes full of mischief.

I opened my mouth to answer when a group of students approached the table.

"Prince Michael! It's been a long time since we've seen your face around these hallowed halls. You've decided to grace us with your presence once more, friend."

I recognized the voice before I saw the face, and shivers shook me. Ugh, no. The *dick* from the hall. He led a brigade of Fae students, leaning on the table on his approach and drawing his brows together in a classic I'm-a-sexy-bad-boy-and-I-know-it gesture.

It might have worked for some. It made me want to gag.

Mike, surprisingly, reached out to shake the dick's hand! Clearly I'd stepped into an alternate universe. "Arlyss Coldwater. How have you been?" he asked.

The girls behind Arlyss crowded closer and I'm pretty sure I heard a coo in there somewhere. Ah, so this was the Faerie version of Mike's fan club. Except this time there were male members too. Even the *guys* here fawned over Mike.

"You're still looking wonderful, as usual, Prince Michael," the closest one said. This one put me in mind of every cheerleader I'd ever met in my life: fair, willowy, confidence out the wazoo, with perfectly styled auburn hair. "The mortal world treated you well."

She tossed her hair over her shoulder. I disliked her immediately.

"As well as can be expected," Mike put in.

I turned toward him, confused at the coolness in his tone, and I saw a stranger. A stranger wearing his face, with cold eyes, a slightly mocking smile, straight shoulders.

The group edged closer still until I could barely move my arms at my sides.

"You poor thing," redhead Barbie soothed, moving closer to almost wrap her arms around him. "At least now you're back where you belong."

"It wasn't all bad," Mike told them. "I made good friends."

Ah, a mention.

The dick—*Arlyss*, I corrected—broke his focus from Mike to sniff the air at the word *friends*. "You catch a whiff?" he asked, ignoring the girls. "Absolutely disgusting." He turned to face me and grimaced, then said in a soft croon, "What the hell is the halfling doing here?"

My hackles rose. I picked at my lunch and aimed for casual and definitely not-pissed. "Friends of yours, Mike?" I asked. Trying not to let any of them see how their nearness bothered me.

These were not good people and my wolf knew it.

I watched Arlyss shudder delicately, at the sight and smell of me I guessed, and one of his buddies piped up for the first time. "I hate it when they open the doors and let the riffraff blow in." The new boy smiled, heartbreaking in his handsomeness, and put a hand on his chest. "Someone call the cleanup crew."

Mike shook his head. "The halfling, as you put it, is my *friend*."

Well, good to know he still had a little bit of his backbone.

Arlyss scoffed and rolled his eyes. "Oh, come on. You honestly expect us, your *true* friends, to believe you'd lower your standards?" His grin widened as he searched for a new insult for me. It must be hard for him, considering he apparently had a head full of rocks. "I mean, come on, Michael. Look at her. She clearly doesn't belong here."

"Do I expect you to take me at my word?" Mike said slowly. "Yes, I absolutely do."

There was something empirical in Mike's face. Something I hadn't seen before. Arlyss turned, and I held my breath as the two Fae boys stared each other down. Arlyss ran an eye over the crown prince and I saw a hint of threat there. Another word, I promised my wolf, and we would—

We would what? Give ourselves away?

"Mike, you don't need to defend me," I said, my voice dropping to a whisper.

"I suppose it's part of your duty to be diplomatic, my prince, but I have to say that befriending someone like *this* seems a bit of a stretch for you," Arlyss insisted, and faced me again. I couldn't breathe. "I hope I wasn't interrupting something between the two of you."

"We are in the middle of lunch." Mike's voice had dropped, devoid of the warmth I always looked for. "Unless you have something important to say? Any of you? Coral, how about you?"

The one on the right shook her head. "Nothing from me."

"Interesting. Very interesting. Although I suppose she isn't terrible to look at," Arlyss purred. "A pretty piece of trash."

Mike jolted to his feet at the word and slammed his hands down flat on the table. I jumped. "If you want an invitation to the Solstice Ball, Arlyss, then I suggest you watch what you say about Tavi. Otherwise, *friend*, we're in the middle of lunch, as I've already said." He surveyed the group, sat back down, and didn't give another second of his time to them. Dismissing Arlyss and the rest of his crew.

Friend. Odd word and emphasis in this situation. Mike had used his status as prince to shut down the bullies. It was sweet, yeah. I hated it.

I hated how he was friends with these god-awful people —the girls who fawned over his good looks, the boys who complimented his status even as they secretly envied him for what he had and they did not. I saw it in their faces. Most of all, I hated how Mike knew how to manipulate them into doing what he wanted. Even if it did stop them from bullying me.

One of the girls slipped into the chair next to me, knocking my backpack to the floor. The clatter broke the tension but I still felt the spotlight on me as I bent to pick it up. No one paid me any attention. Apparently, they didn't care what "trash" had to say.

"So, what kind of plans are in place for the Solstice Ball this year?" the girl asked, flipping her hair over her shoulder *again* with a flick of pink nails. Coral. I stored the name away for later.

It set off an entire conversation about the ball, some kind of celebration I was only just hearing about. I pushed my food around my plate because my appetite was long gone.

"I highly doubt they'll be able to top last year's celebration. Real pixies lighting the ballroom. It was amazing!"

One of them laughed and I used the sound to make my escape, thinking of the way Arlyss had sneered at me. I had no problem taking care of myself. I'd dealt with bullies before. Many times.

Mike caught up to me at the door with his backpack hastily flung over his shoulder. "Don't leave without me," he said, his voice rising slightly. He didn't have to be my friend, but he wanted to be. He'd left the others to follow me.

Part of me warmed at his nearness and my heart skipped a beat. "Sorry. I'm not hungry. I'm going to go find the library and chill there for a while."

"Library it is, then. Come on, Tavi, I'll show you where everything is, since we have time," Mike offered. "Then we can compare schedules. You sure you aren't hungry? You're *always* hungry. You didn't even touch your sandwich."

"I'm fine," I told him, wondering if he would still believe me.

We rounded a corner into the library and in the dim hush I could finally relax. At least here I was comfortable. Here I could let down the shields enough to enjoy the grin he sent my way.

The sun through the windows did nothing to lift the air of darkness in the room, the coffered ceilings catching the light and absorbing it. But the place was clean, kept immaculate. The tables were polished, lamps scattered about lent a soft glow, and the rows and rows of books were a reader's dream. It made the library at the old academy look like it belonged in a regular high school. Stacks of bookcases, shelves filled to the brim with volumes, reached toward the ceiling. I wondered if the other students actually came in here or if the books were just for display. I saw only one other person inside in addition to the librarian.

I let out a sigh of relief the moment the door closed behind us.

"As you can probably tell, no one comes in here much," Mike whispered. "I guess it's your typical library."

"Makes for a good escape," I agreed with a grin. Happy to know we were practically alone. A knot of tension released inside of me.

We chose one of the tables and Mike whipped out a piece of paper, setting it down proudly between us. "Voila, Tavi. My schedule for your viewing pleasure. I mean, we don't really need to worry, since we only have a few weeks of classes left before break. We'll start to panic when the next semester starts because then we'll work straight through until January. It would be nice to have a few classes together, regardless."

I set my own schedule down next to his and pointed, relieved at a few of the similarities there. "Hey, look. We might not have any of the same classes in the morning but our afternoons seem pretty set."

"Great!" When I glanced up, he looked relieved. "And you were worried."

"I think you're putting words in my mouth, sir," I teased.

The sun illuminated dust dancing in the air and set off the gold in his hair, threads of pure light doing nothing to hide the point of his ears. From the way his cheeks reddened, I knew his mind had followed mine down into the gutter. Words weren't the only things he'd put in my mouth. He'd already slipped a tongue in there last night.

Ooh boy, better I not think about the kiss.

75

"Now." Mike cleared his throat and leaned cautiously away from me. "What else did you want to see? Before our classes resume?"

I shoved my worries about lunch aside to enjoy the rest of the day with Mike. The longer we stayed at the academy, the more frustrated I became. No one seemed to want to talk to me unless they were talking smack. The whole school seemed ready to turn against me and no matter what classes I made it through, or how Mike assured me he was there to help, I felt isolated. Trapped. My wolf growled beneath the surface in displeasure and I agreed wholeheartedly.

The other students gathered in small groups and whispered to one another. Mike went to bat for me several times. He'd even insulted another girl during our potions class, calling her a lesser magician than "the halfling" like she should be horrified by her own performance. Or maybe like I should feel better because she was a pure-blood and I wasn't but I did a great job nonetheless.

Somehow, I *didn't* feel better.

Today at the Elite Academy, I saw a Mike I didn't recognize, no matter how many whispers about me he quashed. *That*, more than anything, bothered me. This Mike was colder, snarkier. He spoke down to the people around him, acted better than them. And what was even worse, they didn't seem to know or care. They practically thanked him whenever he spoke.

And yet the moment it was just he and I, he returned to the boy I knew. Funny, kind, compassionate. Ready to lend a helping hand to anyone who asked.

Willing to pull over and help a stranger on the street when her car broke down.

The bipolar performance gave me whiplash. Tears welled up in my eyes before my last class and I wondered if anyone would notice.

They didn't.

In conjuring class, which I'd thought would resemble divination and quickly discovered had little in common with my old favorite class, I chose a seat in the back next to one of the boys who'd been part of Arlyss's group at lunch. He glanced up as I slid into the empty chair at his side.

"Hey, you're the halfling."

But the way he said it didn't make me want to scream.

"Tavi," I corrected. Then tried to grin and found my lips unresponsive.

He smiled before holding out a hand, one I took reluctantly. "I'm Lane. It's nice to meet you. Any friend of Mike's is a friend of mine. You look like you could use one right about now."

I noticed how he'd called the prince Mike instead of Michael. Did he do it on purpose, to put me at ease? Either way, I didn't care. "How...nice of you," I said slowly.

Lane laughed. "I guess you could say I'm less of an asshole than the others. I'm sure they've given you a pretty bad impression of us today. Especially Arlyss. He doesn't know any better."

I found out the reason for his kindness when I glanced up and saw Mike sliding into the seat in front of him. Okay, if Lane wanted to play "be nice to the prince's friend in front of the prince," then I would play along.

"I'll have to take your word on it."

"Definitely. Hey, Mike. Did you happen to see what Professor Zed put up for final paper topics in conjuring?" Lane asked, shifting forward on his elbows. "He made a list for people to choose from."

Mike scoffed and said, "I saw something about the uses for thistles in summoning portals. Like anyone is going to be able to pull one off without laughing."

I didn't understand the conversation so I kept my thoughts to myself.

"I'm not sure if you're going to be excluded from final papers or not, but what topic would you think about taking, Tavi?"

I turned at Lane's question. At least he was making an effort to include me in the conversation. "I'm not sure yet. Maybe I'll choose the thistle topic and see what I can do with it," I replied. *Yeah, right*, I thought, but kept it to myself.

Mike and Lane shared a look and a manly chuckle. "Anyway," Lane said, lacing his fingers together, "we have two weeks to worry about getting those done. Then we can focus on the Summer Games."

Mike cringed and offered, "I don't know. I wish I could sit this round out." He spared a glance at the teacher still preparing for class. "I'd actually hoped my dad would keep me at the academy in the mortal realm until the games were over, then I wouldn't have to worry."

"Maybe the king brought you back *specifically* to take part in the games. You never know," Lane suggested.

"Um, excuse me, but what are the Summer Games?" I asked, shifting in my seat.

Mike looked sick to his stomach but it was Lane who answered me. "It's a big event the school puts on at the solstice. Every student competes against each other. The events are televised. You know, like the humans have the Olympics. It's kinda similar." Lane shook his head and took a steadying breath. "You would not believe how into it everyone gets."

My heart began to race, pounding hard enough to jump into my throat and strangle me. What the hell? I'd already competed to get here! Now I was expected to jump through more hoops? Would they be lit on fire? Hell, maybe *I'd* be lit on fire. At this point, nothing would surprise me.

"Does everyone *have* to compete?" I needed to know.

"Oh yeah, everyone. It's mandatory. Watch yourself." Lane turned to face front as the teacher called for attention. Then he whispered over his shoulder to me. "Be prepared to have all your secrets revealed to the world."

7

Any hint of warmth and joy from my first day drained from me.

"You're joking," I managed to say.

Lane's eyes were shadowed when he glanced at me. "Trust me, I've heard some horror stories."

"He's exaggerating," Mike said.

Except I didn't think he was.

The rest of class passed in quiet agony spent over the idea of the Summer Games. The hours dragged on worse than any other I'd experienced in my life, and I did my best to keep quiet, keep my thoughts to myself. Otherwise I'd go entirely bonkers.

I tapped my fingers against the table in the library I'd claimed for my own during my study hall period, enjoying the pregnant silence and the hour before Mike and I would head back to the castle. I had a stack of books in front of me, reading material the teachers wanted me to look at to prepare me for not only the last two weeks of this semester but the next term. For real, I would be busy enough trying to get through this required reading and fulfilling my room and board obligation without the additional worry about my mandatory participation in the Summer Games...

And how I could find a way out of it.

Honestly, how the hell did I get myself into this mess? Although my shifter half gave me added strength most high Fae could not match, I was in no way ready to compete against pure-blood Faerie students who had been trained for this sort of thing. Especially not in public, televised games.

Hunger Games, anyone? Yeah, I'd read the books. I knew how badly this could turn out for a newbie like me.

I thought about what Lane had said, how I had to be prepared for my secrets to be revealed to the world. Of course, to him it had been a joke.

To me it was a total possibility. And it scared the bejeezus out of me.

Did I have the luxury of being scared? No. I didn't have time for fear. At least, alone in the library, I could break down in private without anyone there to witness and catalogue my misery for later teasing.

I met Mike at the front entrance of the school after the final bell sounded. Or rather I waited for him outside under an arbor of blue wisteria, breathing in the sweet scent and ignoring the strange looks from the other students.

"*Boo!*"

Mike expected me to be spooked when he came up behind me, and I admit his nearly silent footsteps gave him an edge in sneaking up on me, even with my acute hearing. Still, my body gave me the warning in advance. My nerve endings always lit on fire at his nearness.

Besides, I would have recognized his voice anywhere, even a single exaggerated syllable.

I made a show of looking at my nails. "You are going to

have to try a little bit harder if you want to scare me, Prince Michael. I don't jump easily."

I heard him groan and when I turned around, his head had fallen back, golden hair touching his shoulders. "God, please. I can't take it if *you* start using my title, too. Never ever call me by my full name."

"Why? Rubs you the wrong way?"

A little lighthearted energy would do me good and, in the spirit, I reached out to pinch him. The same way he'd done to me earlier.

Damn man. He didn't even flinch. I needed to try harder. "As far as you need to know, Miss Alderidge, I am *Mike*. Nothing else."

We joked on our way to the portal, and on the other side I had to stop to catch my breath. Would I ever get used to this kind of travel? Guess I didn't have a choice there either, because I'd be using it two times a day until graduation.

"Time to get you down to the kitchens." He grabbed me by the shoulders and spun me in the opposite direction, marching both of us away from the portal.

I'd told him about the work-study and the new job I had to look forward to for the rest of my existence. Or so it felt. "No rest for me. Not even time to drop my things off in my room," I said. "Apparently."

I didn't know what specific time I had to report, but I guessed that Mike did.

"I really am sorry my dad is making you work for the palace staff. It's not fair."

"Has he done anything like this before?" I asked.

"Not to my knowledge. Then again, the whole thing with you coming to Faerie and staying in the castle took me by surprise. I had no idea he was going to push you this hard." I felt his breath against my ear and swallowed a groan.

"It's fine," I halfheartedly insisted.

"*No*, it's ridiculous. Stupid and ridiculous."

"Hey, you don't have to get mad for me."

Mike growled. "Mad is putting it lightly. It's like my dad is making you do unpaid labor. If I would have known earlier, Tavi, I might have done something about it. Might have been able to talk to the Elder Council about going easier on you."

"Actually, now I believe they call unpaid labor slavery." He didn't like my joke. "It's okay, Mike, really. It's fine. I'm just happy to be in Faerie. I'm not afraid of a little work. Besides, do you remember Leaves's first introduction at the Halfling Academy? He said we receive a scholarship to pay it forward later. Consider this work-study my version of paying it forward." At least *I* was trying to.

"Okay, with your logic, I can sleep easy at night."

He took me around a corner and down a second set of steps not nearly as magnificent as the first. These were rougher stone without the high polished sheen of the public foyer. Down into the bowels of hell, my mind supplied unhelpfully. Where did they keep the kitchens, in the dungeon? I decided I didn't want to know.

"Hey, Tavi?"

"Hey, Mike." I bumped his elbow with my own to let him know I was listening.

"What are you afraid of?" Mike asked finally, his voice echoing.

"Oh jeez, what a terrible question. Why? Are you going to use it against me?"

He moved closer to my side with a shake of his head. "Absolutely not. You have my word. What are you afraid of?"

My mind immediately flashed to Kendrick Grimaldi and the last time I'd seen him. The only time we'd spoken face to face and he'd cornered me outside the bathroom, forcing his touch on me and telling me he could take what he wanted.

"I don't know. Many things. The dark."

He tried hard to keep his laughter to himself and failed. "Sure, right. Because I've seen you outside at night and you were anything but afraid."

"Well, what are *you* afraid of?" I immediately shot back.

Without missing a beat, Mike said, "Muskies."

"Muskies? What are muskies?"

"They're smoky, insubstantial creatures, notoriously hard to keep your eye on. If you meet a muskie in the woods and you can't see them, well, you're pretty much dead. It's hard to beat them."

The dark side of Faerie, I decided on the spot. There were creatures here they didn't want to tell you about in the schoolbooks. "Thanks for the nightmare material," I said dryly.

"I'm serious. Most Fae are able to smell them before they see them. Muskies smell like rotting flesh left to bake in the sun for days." Mike tapped the side of his nose. "For some reason, *I* can't smell them. Thus the fear."

It didn't seem like he was joking. "What do you mean, you can't smell them? How can they have a smell if they're insubstantial? Can everyone smell them?"

He shrugged. "Yeah, everyone can except me. I have some kind of rare genetic defect, I think. If I ever came up against a muskie it would probably kill me by ambush because I wouldn't be alerted first. So yeah. I'm terrified!"

"This whole thing reeks of a set-up," I told him. "I think you're pulling my leg."

"You've never scented a *reek* until you've come face to face with a muskie. At least, that's what I'm told about the stench, anyway. As you can see, I am still alive, and thus have never met the dreaded beastie myself."

"We can be grateful for small things."

We came to a sudden stop. Mike stared over my shoulder at the doors to the kitchen and the clanging contained within. "All right, we're here. Ready for your next adventure. Are you going to be okay?"

I blew out a breath and pushed the nerves aside. "Of course I will. I'm not a stranger to hard work."

Except in this case...I *was* a stranger to hard work. I'd never had to work a day in my life if I hadn't wanted to, aside from the time I'd been coerced into interning at Uncle Will's firm. My uncle's job as a defense attorney kept us in a comfortable position. To the point where we even had people on payroll to do the cooking and cleaning for us.

God, I would have loved to see Cook's face if I told her I was now kitchen slave labor.

"Give me your stuff. I'll have it taken up to your room for you," he offered.

Shifting, I handed my things over to him, watching him slide the strap over his shoulder like the added weight meant nothing.

"Find me for dinner. And if you have any issues, you let me know."

"Trust me, this will be an experience."

Mike didn't look particularly convinced. I didn't have a good feeling about it either but I wasn't going to say a peep to him about my apprehensions. Much to my surprise, when I held my arms out for a quick hug, Mike moved forward without hesitation and drew me against him.

He'd shared a deep piece of himself with me, I thought as he walked away, trying really hard not to stare at the perfection of his butt.

The guy had a *great* butt.

Some instinct told me he didn't share his fears with anyone else. Mike had been my friend since day one, when

I'd had no one else; broken down on the side of the road, he stopped for me and made me feel welcome at the halfling academy. At the Elite Academy, he was a different person.

I had no friends and an entire school of Fae at my back looking to push me out because I was different. Because I didn't belong.

Where else could I go, at this point?

No need to get worked up. It's the first day. Things will get smoother.

I'd worked so hard to get here only to find a new set of trials and obstacles. I mean, I could run away, but somehow I didn't think the king would let his "grand gesture" of bringing me here be disrespected like that. He would never let the insult slide. Odds were good I'd be in a worse position than where I currently stood.

I waited outside the door for a moment longer before a harried-looking faery with bright yellowy-red hair pushed out and gave me a hard stare. Looking me up and down from head to shoes and scoffing in disgust. "Well? Get after it, then!"

Her slight accent took me by surprise, and obligatory manners had me holding out my hand for an introduction. "I'm Tavi Alderidge. I'm supposed to report here for kitchen duty?"

Could I sound any stupider?

"Yes, clearly I know who you are. I could smell you from a mile away. Nose like a truffle pig." The Fae tapped the side of her nose and I noticed then her eyes were slanted, almond-shaped. Her large bust pressed against the tightness of the apron and her round hips swayed as we walked into the heated depths of the kitchen.

"You could *smell me*?" I asked.

"Yup. You smell human. There's no mistaking it, especially with this much magic in the air. You're so...*average*.

Name's Raelynn. I'm going to be your boss," she said, her voice sharp, harsh. "Now get over to the wash sink because we have a busy night ahead of us and time is wasting."

I followed her toward the exterior wall, still wearing my school clothes. I wondered if they were going to let me take a bathroom break or if I'd be told I should have gone before I started work. No time, I mused, hurrying after her into the constant oppressive heat of the kitchens.

"You have any experience in kitchen duties?"

I could barely hear Raelynn outside the hum of so much magic. It wasn't just in the air, it was in the fiber of the floor, the walls, the ceiling. It permeated everything and quite frankly it made my head spin.

"Um, no, none," I answered truthfully. "My uncle had a professional chef who took care of us. I have no cooking experience whatsoever."

Raelynn led the way through the cavernous expanse of kitchen, the room the size of a modest house for some people in my old neighborhood. Then again it made sense. This space had to serve the entire population of the castle. They'd need the room and the hands to make it happen for three square meals a day. Then I thought about the welcome ball last night. How long had it taken for the cooks to prepare such a feast?

Raelynn reached behind her to tie the stained ends of her apron tighter still. "Honey, you're about to learn real quick. Let this be a warning to you. There's nothing better than learning on your feet in real time. You think you're getting an education up at Elite Academy? Think again."

I really hated the way she said that.

Raelynn gave me a tour of the place from top to bottom, pointing out the different stations and the names of the Fae running them until I had so many nouns and names bouncing around my brain I thought I might pass out. Then again it could have been the heat. Or the smells.

My shirt clung to my sweat-soaked skin and I pulled at the collar as though it would help me breathe better.

It didn't. There was no air down here. I couldn't breathe. A panic attack? I wasn't sure at this point.

"Another thing for you to know," Raelynn said, gesturing for me to follow her toward a large prep station. "While you're working in the kitchen, you will have access to certain rooms, certain stores nobody else has access to. It will be integral to your job and how you perform here. You can't very well be the best if you don't have access to the right stuff. Get me?"

"I'm not sure I do..."

She tossed an apron at me, barely pausing. "I'm saying you have access to the storerooms, stupid, keep up. The palace storerooms don't just house edible foods. They have spell ingredients as well, and certain items in there are dangerous to the uninformed. It's going to be your job to *be* informed. Do you understand?"

Raelynn uttered a few words and I couldn't feel her individual magic for all the power saturating the air. The door opened on a whisper and I knew she'd ingrain the words to the spell in me until I never forgot them.

Should I tell her about my terrible memory? Not the time.

"Go on, take a look inside." She nearly pushed me into the room. "You've got to be smart. Be respectful. Never touch anything if you don't know what it is. Understand?"

"Yes, I understand, you don't need to keep asking me that."

The air inside the storeroom was only a modicum less magic-soaked than the rest of the kitchen but it helped and I suddenly felt like I could breathe. The ingredients were kept in shadow, but the faint light from behind me illuminated rows of shelving filled with glass bottles. I let the coolness sink into my overheated skin and stared up, up, to the tops of shelves I knew I would never be able to reach.

"What kinds of things do you keep in here?" I asked.

Raelynn blew a raspberry. "I think the better question would be what kinds of things we *don't* keep in here."

This room put Uncle Will's pantry to shame.

"You look like the kind of kid who knows better than to touch something if you don't know what it is. Then again, I thought the same about Blossom, and look where she ended up." Raelynn rolled her eyes back into her head, the effect terrifying thanks to the shape of her pupils. "But you—"

"Please. I'd rather not hear any more," I interrupted, turning around and grudgingly leaving the coolness of the storerooms. Whatever happened to Blossom, I didn't want to know, didn't want to think about the possibility of being seriously hurt by the things on those shelves.

They put me to work mixing batter for tomorrow morning's biscuits. Easy, mind-numbing work by any stretch of the imagination, but all I could think about were the Games. Those stupid Summer Games and the strange way Lane had described them. Not to mention the pile of homework my teachers had laid on me even though the term ended in two weeks. That didn't seem to matter to them, and I wondered then if it was because they assumed I was half human. Or if they were just sadists.

By the time I finished, it was dark outside and my arms felt like part of the dough. Raelynn's clap on my back almost sent me face first into the floury mess on my station.

"Good job, Tevi!"

I inhaled a breath that was half flour and half air, and coughed out, "It's Tavi."

"You look exhausted."

What an astute observation. "I could use a little rest."
Except I knew I'd have to devote at least the next several
hours to getting my schoolwork done.

The stirring and kneading had been a killer workout
and I ached in places I never knew existed.

"Girl, you are such a newbie, I swear. It's going to take us
at least a month to get you into shape down here. You go on
and head out for the night. The rest of the girls and I will
finish up here. Take a little something for your dinner.
There should be enough for you to fill a plate to take up to
your room."

Mike had wanted me to meet him for dinner. Too bad
for him I'd still been at work.

And I wasn't going to wait for Raelynn to change her
mind about letting me off early. Dusting my hands off on a
towel, I thanked her and bolted for the door to make a clean
getaway. I pulled up sort when I saw Mike waiting for me
outside the kitchen.

"Have you been here the whole time?" I asked. "You
missed out on eating."

He smiled when he saw me. The kind of big, wide smile
lighting every feature on his face and was almost bright
enough to burn away the aches in my arms. Almost.

"I didn't miss anything. I figured you would be here late
so I grabbed a few things for us. Thought maybe we could
eat out in the garden together, picnic style."

His smile fell at the huge clap of thunder interrupting
us.

Uh-oh.

"Guess we won't be able to have a picnic." To me, finally
being outside of the kitchen and hearing the thunder was a
kind of release. "I love thunderstorms." Maybe I could open
my windows in my room and let some of the fresh stormy

air wipe away the heavy scent of must and age. Nothing sounded better at the moment.

His brows drawing together and his mouth now turned to a long line, he waggled a finger at me in an unspoken bid to join him. We walked to the nearest window and peered outside.

As we watched through the wavy glass, rain began to fall, and lightning cleaved through the evening sky.

Mike stood still.

"What's the matter? It's only a storm." I returned my attention to the weather outside, no longer worrying about the flour covering me from head to toe. "I think they are cleansing. Powerful."

"We don't get storms here," Mike said simply.

I turned to him. "What? There are storms everywhere."

He shook his head. "The land in Faerie is as sentient as the Fae themselves. She waxes and wanes with the seasons, which is how we get summer and winter, but there are no natural disasters. No hurricanes, no storms, no earthquakes. Not unless something is wrong."

A pit of dread growing in my stomach, I asked, "Wrong how?"

He shrugged and looked back at the boiling thunderclouds. "Just...*wrong*."

8

The next day I woke up to what felt like an anchor in my stomach.

Dull gray light filtered in through the windows, the overcast sky outside a perfect contrast to my mood no matter how nice having a quiet dinner alone with Mike had been. The weather put a real damper on my desire to focus, to catch up on homework. I'd been up until well past midnight trying to catch up and failing. And I definitely didn't feel like going down to the kitchen for any kind of *real* work.

Getting out of bed took effort, my body still sore from the bread kneading yesterday. How long would it take me to build up my strength until I didn't feel like an army tank ran me over?

I didn't want to know.

The bad weather continued through the first week of school. At times, it was a minor sprinkle of rain with dark clouds continuing to blanket the sky. Other times, students huddled beneath the covered walkways or locked themselves indoors under the onslaught of a full-scale thunderstorm, complete with lightning, driving rain, and gale force winds.

The angrier I became, the more stressed, the more severe the storm. If I didn't know any better, I'd say the weather echoed my mood, because the other students at school never got any easier to be around. The class work didn't cease. Neither did my stress. If anything, it amplified until I didn't want to leave my room period.

By Friday, I was drowning in homework, aching from my kitchen work, barely sleeping, and infinitely uncomfortable feeling like the smallest, lowliest bug on the totem pole.

It was a new feeling for me. I'd lived my whole life with a secret, yet it never took away from the knowledge of my power. I was a predator.

Until I'd come to this place.

Despite the weather, I had something to look forward to this weekend. My meeting with Melia! It was the bright spot to my week and the one thing keeping me from toppling over into complete meltdown mode. I held onto the excitement of being together with my best friend, kept it close to me like a little light in my heart.

Television seemed to be a pretty popular thing with the Fae—I could never have guessed the extent to which they'd embraced mortal technology—and it wasn't a hard thing to get a small screen installed in my room. Mike had one of the castle staff up within a few hours of my mentioning how I missed the mindless distraction of my favorite shows.

A quick spell brought the screen to life on the wall above my dresser and I watched the news as I dressed.

The weather forecaster sported a small, glistening pair of wings the color of an acorn and a hairdo out of style in 1950, mortal realm time. Classic beehive but with *real bees* buzzing around his head. He didn't seem to care and neither did his co-anchor.

Both of them faced the screen with twin expressions of devastation on their perfect faces.

"I'm sorry to say there looks to be no end to our string of storms." He laced his fingers together on the tree stump desk in front of them. "The land is unsettled."

"Indeed she is, Twilight," his co-anchor cooed.

"You said a mouthful, Ashley. These storms make me think something dangerous is afoot," he replied, shooting her a small frown.

Her gasp was over the top and dramatic but I recognized the genuine worry behind their eyes. "You think?"

"I know." Twilight inclined his head and for a moment the bees paused in the air before resuming their buzzing.

I watched, bringing my folded clothes out from the dresser and laying them across the bed. The storms hadn't seemed too terrible to me, but everyone was worried. Worried to the point where people were starting to mutter under their breath about the weather. Worried enough I saw the king storming through the castle halls with the courtiers and council elders trailing behind him, not making eye contact.

"Everyone out there, stay safe," Twilight continued. "Keep your eyes open for deceivers."

His co-anchor turned toward him with her head quirked. "Deceivers, Twilight?" she asked.

"Exactly what I said, Ashley. There has to be a reason behind these storms. Something is afoot, someone or some*thing* here that doesn't belong. All we can do is hold on tight and hope the land re-balances herself before she destroys us all."

Stomach flipping into surefire puking territory, I waved my hand at the screen, the movement accompanied by a push of magic to turn it off and send it out of sight. I didn't want to hear any more about the weather and the land revolting—because it meant one thing. It meant even the damn earth knew I didn't really belong here.

I sat there on the edge of the bed, trying not to shake. The pit in my stomach opened deeper and let loose a second, powerful wave of nausea. My skin went tight and the rest of me broke out in a strange combination of sweat and chills.

These storms might really be my fault. Not even joking.

After all, they began exactly one day after I arrived in Faerie. I brought my secrets and my half-shifter blood. Now the sentient land was doing its best to expose me for the fraud I was. No, what had Twilight said? The *deceiver*. I'd never had a good nickname before but this one? The worst.

I dropped my head into my hands with a groan, dark red hair blocking out the morning light. If that was the case, then I was doomed.

At least you get to go see Melia, my subconscious reminded me, to try and cheer me up.

It wasn't working. It didn't matter what my subconscious said.

I should have been focused on school and the mountain of homework waiting for me. I was never going to catch up. But as the walls of the room threatened to close in on me, I needed the fresh air. I couldn't stay here anymore. It was almost time to meet my friend, anyway. I'd use the extra minutes to walk around town.

The guards at the door didn't give me a second glance as I rushed past them.

Melia had texted me directions to a little cafe she knew about, and I followed them through the village. A light misting rain continued to fall gently on the ground, catching on leaves and sparkling diamond-bright.

The cobblestone streets sloped away from the castle, with little intermittent steps to navigate the incline. A three-story teal-colored building with a warm red terracotta tile roof sat at an intersection in front of me. I took the lower set of steps, stopping only long enough to bend and smell pink roses climbing up one of the stone walls. Intricate gas lanterns clung to the sides of houses and would be lit at night to provide a homey glow throughout the streets.

Beautiful, I thought. It *was* beautiful here, and if I took the beauty at face value, it was hard not to feel wowed. As it was, even without the slight rumble of distant thunder, there was a darkness I couldn't shake.

It didn't take long for me to get to the cafe, a chestnut-wood and glass building next to a circular pool of water boasting two floating white swans. Bistro tables scattered across the sidewalk intermingled with potted plants. Roasted coffee filled the air and almost dispelled the slight static electricity scent of magic.

Almost.

I hadn't remembered to bring along an umbrella and by the time I huddled beneath the awning at the front of the cafe, I was drenched. A simple spell dried the air around me and brought the moisture from my clothing. My hair... nothing I could do there. It was a soggy mess. Gathering the strands, I knotted them in a messy bun on top of my head as I pushed through the front door, letting it drift closed.

Relief flooded me as I caught sight of Melia's golden-brown curls at a table in the corner. She saw me a moment later, her brown eyes crinkling in a smile.

"Tavi! Get over here, girl," she called out, standing. "I grabbed us a great table and ordered some coffee for us. I hope you don't mind. I know what you like. At least I *think* I know what you like."

I didn't have to fake my answering grin at her babble of speech. Finally, *someone* was happy to see me. I'd never experienced such a rush of feeling as I did then, practically running to her and letting the older girl wrap her long arms around my shoulders. Tall enough to rest her chin on the top of my head. My friend, my mentor. She was an anchor.

"It's good to see you," she said.

"You have no idea how good it is to see you," I replied, voice muffled against her shirt. "A week is too long for us to be apart."

"If I didn't feel the same way, I'd tell you that you were out of your mind. But now..." She trailed off, leaning back to stare at me. "Are you losing weight again?"

Down to skin and bones, no doubt, and those bones were overworked.

"Probably, but not for the reasons you think," I answered. "They have me doing double time in the kitchen and the heat is almost unbearable. I'm a sticky mess by the time dinner rolls around."

Melia took her seat again and poured some more coffee into her cup, making sure to fill mine to the brim as I took the opposite chair. "Girl! Some of the Fae here like it warm, but that doesn't mean you have to deal with it."

"No one else seems too concerned with combating the climbing temperatures." The smell of the coffee was divine. I raised the cup to my nose and inhaled. "I'm pretty sure they're all from tropical climates and it makes them feel at home. I'm the one who suffers."

"Well, see if you can whip up a spell allowing you to control the temperature of the air around you. Then they can all bake themselves to death and you won't look like you spent a week navigating through a desert." Melia held up her cup to prove her point while I felt like smacking myself.

It was one of the first things they'd taught us at the Halfling Academy: how to create a pocket of air around us and control the conditions inside of it. Why hadn't I thought of that spell before?

"What do you think of this place?" Melia asked about the café.

"It's awesome!" I agreed readily. Then leaned back in my chair with a sigh. "Is the food good?"

"It's amazing. They do something different to all their food and drink, as I'm sure you've noticed since arriving. What am I saying? You work in a *kitchen*! The fricken' king's kitchen. But yeah, you get used to it after a while and I'm still kinda missing my instant coffee."

Melia had a weird fascination with instant coffee to the point where she always kept a glass bottle or two in her room. Something about how milk and the bitter coffee combination, she told me, got her day started right.

"It's a funny thing to miss, don't you think?" she was saying. "I almost want to use my key to go back and get some, but girl, it might be a little selfish of me and I'm not sure I want to flex against the travel rules yet. You know? Not sure if they frown on going back to the mortal realm so soon after being granted citizenship here."

I'd missed her speech patterns, I realized. The way Melia took the reins of a conversation and ran with it.

"I'm not sure I told you. My boarding house is right across the street," Melia was saying. She gestured with her cup again and a bit of coffee sloshed over the rim. "I mean, it's a nice place, all things considered, and I get my own room. Gosh, I would have been a little upset if I had to have a roommate after all this time. I really got used to having my own space at the academy."

"I feel it deeply," I agreed.

"I got my first week for free, of course, and now that week is totally done. I crunched some numbers the other day and decided I can't afford to stay here for very long before I need to find long-term accommodations. But I don't want to bore you with money woes." She set her palms down flat on the table. "Maybe after the summer is over, you and I could look for something. *Together*. A little place of our own."

I nearly broke down into tears on the spot, recognizing the hope in her eyes. A rumble of thunder boomed close by. I didn't care. "That would be amazing." I sighed. "You have no idea."

"You serious, girl? You're not saying things to make me feel like less of a needy wuss?"

"No way. Moving somewhere with you would actually be a huge relief to me. The, ah, the Elite Academy makes me feel like such an outcast. Living with a friend might help balance it out."

"Oh damn. You're having problems with the school already?"

Already, yeah. She wanted to talk about feeling like a needy wuss? I personified it! "Not so much problems as an intense dislike of the other students, and the feeling is mutual," I told her. "Plus, like I told you, I'm stuck working on kitchen duty to help pay for my stay at the castle and I really suck at it. *Really* suck. I don't want to do it long-term. I would have to find out if I'd still have access to the academy without being at the castle. I'm not sure if the king set it up as a package deal or not. I feel like there are eyes on me all the time."

Melia took a sip of her coffee, contemplating. "You never know. There are so many intricacies to the way the Fae deal with each other...it is definitely something you need to figure out before making any kind of drastic move. Think about it."

"I don't really have time to think about it."

"Well, I got a job in a store nearby and it's not terrible. Maybe it's something for you to think about down the line."

"Obviously I would have to work somewhere if I wanted

to rent a place with you. I don't think our mortal money translates across the dimensional border." I said it as a joke. Too bad I wasn't joking. "We have to see what kinds of opportunities might be available in Faerie," I finished.

"Good thing you have me on your side." Melia flashed me another wide grin before bending down to retrieve a three-ring binder and a book. "Me and my anal-retentive research."

"What did you do, Meli?"

"I present to you the research I have done on opportunities available in Faerie. I mean, this town is really only known for the king's palace and the schools. There's not much to it outside of those areas." She paused and tapped the top of the binder. "And I highly doubt you want to stay working for the king's palace if you don't have to."

"Absolutely not." I agreed without hesitation. Staying with the king came with too much pressure.

"Most opportunities to carve out a place for yourself in Faerie are found in larger cities or on the coast. I'd say Eahsea is a dead end if you want to make something of yourself."

"What if I *want* to hide under a rock?"

Melia raised an eyebrow and continued. "Maybe for you. The rest of us have things to do and people to see and a life to carve out of nothing."

"Meli." I reached forward and grabbed her hands, feeling too pale and clammy and dead inside next to her. "You need to get out and do something, absolutely. Go start your life. Don't worry about me! I can survive on my own. I don't want you to ruin your chances to be someone because of me. It's going to take me way too long to get through school. I'd never forgive myself if you missed out on an opportunity because you were stuck here waiting."

"I'm not leaving you." She leaned in closer and whispered, "To tell you the truth, I'm a little unnerved by you being pulled into Faerie by the king. I didn't want to say anything to you at first but—"

Her words sent a frisson through me like an electric shock. "What do you mean?"

She shook her head. "I don't know. I have a bad feeling about the whole situation, and the more I think about it, the more worried it makes me. Especially with the rumors I've heard of the corruption in the palace. I know sometimes the Fae Academy for Halflings will allow their brightest students from the first-year class to be schooled in Faerie, but none of them have ever been sent to the Elite Academy. *None.* I even reached out to Professor Marsh to check the stats."

Professor Marsh, my old favorite teacher. Heh.

"I was told the last halfling to attend the Elite Academy was two hundred years ago," I said, the words dry in my throat.

"That much is true, yeah, but that halfling didn't come from the Halfling Academy. From what I've researched, it was a half Fae, half elf male born in the kingdom, and his parents were workers in the castle. There's no record of any half-humans being admitted. *Ever.* Think about it."

Her face said it all, and the hard knot in my stomach grew a little bigger, dropped a little lower. The coffee was too much for me to handle and I set my cup down with trembling fingers.

"Well...Mike did say he thinks his father has an agenda for both of us," I admitted. "Granted, he didn't elaborate."

"See? Plus I can't trust you to take care of yourself," she said. "The last time I left you to your own devices, you became *one* with too many walls and almost killed yourself."

"Oh, har har."

She continued to tap the top of the binder. Around us,

the café was bustling with business. Luckily no one was close enough to hear our conversation. "This does lead me to the big reason I called you here today."

"I thought you genuinely wanted to see me," I replied dryly.

"Make no mistake, I definitely wanted to see you. I needed some girlfriend time. But...I'm worried."

"About me?"

Melia whispered, "I'm worried about you using your transfiguration power without any proper training."

"Trust me, Meli, with the king right above my head, I'm not planning on using any kind of magic any time soon. Especially not a power I'm not supposed to have. You can believe me when I tell you I am not planning on being a wall ever again."

"Fine, I'm glad you're taking precautions. I also might have tracked down someone who can help you."

"What do you mean? Help me how?"

"I've been busy. I found another half Fae, half shifter." Melia kept her voice soft so no one would overhear her. "He's willing to teach you. For a price."

9

Hell. *No.*

No more unnamed, to be determined later prices in exchange for something.

I knew all about the price of extortion for training or information. I'd dealt with the same kind of thing with Barbara, and I knew it wasn't a good idea. It always turned out to be worse than expected.

Melia and I had a light lunch together before I heard the chime of the bells marking the time. With regret, I pushed away from the table and grabbed my purse, putting some money down.

"I'm going to get out of here," I told her. "I've got a lot of homework assignments waiting for me."

Melia stared at me. "Are you going to be okay?"

I forced a grin for her benefit. "Absolutely. Don't worry about me."

"I can't help it. It's part of my job."

"You're not my mentor anymore."

"Doesn't matter. I'll always be there for you, to listen when you need an ear and to tell you how I feel or what I think. And I know you would do the same for me," she said sincerely.

With a final hug, we said our reluctant goodbyes.

I was back under the awning a moment later, deciding where to go because no matter what I'd told her about the homework, my head didn't want me to go back to the palace just yet. Instead I headed to grab some snack foods from the market down the street. There were things I couldn't seem to get from the kitchen and didn't feel comfortable asking Raelynn about. Then I'd have to hear her laughing with her friends about half-humans and our weird tastes.

Melia had to go home and get ready for work anyway, she'd assured me, although I wished we could have had more time together. Being around my best friend did wonders to lift my mood.

When I glanced out from under the awning, I saw the rain had stopped entirely and there were pieces of sunlight trying valiantly to poke through the overcast sky.

Better. Much better.

So, I thought as I walked, Melia had managed to find another half Fae, half shifter. Boy, did she have the nose for finding us. I guess we weren't as rare as I'd thought. She'd given me his number and right now it burned a hole in my jeans, like a little puddle of acid ready to eat through anything it touched.

As if I needed to owe anything to anyone else.

To conceal my shifter nature during my first semester at the mortal academy, I'd had to make a deal with a shifty witch for a potion. A witch who decided she needed to cash in on the favor during my last semester there, and for an exorbitant price. She'd wanted something called the *Augundae Imperium,* an artifact said to leach the magic power from anyone and everything, power stored for later. It had been brought to the castle courtesy of our exchange student guests visiting from our sister school in Canada.

I'd nearly killed myself to get it, because otherwise my witchy bitchy benefactor—oddly named Barbara—threatened to expose my secret. She would have, too, if I hadn't given her what she wanted. I didn't know what she wanted to do with it and right now I didn't care.

So...

If I hadn't learned the dangers of making deals with supernatural beings and owing favors and paying prices from the Barbara debacle, then I really did deserve whatever bad luck fell on me. I wasn't keen to make any of those mistakes again. Melia's shifter friend was going to have to live the rest of his life without meeting me. Too bad.

I paused at the entrance to the market and ducked my head inside to avoid the eucalyptus strung beneath the door frame. I should know what it meant. Part of me must have learned it in school... Nope, not a clue.

Memory like a bucket full of holes.

Despite the glimpses of clear sky I'd caught only moments ago, when I glanced behind me now, the rain grew heavier, like someone beating drums in the distance. It bounced off the tile roofs in a soothing melody and I knew I'd have a long walk back to the castle.

Was it really because of me, I wondered as I perused the shelves for snack foods. Was I really the cause of the abnormal weather? Did the whole land of Faerie know I didn't belong here?

Maybe I was kidding myself.

Yeah, and maybe pigs would sprout wings and fly right off.

Hey, who knew? Maybe here they could, and maybe I'd hack it enough to get through this and out the other side.

Lost in thought, I had a handful of items in tow as I

made my way to the checkout counter, ready to pay...until I heard the laugh.

The terrible, high-pitched hyena cackle of a laugh as familiar to me as my own face in the mirror. *Persephone*.

Of all the times and places to run into her, now *definitely* wasn't good. I was unprepared and looked like a rat someone dug out of a sewer. At least that's how I felt, and I didn't want her to know.

I ducked and hid behind the nearest shelf, my own shopping forgotten as my mind clung to escape plans. Moving products aside, I tried to catch a glimpse of my nemesis. And like the single ray of sunshine I'd seen earlier, there she was, looking as beautiful as ever and surrounded by a handful of other beautiful girls.

I swallowed my groan but couldn't resist an eye roll to go along with it. Even here in Faerie, Persephone had managed to form a new little *meanion* clique. Of course. She couldn't go anywhere without them, after all. I doubted the girl knew how to be alone and actually enjoy her own company.

At least these had a little differentiation in terms of hair color. At the mortal school, she'd only accepted blonds into her friend group. Now I actually saw a few redheads in there. As for her last clique, they'd all been bombshells with the personalities of rocks.

No wonder they chose Persephone Glaski as their leader.

If she was here, then the time had come and gone for me to make my exit. I waited for the most opportune moment before bee-lining toward the register with a couple of items. I could quickly and quietly check out and then run for dear life before anyone saw me.

Halfway there, I heard Persephone say my name.

"Oh my gosh! Tavi? Is it really you?"

This, accompanied by a snicker. Great, I'd been spotted!

When I turned around, I saw her staring at me, with her hands on her hips and her traditional sneer firmly in place. Pert nose, blond curls, heart-shaped face. Yeah, she was a girl to loathe if I'd ever seen one, and not because of her looks but her terrible personality. She'd also been my bunkmate for the past year. We'd hated each other on sight.

Rather, she'd hated me on sight and gave me no choice but to feel the same way about her.

I fixed a similar but slightly less antagonizing look on my own face as I turned to face her. "Persephone. How are you?"

"Oh Tavi, I'm simply wonderful. Isn't this place the best? Literally the *best*." Her friends gathered around her as she spoke and Persephone took delight in telling them loudly, "Tavi is the one who got placed at the Elite Academy. No one knows how. She barely managed to scrape by to get a place in the top five students of our class at the Halfling Academy. Yet for some reason the king seems to think she has what it takes to make it there. She's too good for *our* little school."

The girl closest to Persephone scoffed. "Are you kidding me? How did this cockroach get placed there? Fae children fight their whole lives to get the grades necessary to make it into Elite, and most of them don't succeed anyway."

I swallowed hard and did my best to keep my mouth shut.

"I'm telling you," Persephone insisted, "it's a mystery. She keeps doing well when she clearly doesn't deserve it, because there were far better students who actually deserved a place here." She bent low to whisper to another girl. "There's something seriously wrong with her."

The two eyed me up and down. "Or something seriously right if she caught the king's attention," the one on the left commented.

I winced.

I also caught their meaning behind the statement and blushed. Persephone managed to land a few more rude comments—her specialty—driving home their collective scorn before the group flounced off into the rain under bright umbrellas shaped like flower petals.

"See you never, Tavi," Persephone called over her shoulder.

Just like that, done.

I stood with my shoulders drooped, the fairy at the checkout counter doing her best to ignore me without making it obvious.

I'm an outcast no matter where I go. I indulged in another long moment of standing there trying to catch my breath. Maybe coming here hadn't been a good idea, but staying in the mortal world wasn't either. I knew that for a fact.

Maybe there's nowhere I'll fit in. I'd always be on the cusp of two worlds. Not quite belonging to either.

10

The Summer Games kicked off on Monday.

I'd never felt more dread or anxiety than I did when I stepped out of the portal with Mike and immediately came face to face with the mass of press and news crews waiting in the courtyard.

Holy. Crap. What was I going to do?

"Take a deep breath and pretend like you don't see them." Mike's solid advice, what he'd told me Friday night when speaking about the games, and what he repeated now to make sure I understood.

And for how simple the advice sounded, it was ridiculously hard to follow. No matter how hard I tried to ignore the hundreds of creatures all shouting at once, it was impossible, and each step was an act of sheer willpower.

The news anchors I recognized from the weather report —Twilight and Ashley—were two out of at least fifty crowded around the outside of the school, waiting for a chance to speak with any of the participating students. They definitely waited for Mike himself, every one of them eager for an interview with the crown prince, who would also be competing.

As for me, I'd woken up with a stomach ache which translated into no breakfast and shaky hands and clammy palms. I'd done my best not to stand out today, not to draw attention to myself. Although let's face it, being born with my color hair and bright green eyes didn't exactly put me in a corner. The hair especially. Still, I'd worn neutral colors, dark wash pants and gray shirt, and I'd forgone any kind of makeup. The rich auburn hair I'd styled into a long French braid hung down my back. Casual, innocent. Nothing to say *look at me, look at me.*

I'd thought so, at least, until Mike caught sight of me when he came to pick me up. He'd blinked several times as though he couldn't quite believe what he saw.

"Tavi, you look beautiful. Not that you don't normally look great, but there's something about you today..." He trailed off, the beginning of a smile teasing his lips. "What did you do?"

I'd pushed a stray lock of hair behind my ear. "I showered?"

He hadn't seemed to want to accept my joke. Did I believe the compliment? No way. And while the kind words had been nice, they weren't enough to soothe away the ever-growing knot of anxiety slowly killing me from the inside.

I figured going with the neutral look would help me to not stand out so the press would leave me alone and I could trudge through the games as quickly and painlessly as possible.

A ridiculous pipe dream, yeah, but it seemed like my life was built one pipe dream at a time.

Mike had grabbed my hand the moment we stepped out of the portal. With a bid to be quiet, he'd brought me around the side of the building, hurrying. I highly doubted his plan for stealth would work, but as it turned out, only three of the news people caught sight of us and we already had a head start on them.

"Crown Prince Michael!" the closest pair called out to him. "Michael Thornwood, a moment of your time!"

I caught the sound of harsh laughter under his breath. "Not today." He glanced over at me, still holding my hand. "Places to be."

Instead of going to our homerooms, the entire school met in the auditorium and there I saw the headmaster for the first time. He was about as far from Headmaster Leaves at the Halfling Academy as two Fae could be in terms of physical looks. While Leaves had been young-looking, chestnut-haired, and eager-eyed, Headmaster Cyrus stooped. His white hair was a direct contrast to his ebony skin, with wrinkles cut deep into his skin, similar to bark on an old tree.

His milky left eye lay mostly still but the blue brilliance of his right one caught every student and made it seem like he saw you. He saw you and he *knew* you. Especially the things you wanted to keep to yourself.

His gaze fell on me as Mike and I took a seat in the second to last row and my skin crawled.

I didn't like the feeling his look gave me.

Lane and some of the others were already waiting with seats saved for the prince and his disgusting mortal friend, or so I thought at the looks they gave me. Still, I happily accepted the empty chair and settled in for the welcoming speech.

Headmaster Cyrus called for attention with a pound of his fist against the stone podium, the sound reverberating across the auditorium space. I wasn't sure if he needed the podium to hold himself up or if it was tradition. At this point it could go either way.

"Settle down, students, settle down." He called for attention, his voice the soothing baritone of an opera singer. "I know you are all excited to kick off another year of Summer Games. It is our delight to be able to offer the opportunity to those attending Elite, as there are many others who would die for the chance to participate."

Why did I feel like he spoke directly to me? And why did I feel like I should be grateful? I tried to sink down into the seat.

"Now, if you could focus your eyes on the stage, I'd like to introduce you to your officiant for the Summer Games. Take it away, Magnus Crackenbush."

Cyrus swept his arm out to indicate a broad-shouldered Fae male with two opalescent horns curling out of the back of his skull. Ebony hair waved down to his shoulders, and beneath the light pearl-colored tunic he wore, I saw the outline of black tribal tattoos.

"Welcome, everyone. Welcome to the 230th Summer Games. I know everyone is anxious to get started and kick off the summer solstice celebrations." Magnus shot the audience a dazzling smile meant to put us at ease. While others whooped and screamed to voice their excitement, I shrank even lower into my seat.

Magnus introduced the categories of the competition—something I'd have to get Mike to explain to me later—then went on to speak about the timeline. They would start with two games this week, leading up to the solstice carnival. After a brief intermission, the games would commence once again.

To me, it didn't matter how many games there were or what categories the elders tried to define them as. I didn't want to go through any of it. I wanted to keep my head in my books and push through to the final semester so I could be *done*.

Magnus Crackenbush and his oblivious, lying smile could go take a flying jump as far as I was concerned.

I tuned out the rest of the speeches from a few of the commentators who would be covering the games. I didn't plan on taking part in them anyway, no matter what Mike said about the whole school getting involved. I'd find a way to get out of it, I vowed.

"All right, students," Headmaster Cyrus concluded with a clap of his hands. "Another round of applause for Magnus, if you please. He and his team have put together a dazzling itinerary for this year's games. However, it's time for us to wrap this up. Everyone head to the lunch hall for a special reception to celebrate."

"Hey, Tavi." Mike elbowed me in the side to get my attention. "You totally spaced."

Shaking my head to clear it, I blinked over at Mike, still trying to get my thoughts together. "I'm sorry."

I followed him out with the rest of the student body hiking toward the lunch hall. The moment we were through the wide stone doors I wanted to find a corner to hide in. Surely no one would notice if I snuck away. Would they?

"Stay close to me," Mike was saying. "I don't want to lose sight of you in the crowd. Knowing these vultures, they'll shred you."

I could barely hear him over the rush of voices from his friend group, led by the disgustingly handsome and arrogant Arlyss.

"Do you think Ashley will want an interview with me?" Arlyss asked, practically fluffing up. "I mean, I am rumored to be a front runner for the competition."

"You are," the girl called Coral agreed. "You're sure to win, Arly-bear."

He smirked at her over his shoulder and pushed toward

the visiting press, all wearing badges and with cameramen trailing them.

Was it still too late to hide? I could probably wiggle away from Mike without anyone seeing me, because the moment Arlyss failed to draw the press's attention, the moment they caught sight of Mike himself, they would be here.

His entire friend group—and I use the word *friend* loosely—wanted their fifteen minutes of fame. These were the elite at the Elite, the ones who were upper crust enough to rub elbows with the crown prince on a daily basis. Shouldn't they be used to the cameras by now? To the fame and attention?

Who was I to judge them, though? I just wanted out.

When Mike got pulled off after Arlyss, flashing me an apologetic smile through the push and pull of the crowd, I made my escape. He was the prince, so it was best he kept his distance from me today, I thought. Actually, being trampled by the crowd might be preferable to being interviewed.

I used the sudden upswing in noise to edge toward the food line, grabbing a cookie, taking a huge bite, and chewing thoughtfully. A little wine wouldn't hurt, either. Although I wasn't twenty-one, Uncle Will had never been shy about allowing me alcohol for celebrations as long as I only drank in moderation. There was something subtly relaxing about a good red wine.

Faerie wine proved even more intoxicating.

The flavors were a thousand times more potent here, helped along exponentially through the magic of the land itself. The wine was like swallowing sunlight, the flavors of earth and rain and sweet grapes exploding on my tongue.

I could get used to this. Sighing, I leaned against the wall, letting the coolness of the stone seep some of the heat from my clammy skin. No one would even miss me if I snuck off.

The longer I watched the rest of the students make asses of themselves, the more I felt it safe I'd escaped attention. I was almost out of the woods.

Until I turned to stare directly into the lens of a camera. I dropped the cookie. And barely managed to keep hold of the wine goblet.

The woman squared right up to me, the cameraman peering over her shoulder as she said, "Well, aren't you the most *darling* little halfling?"

11

Muscles tensed, I prepared to flat out *run*. And might have got away, had the woman not latched onto my arm at the last moment. She moved so fast I hadn't seen her hand until her bright red nails bit down on my skin.

I was in trouble.

"So, you're the little one we keep hearing about." She stared into the camera for a moment before smiling at me. "The mortal halfling who has a special *in* with the king himself. We've been waiting to talk to you all morning. How about you and I go over here and chat for a little bit. Hmm?" She steered me toward a nearby table, and when the boy and girl blocking my vision moved aside, I saw a pair of empty seats.

My heart sank. The drab ensemble and no-makeup camouflage hadn't worked.

"It looks like you aren't going to give me a choice," I told her.

The woman practically forced me down into a seat, her gaze firm and direct. A sly smile graced her lips.

Her grip on my arm loosened. She stood close to six feet

tall with chin-length black hair curled around her pointed ears. Her eyes were silver and deep, exceptionally beautiful with her warm honey-colored skin. My hackles rose in self-defense looking at her and I tried to nudge them back down. I sensed a threat.

"Tell me, please, how a halfling like you came to attend the Elite Academy, the most prestigious school in the realm?" the woman began.

"How about you tell me your name, first?" I countered. "It might help."

She monitored me for a moment more before adopting a bored expression. "Selene Montrosse. You can call me Selene. I'm a correspondent."

"For what station?"

But Selene didn't feel the need to answer my second question. Her voice, soft and sharp, cut through the noise of the cafeteria as she asked, "What made you special enough to attend the Elite Academy, halfling?"

Laser focus with this one, I could tell. And although she didn't quite spear me through the way Headmaster Cyrus did, my skin began to itch again.

"Tavi. Alderidge." I resisted the urge to sulk and slump down beneath the table. Another glass of wine would have been welcome. Selene and her cameraman stood there patiently waiting for me to answer, monitoring me for the slightest expression that would give me away.

She wasn't impressed with my name.

"I was in the top five of my class at the Fae Academy for Halflings in the mortal realm," I said. And those horrible silver-gray eyes met my own. Like magic waiting to be unleashed, waiting to make me speak my truth.

I didn't like this woman any more than I liked Perse-phone. They had the same kind of energy of dogged determination to figure me out, and a predisposition to dislike whatever they saw.

"I see," Selene said after another moment. She took a step closer, raising her nose in the air to sniff delicately, and although we were not alone, I'd never felt weaker or more isolated.

Still, I kept my chin held high.

"What about your parents?"

"My mother was Fae. My father was human," I answered carefully. Clearly having to lie, at least in part. I scratched at my neck and watched the hustle and bustle in the cafeteria, hoping they'd get bored with me and hare off for more interesting prey.

The camera continued to run the entire time.

"I'm sorry. You're taping this? Will this be going on TV?"

Selene shrugged, her lips a slash of red in her pale face. "All depends on how it goes and what kind of information you offer."

"And if it goes poorly?" I asked.

She paused, hesitating for a moment before her face softened. "I'm sure you will do fine," she said, and I might have imagined a tiny tremor in her stiff voice.

Until she continued with a series of questions bordering on probing too deep. I decided I really didn't want to know what she was after. If I could keep to myself and avoid her, then this interview would not be repeated. Selene seemed to know more than she let on.

My skin continued to itch and generally feel too small under the weight of my nerves. I didn't think I could be kicked out of this world, since I'd been accepted as a citizen of Faerie, but if the truth of my shifter side came into the light...*who knew*.

Maybe I would be kicked out. I couldn't take that chance.

Through her questions I did my best to come across as

absolutely boring. Insubstantial. Not worth reporting about. I gave her the barest minimum answers and sometimes nothing at all, merely a shrug or a roll of my eyes.

I could tell Selene didn't believe me. To her, I wasn't the ridiculous half-human worthy of nothing but derision. I needed to be inspected. I needed to be figured out for her viewers if she wanted a chance of staying ahead in ratings.

At least, that's how it felt to me. She seemed ambitious.

The moment I caught a break in the conversation, I said, "I'm sorry. If you'll excuse me, I need to use the ladies' room. Nature is calling."

Ready to worm my way out.

Selene and her cameraman had no choice but to let me go. I was out of the room in seconds, grabbing another small cup of wine from one of the refreshment stations and choking it down on my way out.

Jeez, the spotlight didn't sit well with me.

I made it to the restroom and locked the door behind me, ready to hide out for the rest of the reception. Or maybe the rest of the week, depending on how things went past this point.

I remembered Selene's serpentine smile, how her head tilted to the side as she continued to question me.

Maybe living in Faerie had been a bad idea after all. Coming from the mortal academy to this one was like jumping from bad to worse because I hadn't known any better, and yet I was expected to smile and be grateful the entire time.

By the time I got back to my room later in the evening, I was a wreck. The long days were wearing on me. With school, then working in the kitchens...I couldn't keep up. I'd grabbed a plate of food on my way out from work and settled on my bed, prepared to do homework until I passed out.

Instead of sticking to my plan, I stared at the food, my appetite gone. I was so tired. Too tired to even want to eat, if the half-hearted grumbles from my stomach meant anything. And I was super tired of being assessed and found lacking. Tired of being evaluated because of the blood in my veins.

"Tavi, *you are hungry*," I tried to tell myself, knowing I'd need the food to get me through homework. "You want to eat because you need to keep up your strength to make it through life."

I knew the roasted chicken would taste delicious, as well as the green beans, the freshly baked brown bread, and the assortment of cheeses Raelynn had made sure I'd taken to sample. How could I be a good cook if I didn't know the basics, after all?

I'd probably never be a good cook but I'd given up fighting her on the point.

My thoughts drifted toward Selene and her interview. I'd never felt so laid bare before, with her insistent and probing questions. Just as I'd never been faced with a plate of food and *not* wanted to eat it. Things were definitely going wrong for me. Glancing out the window, I watched the storm clouds continue to roil, the faint outline of the moon barely visible through the gray. Storms, rain, and the land still unsettled. I had no idea how I was going to continue to balance all of it.

I wish I were back at the Halfling Academy.

Oddly, the thought surprised me.

At least there I'd been at the top of my class and surrounded by friends—and if not friends, then good acquaintances. People like Melia who knew my secret and still liked me in spite of it. Or people like Nora, the shy quiet girl who'd been part of my first-year class.

I set the plate of food aside and headed for the bathroom. No way was I going to make it through my homework like this. I couldn't even focus on eating!

Though the bathtub called me, I settled for a quick, hot shower before seating myself at my desk to work on an essay for potions class. Pen in hand, I stared at the paper, tapping, definitely ready for the words to write themselves. Wasn't there a spell for that?

What was the point of learning to use my fae magic if I couldn't work a spell to drag my thoughts from my head to the paper? Absolutely ridiculous.

It drew a laugh and I stared at the empty sheet waiting for my words. Words I didn't have because I was fresh out of them. I didn't have a thing to say about potions, and honestly? I didn't want to. End of term was right around the corner. I didn't understand why I had to do this work like the rest of the students who'd spent the full semester at Elite.

Time passed as I struggled to work. A rustle at the window provided the perfect excuse and I turned around to see the crow sitting on the windowsill.

With half a page written, I decided it was the perfect time for a break.

There was no fear in the animal's eyes. Only a strange curiosity as it stared at me, its head tilted to the side and its beak snapping to get my attention. Kind of a *hurry up, I'm waiting* motion. I had no clue if it was the same crow who had shown up with the wolf amulet—the amulet currently hidden under my mattress. They all looked the same to me.

"Well, hello again, you. What are you doing here? Are you hungry?" I grabbed a piece of uneaten green beans from my dinner plate and approached the window.

A meal between friends, I mused.

"Do you want a green bean? It's okay. You can have it." I chuckled as the crow squawked once, a sound I took as a yes. "I don't know if you're hungry or not but it's better than letting the food go to waste."

I tossed the green bean to the bird and watched it snap up the vegetable. Then I saw the rolled-up piece of parchment clutched in its right talons.

My lungs seized. Oh no, something new this time.

"Why do I always feel like you bring bad news with you?" I gently scolded, trying to keep my voice soft. "Remind me to see if I can bribe you into bringing good news. Okay?"

A cocoon of peaceful silence seemed to pulse around the two of us as I fed the crow the rest of the green beans. Again, I peered down at the scrap of paper.

Eventually we worked up enough of a friendship that I reached out to run my hand across its wing. And it let me. Softer than I'd imagined. The bird closed its eyes.

"Thank you for coming to visit me, and thank you for being so trusting." I held up my hands. "No more food. You ate it all."

The bird released the parchment. The paper fluttered to the floor and I opened it as the crow flew away, having delivered what it came for.

The note appeared to be handwritten, though it was unsigned. I saw my name at the top.

GREETINGS, TAVI

Someone knew I was here. Someone knew which room I'd claimed.

My heart turned to ice as I read.

WE KNOW YOUR SECRET, AND YOU ARE NOT SAFE HERE.
RUN.

12

Run. I couldn't get the word out of my head and I stood statue-still for a long moment, a soft breeze blowing in from the open window. *Run.* But where would I go? Was I in some kind of danger?

Damn. *Damn.*

What was I going to do now?

The ice crept from my heart to my veins and stayed with me until the morning sun slid over the treetops. Sleep refused to come, of course, and although my stomach ached from not eating, my appetite had completely disappeared without a trace.

I stared at the ceiling, with the sheets pulled up to my chin. Feeling like dirt. I'd burned the note in the fireplace, summoning a flame with ease. The magic did nothing to loosen my limbs and the tension stored in every fiber of my being.

Run.

I wondered who had written the note, and how they'd gotten the crow to do their bidding. Where did they expect me to run *to*?

And why? Another frisson swept through me as I

remembered the Augundae Imperium. Or rather the fake Augundae Imperium. Funny that I hadn't heard anything else about how it had mysteriously disappeared once we crossed through the portal from the mortal realm. Did they suspect I was behind that?

Was that why the king was keeping me here in the castle, close and under direct supervision? And if that wasn't it, what else could it be? Had someone discovered my half-shifter secret?

Too many questions with no answers.

I was a distracted mess that day at school. Mike found me for lunch, surprising me with the fact it would be just the two of us eating instead of his usual clique.

"Are you sure you're okay?" he asked for the thousandth time. "You're pale."

"Yeah, I'm all right. Not hungry."

He'd chose a table for us away from the majority of the crowd, and the suspicious part of me, larger lately than normal, wondered what was up with him. Why he wanted us to be alone.

"Now I *know* there's something wrong. You're never not hungry. And this food?" He gestured down to his plate. "It's amazing."

My gut churned. "I'm sure my appetite will return soon," I said, settling across from him with a half full tray of goodies I still couldn't eat. I forced a laugh for his benefit, ending on a snort.

The sound seemed to settle his worries because Mike stopped pushing after that.

He seemed to be his old self again, talking and joking about classes and how he was going to have to bribe someone to keep up his good grades from the mortal academy. I couldn't even appreciate his humor at the moment.

Who had sent me the note? How did they know my name?

How did they know *where I sleep*?

There were a lot of things about this realm that made me feel unsafe, but this took the cake. What did this face-less, nameless person know and how could I find out? I needed to protect myself.

"Tavi, hey!" Mike snapped his fingers to get my attention. "You spaced out again."

I shook my head, setting down my fork and glancing at the still full plate. "I'm sorry." I meant it.

"This is the fourth time I've tried to tell you the same story and you're still ignoring me."

"I know, and I'm really sorry. I haven't been sleeping well."

Mike appeared concerned. "Is there something wrong with your room?"

"Gosh, no. My room is fine. I'm a little preoccupied with the newness of everything. It's taking me a bit longer to settle in than I'd hoped."

"Understandable." He pushed a piece of gold hair behind his ear, his expression sympathetic.

"Trust me, I would tell you if there was something both-ering me with my room. Everything is great there."

"Is it classes? Work?"

"I guess you could say I'm still adjusting."

Mike took my answer at face value and went on with his story, though I knew he was aware of my every glance around the lunch space, every movement I made, the things I said and moreover the things I did not.

He was worried about me, although he wouldn't push the issue while we were surrounded by people. Fine by me. I didn't know how to explain my situation to him, not in a way he would understand. Especially considering he didn't know my *biggest* secret.

My wolf prowled close beneath the surface and a constant stream of magic kept her from taking over entirely, taking over so my worried mind wouldn't have to stress double-time.

Classes passed slowly into afternoon and the kitchen was bustling when I arrived for work after school.

Raelynn met me at the door, with grease stains on her apron and a scowl deepening the lines on her forehead.

"You better suit up and grab an apron, Teri. I mean it. We don't have time for you to muck around," she barked out immediately.

"It's Tavi."

I don't know why I bothered to correct her. She had a new name for me every afternoon and by this point it seemed this was all part of a game she played. Still, I guess I had my part to play in it too.

I did as she asked and drew an apron down from one of the wooden pegs near the storeroom. Melia had been right with her idea about creating a small vacuum of space where I controlled the weather. The kitchen got hotter by the minute but a few whispered spell words and I was comfortable.

"Get a tray and put a smile on your pretty face," Raelynn instructed. She went so far as to shift her fingers in the air in an exaggerated fashion, her mouth going along with the motion. "We're taking tea to the Elder Council. Or more specifically, *you* are going to be taking the tea. I'm management."

I swallowed over a lump the size of a boulder in my throat. "*The* Elder Council?"

"Yup. You've heard of them? They are the governing body working directly underneath the king and queen to uphold the law in Faerie. And it's a huge deal to serve them tea. I'm sure you understand. You're a pretty girl. Your presence will be greatly appreciated as long as you keep your mouth shut." She worked as she spoke, pushing me this way and that in preparation. "Put up the hair. I don't want you getting any of it in the cookies."

I knotted my hair on top of my head in the best bun I could make considering the lack of time, and joined a line of three other pretty kitchen girls. We each carried a tray with a pitcher of hot tea, cream, sugar, and a plate of either cookies or warm scones with butter.

One of the other girls, older than me and a master at kitchen wizardry it seemed, took the lead. Thank goodness, because I had no idea where we were going or what to expect.

Raelynn swatted me on the behind on my way out the door. "Behave yourself!" she called out.

Like I had any other option? At the very least, my confusion would keep me silent. I wouldn't be tempted to say something regrettable or stick my foot between my lips this time.

We climbed a set of curving stairs toward the main floor of the castle and turned left, away from the main throne room. The girl leading the procession knocked on one of the doors and waited a moment longer before entering.

I saw King Tywin and Queen Laina seated around a circular table engraved with ancient runic symbols. The sight of the royals clanged through me. Only a week ago, I'd stood in front of them being welcomed to this land. Being asked by their son to dance.

No—no, I couldn't think about Mike right now. Especially not when I had immediately broken out in a cold sweat.

The council and the two royals hardly noticed the

servants enter. We were the help. Not worthy of notice. Thank goodness I'd put my hair back and wrapped it with a black bandana to keep the strands at bay. At least it made me less noticeable.

I followed the lead of the other kitchen workers and set the trays down on smaller serving tables lining the perimeter of the small chamber. Even the king ignored me, though I knew for sure he recognized my face after hand-picking me from the Halfling Academy.

The council did not pause their talking at the new arrivals.

"We still have no idea where the artifact is. It disappeared without a trace. We haven't been able to pinpoint the exact time the fake was put in place." The speaker, who looked oddly familiar when I glanced up, banged his fist on the table for emphasis. "I knew we shouldn't have trusted Cote with its protection."

"What else would you have us do? An item of such importance was bound to garner attention!" another one of the Elder Council exclaimed.

The king watched the dialogue silently.

I realized with a pang of fear they were discussing the Augundae Imperium. The same artifact Barbara the witch had forced me to steal for her. I'd used my powers of transfiguration to get through the walls and the layers of magical protection surrounding the artifact.

I thought of Barbara the last time I had seen her. The glee in her eyes as she had grabbed the Imperium from me. Her purposely neutral statement about why she wanted the artifact.

Where it was now, and what Barbara had wanted it for, I had no idea.

Oh God, with this many magical powerhouses in one room...*please don't let them smell the guilt on me.*

My gut plummeted through my shoes and into the bowels of the castle.

"I'm still not clear how no one realized the Imperium was a fake even before they brought it through the portal," one of the council members blustered. "We questioned the teachers from the Canadian Halfling Academy at length and none of them knows anything about the disappearance. They were subjected to truth spells yet no one knows how the Imperium was stolen or even *when*. It's a mystery, Your Majesty."

"And no mystery goes without an answer. We need to figure this out before chaos ensues." King Tywin did not rise from his seat. He kept his voice modulated. No one seemed to notice the way his mouth tightened. "What do we do? We can hardly beat the Unseelie uprising without the Imperium."

The Unseelie? My mind struggled to keep up. Wait a minute. Hadn't Mike told me there were no more Seelie versus Unseelie courts? Or...no, he'd said his family predated the courts. Confusion had my hands trembling and the porcelain tea set rattling.

The man next to the king agreed. "There will be no way to take out Dorian Jade without the power of the Imperium."

The what and the who?

I'd just set my tray down and the girl in front of me nudged me. We had to leave now. Part of me wanted to stay behind and hear more. To hear what the council discussed in furtive tones, what the king and the queen didn't want the rest of their citizens to know regarding the disappearance of the Imperium.

And I guiltily wanted to raise my hand. *Right here, Your Majesty. I know where it went, who has it now, and who took it. All me.*

If there was ever a time for me to be quiet…

I shouldn't have heard what I did, I thought as we made our way back down to the kitchen. The girl who'd nudged me to leave now clapped a hand on my shoulder and offered me a sunny smile. The first one I'd seen since I started working in the kitchen. "You did well," she told me in a lilting tone. "Most people freeze when they are in the presence of the king."

Except I wasn't most people. I'd had the crown prince's tongue in my mouth.

"Thanks," I struggled to offer in return.

After work ended for the day, I waited outside the kitchen doors for Mike, as he'd asked. He'd wanted to have dinner with me. The reason? I needed to make it up to him for ignoring him at lunch.

Pushing sweaty hair behind my head, I giggled. I was a hot mess but I had a date with the prince, one he wouldn't let me squirm out of because he was concerned about my eating habits.

Had I mentioned lately how wonderful he was?

It took him another fifteen minutes to show up but at least he was there, hurtling toward me, winded. "I'm sorry I'm late," he said immediately. "I was trying to get down here as fast as I could but I was caught in the hallway. There were people I knew and I couldn't make a clean break for it."

I waved it away. "It's fine. Hey, I have a question for you."

"If it's what we're having for dinner, I'm not going to answer. It's a surprise." He glanced down at the picnic basket over his arm and if it was possible, my heart melted even more.

But I had to ask before I forgot. "It's not about the food. Who is Dorian Jade?"

Mike stopped to stare at me. I could see his hesitation clearly. Taking my measure and trying to decipher what I knew and why I'd be asking him about the name. Finally, he sighed, then placed his free hand on the small of my back to guide me up the staircase. "I guess dinner will wait. Come on, Tavi. It's easier if I show you."

Instead of going to the dining hall, he brought me up two flights of stairs to the castle library on the second floor in the wing opposite the one where I stayed. He pulled at the vine-shaped iron handles. The muscles of his arms shifted and clenched as he pushed hard to open the doors.

"As I'm sure you can see, this is the royal version of our favorite room at school," Mike said in a hushed whisper. "But clearly no one spends any time in this room."

"Then why have it? Doesn't the public have access?"

He shifted aside to let me enter then closed the doors behind us. After making sure we were well and truly alone, he let out another sigh. "No. This is for royal access only. Oh, and the Elder Council, should they choose, although I think they have their own private resources somewhere else."

The patchy sunlight from the windows, with a view to the west, deepened into shade the further we stepped inside the room. Candelabras and gas lanterns burst to life as we moved past them. The white marble floor wound around high shelves, with large tables set here and there, accompanied by throne-like chairs.

Mike waved his hand and flames burst to life inside the cold fireplace. Far in the distance I could see windows leading out to a small mezzanine. And in front of me, books.

"The servants keep the place clean, but I'm relatively sure we're the only other people to come in here in years."

"Now you've shown me this, I'm not going to want to leave," I whispered, in awe. Although we were the only ones here with no librarian ready to breathe down our necks for being too loud.

Old habits die hard.

Mike led the way toward the left side of the room. He set the picnic basket on one of the empty tables he passed. "You know you can use this room whenever you want. Even though it's supposed to be royals only, no one would ever notice. It's at your disposal." Then he gestured toward the wall and the black tapestry draping from floor to ceiling. "You see this?"

I shrugged. "You're telling me the servants clean the drapes, too?"

"They do, but that's not the point." He pushed the black tapestry aside and underneath I saw a wall painting of a map. Old, I knew right away. Probably older than many of the books kept inside the library.

"So, this is Faerie in its entirety," Mike said, ripping the wall covering down and letting it pool on the floor. Half of the map had been blacked out, darkened with some sort of spell leaving a charcoal-gray haze over the paint.

I lifted my fingers to touch and found the air around the map thick and impenetrable.

Mike took my hand and moved it down, to the lower left corner of the map. He pressed my fingertips to the wall. "This is Eahsea, and the king's palace. A great forest separates our town from the majority of the cities in the land. The busiest ports are along the eastern seaboard. My father has assigned lords and ladies to oversee those areas though all are under his command."

"Why can't I see the other half?" I asked. "There's clearly some kind of spell in place."

"It's strange. I'm not sure exactly when it happened, because the other half of this map wasn't always blocked off. Maybe my father did it, maybe not. But, ah, twenty years or so ago, rebels stirred up resistance and constructed a magical wall between what they claimed as their half of the land and ours." Mike pointed to the demarcation line where the strange mist seemed to darken along the edge of the forest. "Our people aren't allowed to pass over the wall."

"Our people?" I wanted clarification.

"I suppose you could call us the Seelie." Mike turned to stare at me with his lips quirked. "It's a little confusing, I know. For a while it was kind of a joke. You asked about Dorian Jade? A few years ago, Dorian Jade rose to power in the rebellious half and declared their side to be Unseelie and made himself a king."

"Wait...you said your family doesn't belong to either court."

"For centuries, the Fae under my father's leadership have worked to cultivate an image away from those black and white lines. No more light and no more dark. One people. Then along comes Dorian Jade and he throws things into chaos."

Well, news to me. "Faerie used to be one kingdom and now it's two? I don't get it. I thought your father..." I trailed off, turning my attention back to the map. Trying to put the pieces together and failing miserably.

We hadn't been taught about courts in school. None of the Faerie History professors mentioned Dorian Jade, or a wall. I would have remembered.

"Pretty much two kingdoms, yes. Dorian Jade is too powerful for anyone to make a move against. At least, not right now."

I froze where I was, my limbs suddenly unwilling to cooperate no matter how I tried to make them work.

"Hey, Tavi, it's okay." Mike's voice reached me through the brain fog. "I'm not sure where you heard about Dorian Jade, but you have nothing to worry about."

Did I look worried?

He tapped his fingers against the map. "I mean, there are plenty of wonderful spots on our side of the wall. Plenty of places of beauty which Dorian Jade's fake monarchy can't touch." He then stepped back toward the table holding our picnic dinner. "I haven't been a part of the conversations with the Elder Council but Mom mentioned something about them having a plan."

Oh God. Maybe that's why the king and queen had wanted the Augundae Imperium. They'd planned to use it to take down Dorian Jade. And because of me, they didn't have it.

Some crazy hoarder witch with a smoking addiction did.

There were the storms to think about, still raging on without an end.

I couldn't focus any longer, my desire to know more about Dorian Jade completely forgotten along with what little had remained of my excitement over a dinner alone with Mike.

At this rate, I was going to single-handedly destroy Faerie.

13

I learned pretty quickly that being a part of the Elite Academy meant all of our training tasks were televised for the realm's entertainment.

Lane, in an uncharacteristic show of genuine concern for me—I think I might have turned green at some point the morning of the first game—assured me there was little possibility of actually dying. The world was watching and the television networks didn't want the students hurting themselves any more than necessary.

Any. More. Than. Necessary! He'd actually said those words.

Although, Lane finished, some of the tasks *could* get dangerous. *Particularly* if the student was a halfling who didn't have the skills—like I wouldn't recognize the little dig he threw my way.

Great. Just put a big sign over my head with flashing lights. HALFLING WITH NO SKILLS ABOUT TO GET KILLED FOR SPORT.

Maybe I'd make headline news.

Except, I thought on Wednesday morning while we waited for the first game to start, I did have skills. Or rather my wolf did. And although she was literally gnashing her teeth for a chance to rip the competition apart, I knew I had to proceed with caution and think every step through.

No wonder he said I looked a little green. I was sick to my stomach.

The moment Mike and I stepped out of the portal on Wednesday, we walked straight into chaos. The outside courtyard of the school was pure madness. There were cameras everywhere, and although I'd mostly gotten used to the permeating scent of magic, the air today was filled with expectation and excitement.

There were no classes. The games would take up the entire schedule for the day, and with Magnus Crackenbush standing on the front steps of the academy, calling for attention, I knew I'd rather write a thousand papers for potions than go through this.

Mike clapped me on the shoulder and I could feel his excitement. "This is it, Tavi. The first set of Summer Games! Are you ready?"

I swallowed hard. "No, I'm *not* ready."

"Aw, come on, I've seen you play Capture the Scroll, more than once. As long as we make sure you don't roll your ankle again, I'd say whatever the first game turns out to be, you will do well. Trust me."

"Yeah, but Capture the Scroll was a *game* game."

"So are these," Mike said with a smile. "The first category was resourcefulness, remember? Honestly, it could be anything."

I wish I had as much trust in myself as he did in me. And he looked so excited. So ready to dive right into whatever terrifying and potentially deadly game awaited.

I probably would have stayed in place and grown roots if Mike and his cronies hadn't ushered me along. Well, *Mike* did. Arlyss and Lane were only around to make sure they stayed in the spotlight, although we had all fallen into a comfortable place where they mostly ignored me and I pretended I didn't care.

The school remained gathered in front of the academy building with Headmaster Cyrus leaning against one of the stone columns looking like he was about to keel over and take a nap. The startling snow-white hair of his beard and hair trailed down to the belt keeping his trousers up, while the billowing sleeves of his robes hid most of him from view.

Cyrus called for attention the moment the professors manning the doors assured him we were all gathered and we were ready to proceed.

"Welcome again, students." His voice rang out above the crowd and within seconds he was met with complete silence. Even Mike stilled beside me with his attention focused completely ahead. Practically trembling with excitement, I saw. I shrank closer to him.

"I'm sure you are all excited to begin the Summer Games! Here to speak to you more on what to expect this fine morning is our games officiant, Magnus Crackenbush. Take it away, my boy."

The horned man strode to the center, relishing the limelight and the crowd's reaction. Today he'd chosen to dress in a robe the color of a spring crocus, a color that should have looked feminine on him. It didn't. Instead, it drew attention.

"As your headmaster stated, *welcome*," his deep voice boomed out. "Be prepared for untold delights this year, ladies and gents. My team and I have put together an entirely new program unlike anything you've ever seen before. Today, we embark on our first game to test your resourcefulness. Try to think of this less as a test and more of a way to show your prowess. Prove to the world, to Faerie, why you belong at Elite! Make us proud. Now, without further ado—"

He broke off in anticipation and I felt my stomach sink

further toward the ground. This was it. This was the big moment.

"There's no way I can back out of this, right?" I hissed to Mike. "No lifeline I can call for a time out?"

His eyes were bright as he shook his head, his attention completely focused on Magnus and the big magic he was about to do. "Nope, none. It's go time."

Power crackled over my skin until every fine hair stood to attention. My wolf, lurking beneath the surface of my consciousness, opened her eyes as well, preparing. Ready and tense and waiting. Whatever Magnus and the rest of his team had in mind, they were launching it, now.

The other students around me raised their collective voices in a huzzah and I closed my eyes to try and drown out the immense pressure in the atmosphere.

Though my vision had blackened when I reopened my eyes, things finally cleared and—I didn't know where I was. The courtyard and the school were gone, along with everyone else except students, and I found myself standing in the middle of green grass.

A heavily wooded jungle sloped away from me in every direction and the rest of the familiar landscape melted away into blue peaks of mountains. Moss-covered rocks punctured the ferns and low shrubbery, and in the distance, I saw the towering trunks of palms, giant red cedars, kapok and rubber trees. The wind now smelled of water and achingly sweet flowers.

We'd been transported into a rainforest. And it was growing larger by the minute. I couldn't tell what was real and what was an illusion.

Magnus's voice came as if from a great distance. "Now, students, for this first game, you are expected to navigate through the jungle to find the hidden temple. Only once you are inside the temple will you be able to get back to the school. You are not only allowed but *encouraged* to use whatever magic is at your disposal—with one rule: Do not harm your fellow players. Remember, this is a test of your own prowess. Good luck!"

The voice faded away, and when I glanced around again, I saw I was alone, utterly alone. My heart thudded in panic. Where the hell had everyone gone? Spinning around in a circle, I tried to spy some glimpse of the massive student body surrounding me just seconds ago. I swore I could still hear the lingering strains of cheers in the background but soon even those noises were drowned out by the caws and cackles of tropical birds.

"Mike? Where are you?"

No answer.

I had no idea where I was—if I *was* anywhere, and not just part of a massive illusion or magic trick. No choice at this point but to follow the game rules.

I pushed off through the foliage, hurrying deeper into the jungle. It was like being in the middle of the Amazon River basin. Heat and humidity pressed down on me and soon my sweat-soaked clothes clung to my skin. I tried not to think about the oppressive heat, stretching my neck to inhale the cool breeze. Nope, now my lungs were boiling. Shortness of breath made it kinda impossible to ignore the scorching temperature after all.

A hidden temple, huh? *This is a freaking death trap!*

Letting my shifter senses do the thinking for me and desperately trying to smooth out the tension and anxiety I carried, I pushed forward. My wolf led the way.

The jungle held secrets, for sure. Several times I had to run in a completely different direction at the roar of unseen predators, where even my wolf didn't know what we were up against. A peal of thunder rocked in the distance. Was it natural? Or had the outside world of storms somehow managed to penetrate this illusion?

I stumbled across a giant Venus flytrap which snapped at me as I passed. A spell calmed it long enough for me to avoid tendrils creeping across the dirt, ready to drag me into its gaping maw. A giant spider nearly grabbed me from overhead a time or two, and I narrowly ducked in time to avoid the hissing strike of a snake longer than I was tall.

Ripping off the spider's legs bothered me the first time I did it. But when those pincers grabbed my own leg and I had no choice, the second time around I didn't care overly much. It was a game, right? A stupid game for the amusement of others and the torment of, well, me mostly.

This is dumb as hell, I thought, securing my sweaty hair to the top of my head with a band from my wrist. I hadn't been planning on a jungle trek when I woke up this morning and if I had I would have packed myself some damn water. I sure didn't trust anything I'd manifest from this place. More than likely I'd spell myself some water contaminated with microscopic creepy crawlies. I had enough to deal with at the moment without adding to my misery.

I pushed aside a wide branch covered with garnet-colored garlands of flowers, then fell into open air when the ground suddenly ended. Spines pricked my skin and rocks did their best to bruise me as I slid down a sloping hill on a scream, landing on my tailbone hard enough for me to see stars, the breath knocked out of me.

I blinked a couple of times and tried to move my arms. Though it took a bit to get air back into my body, I finally managed to push up to my feet. Hot, dirty, and thoroughly irritated. A little pained but alive. Were the other students having such a hard time with this?

And trust me, I'd already tried a tracking spell to find the temple. I'd tried every piece of magic I could think of to find the damn place and none of it had worked. A test for resourcefulness my butt.

So, I trekked on through the jungle until the trees coalesced into a dense curtain of green and I eventually lost my way.

I knew time passed from the angle of the sun through the leaves. I came across other students only a handful of times, and most of them took one look at me and scoffed. One went so far as to tell me I was going to fail, before striding confidently away and not looking the least bit sweaty or irritated or dirty.

Just me, then.

Although I knew I looked a hot mess, I doubted it was my appearance that made the other student act this way. It was my blood.

Alone, I continued through the brush and soon even my wolf was ready to throw her paws in the air and call it a day. If I'd been able to shift without worry, I might have let her take over fully, though I didn't have a scent to track. At least then I might—

I tripped over a rock, flying forward on my hands and knees. Except the ground didn't remain solid when I landed.

I began to sink.

What the—

Quicksand.

"Shit, oh *shit!*" I managed to get out as the sand quickly spilled over my head and filled my mouth with pure white grains.

I never had a chance to even scream.

14

Each grain of sand did its best to choke me, lodging between my teeth and flowing toward my throat.

But the quicksand soon spat me out on the other side. I dropped through the darkness and hit a stone floor. Hard.

This time there was no mistaking the snap of bones in my arms.

Sadly, I was no stranger to broken bones, and despite my healing abilities, this one wasn't going away anytime soon.

Coughing, trying not to choke on the sand, I struggled to breathe against the explosion of pain in my arm.

It was time for the old *think, Tavi, think* game. Hopefully I could figure out a way to get out of here fast.

It took way too long before my frightened mind calmed long enough for me to utter a spell expelling the sand from my body. I lay on the ground for the longest time, rubbing my tongue over my teeth, looking for anything grainy the magic might have missed.

Something more than my ego had broken today, for sure.

Luckily it hadn't been a very long way down before the ground caught me.

I wiped the sand away from my mouth with my good arm and took a look around. Underground, certainly. There were dim shafts of light coming through what looked like openings where tree roots had burrowed down through the jungle soil. The roots met with stone built up in a wall.

I was underground in some kind of...

Oh. My. Had I accidentally found the temple?

A swift burning sense of hope had me scrambling to my feet. Had the quicksand been a miracle in disguise, bringing me right into the temple I was supposed to be looking for?

Dumb luck, maybe.

I cradled my broken arm against my torso, my mind flashing back to the last time I'd hurt a limb. It happened more often than I would have thought for a person like me. Then, Mike had been there to heal it for me. Now I was all alone, and although I knew a few spells to deal with cuts and swelling, I wasn't advanced enough to deal with broken bones. I couldn't take the risk of making it worse than it was. I didn't have the strength to waste on trying.

With no choice, I started walking, looking for...I didn't know what. Something to take me back to the school. A magic portal or something?

I had no idea.

Shaking off the pain from the snapped bone, I used protruding vine-like roots to pull me along the corridor, my eyes scanning my surroundings for signs of anything else prepared to hurt me. Snakes, spiders, traps hidden in the walls themselves. Maybe a magical bomb of some kind.

I fully expected one wrong step to send spikes shooting out at me, like in the movies. I was definitely no Indiana Jones, and honestly, I'd never wanted to be. I just wanted to make it out of here alive.

My skin pebbled the longer I walked through these strange chambers. At least the oppressive heat from above was more tolerable underground. There was no magic, no strange gut sensation giving me the right direction to go in. Light still slanted in from above and illuminated swirling dust in these empty tunnels.

I saw no signs of anyone or anything else. Thank God, because just thinking the word "tunnels" had my imagination running wild.

Grimacing, I rubbed my tailbone with my good hand, walking for what felt like hours through dark caverns. The walls were coarse, the ancient stone cracked. I didn't want to make too much noise and draw attention to myself since there was always the possibility I wasn't entirely alone. I pursed my lips and kept moving.

I strained my mind for some kind of clue I might have missed. Some way out of here or a secret clue in something Magnus had said to the group. When the hallway came to an abrupt halt, a dead end, I had to reverse and start all over again.

Taking a deep breath, I rested for a moment with my good hand on my hip, eyes narrowed. At least the building wasn't crumbling. This wasn't some kind of ancient temple where the jungle had done its best to eat away at the structure and reclaim it as part of the landscape. There was no lichen blemishing the walls or stone beneath my feet.

"Okay, Tavi," I said out loud. "Think. Think, Tavi."

The small hairs on the back of my neck rose again and though I whirled around, I still saw nothing behind me.

My brows drew together. One thing was obvious. No matter what kind of tricks my mind played on me, I was alone here. Had I come to the wrong place after all?

Hours passed and I felt like I was walking in circles.

Another turn and the crack of falling stones had me

hurrying forward. Boulders dropped, collapsing part of the floor where I'd been standing. The wall crumbled, leaving nothing but vines, roots, and hard-packed dirt behind.

I coughed, waving away the dust until the movement jabbed at my broken arm.

An unease settled inside of me, coating every nerve in my body.

I couldn't explain why the disconcerting sensation of being watched got to me. I had to be even more careful, I told myself, turning to study the rest of my surroundings. Shaking my head, I tried to walk forward again, my legs unwilling to cooperate.

The fall into this strange place was odd. How unlucky was I that I'd managed to stumble into quicksand and ended up here? I hadn't found another opening to try and climb out. I'd tried hugging the walls to find a way through but the shadowed depths all blurred together. No distinction. Nothing to tell me I was headed in the right direction.

Hey, at least the ceiling hasn't collapsed. My subconscious tried to be helpful but part of me wondered if the thought wouldn't bring about that very thing.

"Your time is up!"

Magnus's voice sounded like a loudspeaker overhead, and the unexpected magnitude of his words echoed through me, sending me screeching down on my knees with my good arm covering my head.

"The remaining students should brace themselves for the trip back," Magnus continued with amusement in his voice.

Um, what?

The magic swept me away a moment later, enveloping me in a cradle of warm air, completely opposite from the first trip into the jungle. Like a mother's embrace.

Or so I thought until the force of the spell sent me

tumbling when my feet hit solid ground again. I fell hard, barely managing to keep from hitting my broken arm on the way down.

When I finally opened my eyes, I was in the academy gymnasium with ten other dirty, battered students. Surrounded—*inevitably*—by the rest of the student body and the games crowd.

Including all the press. With their cameras. And their microphones.

Oh, just kill me now.

Heat flooded my face and I knew the attention was turned on me. I struggled to my feet, losing my balance and toppling back over when my knees refused to lock. Boy, this wasn't good. I scanned the approaching press for any kind of familiar face and saw nothing but smirks staring back at me.

"Tavi! Tavi, hold on."

And there was Mike, bursting through the crowd, not a golden hair out of place on his perfect head.

"Mike…"

He grabbed the hand I held out to him and helped me to stand, his face white and stricken. I was grateful when he grabbed me close, keeping me cushioned against his chest.

"What happened? I looked for you, where were you?" he asked on a rushed exhalation as he tried to get us out of the gym.

I shook my head. Leaning into him. Anxious and scared and comforted at once. "I don't know. It was like nothing I did worked. I was out there for hours—" *Had* it been hours? Or was the magic playing tricks on me?

"Your arm!"

"Yeah, I took a spill through quicksand."

"I'd always heard a student could get hurt or even die in the games. But I didn't think the school would actually let it happen. Hey, ignore them," he insisted as the press corps continued to hound us. "Don't pay anyone any attention. You look at me. Tavi, look at me." He leaned back only long enough to make sure he had my complete attention before cupping his hands around my broken arm.

A flash of heat found its way from his fingertips straight to the bone and in another second, I knew the broken pieces had knitted themselves back together. His magic tingled familiarly through me.

Wow, I needed that.

"It's okay." Mike brushed away a tear when I glanced up to meet his eyes, then chuckled. "You have nothing to be upset about. Are you all right now?"

I finally managed to say, "Yes. Yes, I'm fine. Did you make it through and find the temple?"

Mike grinned. "I did. I'm sorry you didn't." His head swooped up at the increasing noise level, the press moving closer to speak with the handful of students who hadn't passed the game. He narrowed his gaze at them. "Come on, let's get you out of here. I'm not going to stick around while they ask a billion questions."

Each step still hurt as Mike ushered us out. The darkened hush of the hallway was a balm.

"I know what will cheer you up," he said. "How about you and I go to the Solstice Carnival this weekend? It will give you something to look forward to, away from the chaos of the games and the stress of school."

I could barely look at him through my awkwardness. How could Mike still want to be so nice to me after my utterly miserable fail during the first game? "You want to go with *me*?"

It came out all wrong, a bleat of sound, and I shook my head.

"I mean, yeah. Duh. Of course," I finished lightly.

If I didn't know any better, I'd say he looked relieved.

"You're going to like the carnival," he insisted. "It's fun. Lots of food, carnival games, sideshows. It's really a big party to celebrate the approaching summer. Like the Fae really need an excuse to party."

He was trying to cheer me up by talking about the festivities instead of my failure during the first game. I didn't mind. In fact, I appreciated the light turn of conversation, as well as the lengths he went to in order to protect me from the crowd.

"It sounds great. I'm looking forward to it." A party would definitely be a good way for me to shake off the tension of these last few weeks. Plus, greasy food and spending time with Mike? What a way to lift my spirits.

We rounded the corner into the courtyard and found it nearly empty, most of the students sticking to the gymnasium for interviews and, no doubt, to tease the losers who hadn't made it through to the next round.

How had Mike managed to remove me from the equation? He must have used his princely authority to keep everyone from following us.

"Well, what about the Solstice Ball next weekend? Do you want to go with me to that too?" When I jerked around to stare at him, he was staring down at his sneakers. Was that...shyness? From the Crown Prince of Faerie? No, I must have hit my head harder than I thought.

Ah, the ball. I blinked once. "You mean, like a date? An official date?"

Gah, why couldn't I keep my mouth shut? I shouldn't try to put a label on things. Talk about awkward.

Mike walked toward the portal, the soles of his sneakers scuffing against loose stones. "I know it's still more than a week away but I really don't want anyone else to ask you. Because then I'd be stuck going alone."

More like the opposite. I would have been super lucky to

find a date if Mike hadn't done the asking, in this case. "Oh, I doubt you'd be alone. What about your fan club?" I rolled my eyes. "Like the prince would ever attend a dance alone."

"But you'll go?" he pushed. "With me?"

"You know I will. It will be my first Faerie ball. Now I have to go dress shopping."

"There's the spirit! You're going to have fun. I mean, I know things have been a little tough for you since you came to Faerie. It's a big transition. But the Solstice Ball is awesome."

I'd have to see if Melia would go with me Saturday morning.

When I raised my gaze to him, Mike was still looking at me. And I couldn't help but smile. Mike was one of the only people who really saw me. Not the dirt and the grime, the failures and the triumphs. He saw me. For me. If those things weren't enough to make me want to kiss him, he was also drop dead gorgeous.

I didn't regret saying yes when he asked me because I wanted to think about how much fun we would have instead of the possibility of it ending badly. Maybe this really was a date.

Yeah. Wishful thinking.

But his smile matched my own and for a breath of a second, we both leaned closer.

"Crown Prince Michael! Michael Thornwood. Over here!"

A hand grabbed Mike by the shoulder and whirled him around to the mass of Fae reporters and their cameras.

"Michael Thornwood, a moment of your time for an interview," one of the reporters stated.

Mike turned back to give me an apologetic shrug. "He's one of the reporters employed by the royals. It wouldn't look good for me to refuse." Not like he had a choice.

This time, I wasn't to be left out.

A throat cleared and when I shifted, I saw Selene staring at me, slinking forward. I swallowed a huge breath of suddenly stifling air. She was worse than the snake from the rainforest. At least it gave me a warning before it struck.

I spared a last look at the gold ring in the cobblestones, the portal back to the castle. Escape was so close.

She crooked a painted finger in my direction. "Come on, Tavi. Let's have a chat."

15

The pit in my stomach grew to gargantuan status and I was surprised I still managed to walk and talk at the same time. We found an empty bench a few yards away. Good, because I didn't want to lose sight of Mike.

I sat as still as possible under Selene's direct, bordering-on-hostile gaze. Wanting to turn away and bang my head against the nearest hard surface. I glanced over to her cameraman, but his face was neutral, stuck behind the lens.

As if an interview wasn't bad enough, I still wore my clothes from the game, while Selene was dressed in an immaculate white dress that clung to her curves and brought out the beauty of her full-blooded Fae features. Not a single black hair was out of place on her head.

Well, talk about a skewed balance of power. She was the princess and I was the dirt underneath the wheels of her carriage.

Selene cleared her throat to draw my attention. "Tell me about the first game," she prompted. "Tell me how you felt when you discovered you were alone in the jungle."

Don't squirm. Don't give her what she wants. "I'm not sure what you mean. Every student was alone in the jungle. Doing their best to find their way out," I said with a forced noncommittal shrug.

She wanted to corner me and use the element of surprise? I'd show her I wasn't the stupid failure everyone at Elite thought I was.

"Yes, but not *every* student here was handpicked by the king to attend the academy. *You* were." Selene tilted her head to the side to peer down her nose at me. "And yet you didn't finish the game. You were one of ten who did not make it to the temple before time ran out. I want your take on the experience."

The way she spoke, the way she made mental notes on my smallest movement...it was clear Selene knew something was up with me. Something different. I almost felt at this point she shadowed my every move, trying to uncover my secrets.

Maybe she was. Maybe she wanted me to be the story of her career because her extra senses told her I didn't belong in this world.

Lane had warned me to expect to give up all my biggest secrets in this competition. I hadn't thought it would be this soon.

And I hadn't expected it would come in the form of a beautiful Fae woman.

I told her what she wanted to know, my impressions of the first few hours of the competition. Selene prodded me into giving more than I wanted and a few times I had to rein myself back in before I said anything she would take the wrong way.

I wasn't sure how, but I knew it was a possibility.

"You said you fell through the quicksand? How terrifying," Selene pushed. Her features softened but I wasn't convinced. It was purely for the camera, and I barely bit back the nasty things I wanted to say to her. She didn't seem the least bit concerned. "What happened afterward?"

"I fell down into some kind of underground cavern and hurt my arm. Afterward, I simply followed the tunnels, trying to find my way out," I told her. Shifting away before she noticed my now not-broken arm and tried to figure out who'd healed me.

"And yet you never did?" she asked.

I shook my head. "No."

"I along with the rest of the world saw the moment you re-emerged in the gymnasium. A certain young gentleman, prominently known, bent over backwards to attend you himself, did he not?"

"Uh..."

I dug my nails into my palms.

"Prince Michael Thornwood. The two of you appear very well acquainted. In fact, if sources are to be believed, you danced together quite often during the welcome home dinner the king and queen threw for him."

Oh God. She knew! "Mike and I met at the Halfling Academy," I said evasively. Blood rushed to my head. "We're friends. Classmates."

Selene leaned forward. "Such good *friends* he would personally heal your broken arm? It's quite an intimate act, to heal someone."

She knew about the arm too?

The world spun around me, narrowing on the reporter's arching brows. "I don't believe so. I've had past injuries attended to by a school nurse and I don't think that counts as intimate," I argued. My skin itched once again, to the point where you'd think I'd be used to the sensation. I couldn't wait to get out of this meeting. She wanted to get a rise out of me and I was determined she would not.

But I knew Selene wasn't finished with me yet.

"Still, it is rather interesting, the fact that Michael Thornwood is most often seen in *your* company." Selene folded her hands on her lap. The picture of innocent curiosity. "You must be quite close. Does his position as next in line for the throne have something to do with your willingness to be around him?"

My lungs constricted.

"As I said before, we're just friends. He understands this is a difficult time for me, with my transition from the mortal world, and he is helping me the best he can. He is a good person. He will always help out a friend in need."

There, let her chew on *those* words for a while.

Selene shook her head as though trying to dispel her surprise, scribbling on her notepad, barely breaking eye contact. She asked me a few more questions lasting an eternity, the whole while appearing dissatisfied with my answers.

Fine. I didn't care how she felt.

At last the interview was over, and with a look she had her cameraman turning off his camera.

I was about to get up when Selene grabbed my chin with a hand, squeezing. Her touch was cold. Hard. Bruising.

She told me simply, "I know you're hiding something, Tavi Alderidge. I can sense it. And I intend to find out what it is."

The moment Selene released me, I bolted through the portal without waiting for Mike to finish his interview, calling the magic that would allow me to pass through from one area to the next.

And when I reached my bedroom to hide, blessedly alone, I let out a guttural scream, hands clawing into fists at my sides and with such force I felt the press of claws as my hands transfigured themselves.

The release did nothing for my nerves. My palm pressed against my forehead instead of going through a wall and it took much longer than normal for my breathing to return to normal. I wanted to cry. From desperation. From anger.

I lay in bed the next day, giving serious thought to staying home from school and skipping my classes. What was the worst that could happen, honestly? No one would miss me. Only Mike and our professors knew my name, and they only got it right half the time. The other half they didn't bother to look at me or call on me when I actually raised my hand.

The one thing forcing me out of bed every morning? I wasn't sure how absences were handled at the Elite Academy and if one this early in my tenure would count against me.

Although maybe if I pretended to be sick, I could get out of having to take part in the second game. A girl could wish.

I hurled myself at the bed and rolled over on a groan to punch my pillow. Then gave it an extra punch for good measure, though not hard enough to tear a hole. I'd worked too hard to get to Faerie—I couldn't screw things up now. No matter how much I wanted to back out and just sleep.

My body ached and although I knew there was a potion designed to heal those kinds of ailments from the inside out —we'd covered them in our classes—my brain felt too foggy to retrieve any of the information.

Pretty much I was as good as useless.

Despite it being the first day of the games, I'd still had to work in the kitchen. Raelynn definitely threatened physical repercussions if I didn't show up. I'd dragged myself to bed around nine, skipping dinner in favor of a good old-fashioned blackout.

I didn't wake up until the sun rose, and if I dreamed, I didn't remember.

Mike came to get me, as he did every morning, and although he remarked on how pale I looked, he said nothing about my hesitation in following him to the portal. And I didn't give him a reason to. We went to school as we had the day before, again greeted by the press and this time ushered into the auditorium by the professors.

Ready to be briefed on the second set of games.

I wasn't sure how the others kept their excitement at peak levels. Maybe the only person who felt the dense pressure of dread...was me.

"Exactly right, everyone. Settle in. Make yourselves comfortable." Today Magnus the officiant greeted us alone. Headmaster Cyrus had taken a seat in the first row like a spectator.

"Are you ready for this?" Mike whispered in my ear.

I mustered up a weak smile for his benefit. "Oh, sure. Never been more ready in my life."

"Today we have something very special planned for you. A chance for you to really flex those magical muscles," Magnus said, rubbing his hands together. "And perhaps a chance for those of you who didn't finish yesterday to redeem yourselves."

Why did I feel like all eyes were suddenly on me?

"Prepare for Game Two!"

Magnus sent a wave of magic across the auditorium, and this time when I opened my eyes, Mike stood next to me.

For a second.

I opened my mouth to ask him what was going on, but his form began to waver. As I watched, he began to disappear, until I was alone again.

The officials didn't waste any time, I thought with a shiver, rubbing my hands together. The first game had been barely twenty-four hours ago and already we were in for a storm of crap. What would today bring, I wondered.

What theme would this game test?

Like a magically powered loudspeaker, I heard Magnus overhead. "You are each in your own private space, students."

Yeah, he had that right. I stood in one of the courtyards outside the castle. A stone fountain bubbled merrily, the surface of the turquoise water filled with floating pink and white roses.

"Now," Magnus said with obvious glee, "there are fifty relics hidden in the clouds in the sky. You have two hours to be one of the fifty students to grab a relic and win the game. Use whatever means are at your disposal to reach them. Your time begins now."

More advanced Fae would know spells enabling them to fly, while others, like Nurse Julie back at the Halfling Academy, had been born with wings. I only knew a handful of students with wings. Surely, they would be the first to reach the relics and claim them. As for the rest of us...

I groaned, head dropping forward until my chin hit my chest. As a half shifter, I had the power of transfiguration; a rare magic found only among those with shifter blood. I could literally become a bird. Like the crow showing up at my window. I could go get one of the relics and be done in minutes.

But because transfiguration was so rare, and only showed up in shifters, I couldn't use it. It would be a dead giveaway.

I wanted to beat my head against something hard. Anything would do.

Down a short flight of steps, the rear lawn stretched out like a flat plain toward the towering trees of the forest border. I couldn't see any other students around me but I sensed them, like a niggling sensation in the back of my mind. It was like we were cut off from each other to do this task. Maybe that was why I'd seen Mike for a split second before he disappeared. He could still be right beside me and I would never know.

Stepping onto the grass, I took a deep breath, staring skyward. I had a pretty good grasp of elemental magic, though it was introductory stuff. I wasn't sure I could actually use air to levitate myself into the clouds without ending up plummeting back down to earth.

Forget breaking another arm. I'd be a pancake.

Still, it was worth a try. Since Fae were inherently connected to the land, elemental magic came easier to us than anything else. Of course, there were those who felt more connected to air, say, than water or earth or fire. For me, given my halfling nature, I'd always worked better with earth. Which was probably why I wanted to stay with my feet planted on the ground.

I stretched my hands out at my sides. Wiggled my fingers. A thought brought the wind to me, a brisk breeze unable to even get my feet off the ground.

Okay, apparently I needed to try harder.

I kept uttering the spell words until my throat ached. The wind pulsed around my body with enough strength to send my hair flying into a halo around my head. The magic brewed inside of me, calling the elements, using the strength of the land itself to aid me.

Come on.

Still, it was never enough. I managed to get my feet a few inches off the ground a few times but nothing like the strength needed to get me into the clouds.

The more time went by, the angrier I became.

"This is ridiculous!" I yelled out. Thankfully alone. I assumed.

How was this possible? I'd done better at the Halfling Academy than I did today, even with my bucket full of holes memory! I could harness a ball of pure air with enough force to knock things off of shelves. I manifested fire out of nothing and water from a stone.

But I couldn't do *this*? There were probably a dozen artifacts above my head right now and I couldn't reach any of them.

It felt like no time at all before Magnus's voice sounded again over the magical loudspeaker. "All right, folks! All fifty relics have been obtained. Time to head back. Game two is officially closed!"

The magic pulled me back to the auditorium, my chin dropping to my chest.

I'd failed. *Again*.

16

"Tavi! Tavi, over here."

The moment I manifested back in the school, the first thing I saw was Selene running toward me.

"I'd like a word with you."

I waved a hand to cut through the air and turned in the opposite direction. "Leave me alone," I snapped. I wasn't in the mood.

With the end of game two, the school had officially let out for solstice break and I didn't plan on sticking around to see what anyone thought of this. All I wanted to do was go back to the castle to bury my head in my pillow and not come up for air for a few hours.

But Selene, with the tenacity of a mother securing a mate for her single daughter, tracked me out of the school and down the sloping steps towards the village. I wondered if I put on a burst of speed if it would help me lose her. She knew the place much better than I did, so probably not.

"Hold on a minute. I want to talk to you," she called out. "It's a little hard to keep up in these shoes."

I listened to the click of her heels on the stones. "Haven't you bothered me enough? Or do you want to do a full-length feature on how the poor little half-breed can't manage to finish a single task?"

I wanted to scream again, barely able to keep the hysteria to myself.

It wasn't until she reached me that I noticed she didn't have her cameraman with her. Selene finally caught up and took me by the shoulder, leaning close to say, "Don't you think it's strange you couldn't do those two simple tasks?"

Knowing I would give her my full attention and stop walking.

Knowing her words would do the trick this time.

I stopped in shock, my spine straightening at the weight in her words. "What do you mean?"

"Why do you think you're at the Elite Academy, Tavi, when it seems like you don't have the skill set to be there? It's like they're proving a point, isn't it?" Selene continued, her voice dropping low. She took another step closer until if I turned my head, our noses would touch. "Like you've somehow been maneuvered into a situation where you can't win. It must seem strange to you."

I finally turned around to face her. What was she getting at?

"You...you think I've been forced to lose on purpose?"

Today Selene had adorned her curves in a dress of pale yellow, softening the harsh lines of her face and hugging all the right places. If I hadn't been on the receiving end of her interview, I might have said the picture she put together looked soft. Trustworthy.

I knew better. She dressed in a way she knew would get the results she wanted. Where had she stashed her minion with the camera *this* time? Maybe he lurked around a corner waiting for me to slip up and give him something juicy. I wanted to turn around and scour the hidden places around us but Selene kept hold of me to make sure I didn't bolt off again.

Sadly, I also needed to know what she knew, so I wasn't going anywhere.

"This isn't on the record," I said immediately. "Whatever you have to say to me, we say it on our terms and not for the rest of the world to hear."

She looked at me like I had told her I had an attached twin hidden in my shirt. "Yes, it is on the record."

I wasn't in the mood for her games. "Okay, your choice." Shrugging, I turned to walk away.

"Okay, okay. *Fine*." Selene jogged to keep up with me, saying the words with a roll of her eyes. "It's all off the record. I promise."

I didn't put much stock in the promise of a Fae like Selene because I knew there were always loopholes. Still...

I faced her, right there on the steps leading down to the village, and although I heard the school's commotion in the distance, it was like we were the only two people in the world. A short spell ensured a bubble of silence protected us to keep us from being overheard.

"Why don't you tell me what you know? Why do you think I was made to attend the Elite Academy on purpose?" I asked her right off the bat. What kind of suspicions did Selene harbor, to the point where she felt compelled to seek me out?

Selene blew out a breath and for the tiniest fraction of a second, her mask of cool detachment slipped. I noticed a single hair out of place today, just one sticking straight up. Was she slipping?

"The tasks this year are relatively tame compared to some in the past, Tavi. Tame enough most of your class-mates are making it through these games with little effort.

162

It's strange to me the game officials chose these tasks the year the school brings in a halfling."

"You think they dumbed the games down...because I'm here?" I clarified.

"I think they dumbed down the games to make your failure seem epic. A direct and stark contrast to the other students, designed for you to stand out. Just as I believe there is more going on than meets the eye." Selene stopped, heaved a sigh. "Look, our viewer numbers are way up because more than half of the realm wants to know how the half-breed is going to do. We've never had better ratings than we have since we began to cover your activity during the games. It's incredible."

I scoffed. "Well, then, I'm sorry I'm letting everybody down."

"Oh no," Selene hurried to correct. "No one is let down. If anything, the worse you do, the happier the people are. Don't you understand?" She spoke slowly to get through to me. "No one wants to see you succeed through the games. Although there are a few we've polled who are rooting for you."

A hard knot settled beneath my ribs and I rubbed at the suddenly sore spot. "I don't get what you're saying. People love that the tasks are easier and I'm still failing? No," I said.

"I'm saying," Selene explained, "I think someone is purposely choosing tasks that look easy but require higher levels of knowledge. To keep you from advancing. Perhaps there is even a spell in play to prevent you from accessing your power. Do you understand?"

"But...why?"

"I don't know, Miss Alderidge. You tell me. What is so special about you?"

At the moment? Nothing besides a truly spectacular rise

of acid reflux. "Your guess is as good as mine. Still, if you're right, then someone purposely wants me to fail."

"It would seem."

Selene and I chatted for a few more minutes but the bulk of the conversation had already occurred. We said our goodbyes and I walked across the village toward the castle instead of returning to use the portal. Weirdly enough, I didn't hate her for what she'd said. Neither did I think this another chip she'd played in her game. If Selene even had a game. If I boiled down her essence, what I understood about her, she wanted the ratings. Which meant she'd have no reason to talk to me about her suspicions and let me on to what she knew, which might lead me to do better in the games.

Right?

I still had my kitchen work to do. And afterward, although part of me knew I should have stopped to talk to Mike about his experience with the game today, I went straight upstairs. I needed alone time, and a moment for my racing pulse to settle and my thoughts along with it.

Grabbing a plate of food, I returned to my room for a shower, homework. Maybe even a little television. But I quickly turned the TV off when every channel broadcasted coverage from today's game. I didn't want to see myself on there, failing to produce even a small breeze.

The roast beef sat heavily in my stomach and I laid a hand across it to comfort myself. Emotional eating, check.

Two assignments done and a mountain of reading still to do. Check.

I should take the accomplishment as a win instead of brooding on what I hadn't done. And normally I would, but for some reason, since coming here I had a hard time staying positive. Then I thought about Mike and the carnival waiting for us. A *date*, and one I could not mistake for anything else.

A tap at the window caught my attention and when I turned in my chair, I saw the friendly neighborhood crow waiting for me.

"Oh hey!" I said to it. Rising with a smile. "What are you doing here? I'm sorry to tell you I ate everything tonight. Not even a scrap left for you."

But the crow wasn't interested in food, and it wasn't interested in hanging around. It dropped off a second piece of parchment before quickly taking flight, disappearing into the navy and ebony sky.

My heart flipped as I bent to pick up the paper.

SOMEONE ELSE KNOWS YOU'RE HERE. SOMEONE OTHER THAN ME.

PLEASE, TAVI. GET OUT BEFORE IT'S TOO LATE.

17

I t was a good thing I didn't have school the next morning, as I spent most of the night either in full-blown panic mode or having nightmares.

Who knew I was here? And what would they do to me if I stayed?

My mind conjured up every terrible thing it could think of to keep me hyperventilating until my head felt light and I almost passed out. Someone from the Grimaldi pack had seen me go through the portal into Faerie. Had they found a way to sneak in undetected?

That led me to thinking about the Augundae Imperium. Did Barbara still have it in her possession? Was it Barbara who had gathered enough magic to follow me here?

So many questions. I felt like I might never sleep again.

Saturday kicked off the Solstice Carnival celebrations in the large meadow behind the castle. The caravans arrived in the early morning hours before the sun even rose. Through my window I watched a team of hundreds of Fae setting everything up. It took most of the day, and by mid-morning, I could smell the food cooking. There were vendor tents stretched to the edge of the forests, with wide green paths between them.

By nightfall, the lights were strung and the midway rides up and running.

The carnival was a nighttime thing, or so the girls in the kitchen told me. The moment the sun dipped below the horizon, I knew Mike would come and fetch me.

I'd decided I'd had enough of him coming to fetch me from my room and said I'd rather meet him in the gardens instead. I didn't want him to always feel like he had to come and drag me from my room to go anywhere.

No mystery there.

The whole mess of the last week—and let's face it, the first one too—had me agonizing in front of the bathroom mirror for what felt like a good hour because I wanted to look pretty. Not just for him, but for myself. I wanted to dress in something I knew made me feel good and spend one night, *one*, without worry. I wanted to focus on having a good time and letting the rest of the crap fall away.

I put on my favorite white tank top with pearl buttons down the center and a pair of khaki-colored linen shorts. Completed with sandals and a loose wave in my hair, I was satisfied with the makeup and the look.

So was Mike, apparently.

Heat curled in my stomach as his eyes widened and his mouth rounded on a whistle. "It's nice to see you looking relaxed," he finally said. As though it had taken him a little bit to figure out what to say and find his voice.

I tugged at the bottom of my tank top. "Yeah, I'm looking forward to tonight. I remember going to carnivals when I was a kid. I always had a good time."

Of course, I'd gone with other shifter kids. But Mike didn't need to know that and it hardly mattered anyway. I tried hard not to gawk at him, dressed in a black shirt casually unbuttoned at the neck to show his tanned skin underneath. Black slacks that accentuated long legs and trim butt. Tried not to gawk and totally failed.

"It's going to be an experience," he told me as we walked down the marble steps toward the green. "The entire town and most of our neighbors turn up for the Solstice Carnival. There are so many things to eat."

"Mmm, carnival food." I smacked my lips.

"Not only the things I've read about for mortal fairs. There are also Fae delicacies you can only get during the solstice."

The man knew the way to my heart, no doubt about it. I couldn't wait.

We walked from the gardens down onto the lawn and soon the sounds of the Solstice Carnival grew loud. The lights were blinding, a draw for not only students but everyone around. Would I see Melia here? I hadn't even thought to invite her. Of course she'd be here. Excitement quickly pushed any lingering guilt aside.

The people were prepared for an occasion, both high and low Fae hustling around with their arms full of bouquets and food. There were streamers and banners and laughter in the air.

"Are all celebrations in the realm like this?" I asked Mike.

He turned to face me, smiling. "Not *all* of them."

Something in my chest started to tighten until I forced out a breath. To have the time alone with him...it was everything I needed.

Mike swept his hand out and I took the gesture as an invitation to lead.

"Come on. You choose where we go next. You're going to love the food."

I opened my mouth but felt all the wrong things ready to come out. So I shut it, smiled, and tried to take in the sights as we strolled through the balmy night. I tried not to worry about the people staring at us or what they might think. I gestured toward the vendors and invited Mike to talk about this, about his people. About what he loved.

The revelry had its own beauty. People danced and ate. There were rides designed to steal your breath and a thousand different treats to try. Mike was right. I did love the food. Somewhere in the distance there were drums. There were strings and horns and harps. Music filled the air to the point I couldn't help but want to dance, feeling my joy returning, all for the love of the sound.

Of life.

Mike and I lingered at the edge of it, caught between making jokes and watching the people. After we tired of watching, we joined in and went on every ride the carnival had set up, Mike holding my hand as we went. We played faerie games and ate all kinds of things I could never even begin to imagine. Seeing Mike tip his head back to laugh gave me more joy than I almost felt I deserved.

How had he gone a year without this kind of happiness at his fingertips? In comparison, the mortal realm was dull and boring. Stagnant.

Finally, he caught my gaze and said, "You haven't seen any of the sideshows yet! All those tents back there? Palm readers and tarot cards galore."

"And you haven't won me a prize. Shame on you!" I pointed toward the curved bow and arrow set serving as top prize for one game. "I thought for sure you would have this game in the bag. Come on, Mike."

Keeping eye contact with me, he proceeded to breeze right through the game as if he could do it in his sleep. A victory bell went off.

I chuckled and shifted closer to him. "Okay, you've made your point."

The small warmth in my stomach, the one that always burst to life when I saw him, grew larger and stronger the more time we spent together. And I didn't ever want it to go away.

Mike waited until I'd accepted the bow and quiver of arrows—an odd prize, but cool—before putting his hand on the small of my back. "Come on, Tavi," he said. "There are plenty more things to see before the night ends. I want you to have your fill of what Faerie has to offer."

And maybe I wanted to have my fill of *him*, too. For as long as we had together.

Around midnight, Mike led me toward one of the oracle booths on the outer limits of the solstice celebrations.

"This is the last one," he promised with a laugh. "You look like you're about to pass out."

I was hot all over in a good way. It would never get old, I decided. I hooked my arm with his, peering at the people walking by. I felt Mike's eyes on me as we passed between the tents, and I tore my gaze from the lights, watching the shadows pass over his face. Suddenly the cheers and music of the carnival felt very far away. It was only the two of us. No one else in the world.

My exhaustion slipped away with the acknowledgment. If Mike had asked me to, I would have stayed awake with him for the rest of the night, making our way through the labyrinth of revelry and happily getting lost.

"You must have been to so many of these," I managed to say, dragging my gaze away from him when heat burned my face.

"Oh yeah," he agreed in a husky voice. "And I still look forward to them every year. I hope they never stop."

"You're not too bored doing it all again with a newbie like me?"

He shot me a look. Like I had better be kidding. I laughed softly and a calm silence enveloped us for a moment until we found our groove with each other again. And listening to Mike's laugh I stopped hearing the celebrations around us altogether. We walked close enough to touch continuously, his fingers grazing mine. Warm and sturdy. He stroked his finger down mine and I shivered.

"Ah, here she is."

I hadn't realized we'd arrived at the booth, and I whirled around to look at the striped purple-and-pink tent. I read the sign: "Madam Muerte?"

Mike handed me a few gold coins. "Here. This is on me. She's a real hoot. I went to her last year and she had some wild things to say. You are going to enjoy this."

I wanted him to elaborate on what he'd heard but a hiss of sound interrupted us. The curtains slid aside and a short brunette woman beckoned us forward. "You're here to get a reading from the great Madam Muerte?" she asked in a low croak.

She reminded me inexplicably of Barbara. A young gypsy version of Barbara.

The woman sat behind a table, with a long cord of black-and-white hair secured in a braid behind her, the top of her head wrapped in a red scarf. She'd tinted her cheeks a bright shade of rose to match the scarf, with several lines of gold hoops threading through both ears.

For some reason, looking at her, I didn't want to go in. The gold suddenly burned my palms and I struggled not to wipe my hands on my shirt.

I shook my head and said to Mike, "You know what? I think I'm okay. I'm actually getting a little tired."

"Trust me, this is going to be fun. It will only take a minute," Mike insisted. He pushed me forward when my heels wanted to dig into the ground.

"Are you sure—"

The fortune teller didn't take my hesitation for an answer. She reached out and grabbed me by the wrist, pulling me into the stifling tent.

"Come, girl. Don't be afraid." Her voice came out in a drawl of sound. An accent I could not place for the life of me, like a mixture of Romanian and Spanish.

But why? I wondered, drawing in the scents of sandalwood and other burning incense, the smoke going straight to my head until I had no choice but to take the seat across from her. Dizzy, I watched her sit in a flounce of fabric. Eagle eyes drank me in, assessed my measure even as she reached out to grab my hand.

"Come closer." She pulled at me, and where she touched, my skin felt like ice.

I needed to get out of there.

"What do you see, Madam Muerte?" Mike asked, standing behind me. "Anything interesting?"

The carnival worker paused to inhale. "The universe unravels her secrets to me. What is your name, child?"

I didn't want to give it to her, although Mike happily supplied it seconds later. Drat it!

Neither one of us expected her to go into convulsions the moment she closed her eyes. Her breath exploded from her chest.

"Terror! Pain. What have you done, child?" Her hand clutched mine, her fingernails digging in deep, the rest of her shaking. "What have you *done*?"

She would not let go of me no matter how hard I tried to pull away. Any harder and I'd bleed.

"Um, Mike? Is this normal?" I asked desperately.

"The catalyst to the end is here. The coming of the end is here. What have you brought with you, when you crossed between worlds?" Madam Muerte gripped me harder and leaned forward until her face loomed inches from mine, her eyes boring into mine, searching, searching. Her voice rose on a screech. "Stormy skies! Secrets! Great prophecies!"

Oh God, she was talking about the Augundae Imperium. I'd heard it was meant to fulfill a prophecy but I'd ruined everything by stealing it.

"You've brought the end with you! You have doomed us all. You are the storm, the fulfillment of the Faerie Prophecy."

My stomach flipped. "Mike, help!" I couldn't take any more.

For an older Fae she was surprisingly strong and I found I couldn't break her grip on my own. Mike rushed forward to free me from the mad gypsy.

She began to chant, her eyes rolling back into her head:
At 'croaching light of black moon morn,
A shifter child shall be born.
An innocent and pure of heart
Born to rip the Fae apart.
Born to rip the Fae apart.
A wicked end, downfall's start,
And falling into endless night,
Shall bathe the blood with sweet delight.
And as the light of day is done,
The fearsome battle—

He didn't waste another moment. The instant the connection broke he grabbed me and hurried both of us out of the tent. My heart pounded until I heard nothing but my pulse in my ears. The words had sounded familiar to me, but I couldn't remember where I'd heard them. In a book somewhere, maybe?

It didn't matter. Nothing mattered while I still felt her grip on me. Mike pushed me between tents a good distance away from the still-screaming Madam Muerte.

"Calm down," he soothed.

I slapped a hand on my chest and felt my heart close to bursting. "Calm down? Are you kidding me right now? She nearly gave me a panic attack." I glanced over my shoulder and swore I saw the tent shaking.

"I think the feeling is mutual." Mike tried to give me a hug but I didn't want to be touched. Not with those words circling in my head.

"What the hell, man?" I reached out to slap at him lightly when he got too close. "She was *terrifying*."

I couldn't stop shaking. I couldn't stop fidgeting, too much energy inside of me. The words...what had she said? Something about a storm, and a prophecy? Something about a shifter child being born—

The realization washed through me in a tidal wave of pure ice.

The Faerie Prophecy.

I'd read about it in one of the books at the Halfling Academy library, but I hadn't actually finished it. I'd thought it too obscure and just scary enough to make me not want to read to the end. Did Mike know about the prophecy?

When I turned back to him, I caught him studying me, with his hands in his pockets and his brows drawn down in concern. "Hey, don't take her seriously. She's known locally as a crackpot."

"You said it would be *fun*," I argued.

"Well, I didn't think she would start screaming about the apocalypse! I'm sorry."

Oh God, had Madam Muerte actually said the word

apocalypse too? I could no longer be sure of anything. My mind was zipping with thoughts all jumbled together. But the main thread was a feeling of dreadful guilt. As if I alone was responsible for so many terrible, terrible things.

I tried to shake off the fear and worry but failed miserably. My fingers trembled and the rest of me felt like spaghetti left too long in the pot. Loose, without balance, without strength.

"Hey, you look pale. Are you sure you're okay?"

My head still swam and before I knew it, Mike had his hands on my shoulders to keep me steady and continued to talk in a low, soothing voice.

"Tavi, breathe it out. She didn't have anything real to say. It's all for show. Sport. It's a carnival, remember?"

The food and treats we'd had earlier sat heavy in my stomach now. "She really creeped me out." I closed my eyes and tried to do what Mike said, finding it hard.

"I know. She's absolutely nuts. You can be sure I'll let Father know about her. If this is the kind of act she's resorted to in order to draw in gold from the people, then she has no business being in Eahsea."

The deep breaths were starting to work and I finally calmed down enough to tell Mike, "No, you don't have to talk to your father about her. I'm sure she was just putting on a show. It's fine. I'm stressed enough I started to take her seriously." I offered up a weak smile. "Probably doing her best to play the part and earn her money. Right?"

He nodded vehemently. "You're right. Nothing to worry about."

Except her spiel about the storms. About secrets. Those rang dangerously close to home for me.

I raised my gaze to meet Mike's, holding on to him. Watching as the tension slipped from him and his smile grew warmer. Sweeter.

"Tavi?"

"Yeah, Mike?"

His eyes went dark. "If I kiss you...are you going to run away again?"

My breath hitched and I shook my head, feeling helpless. "No. Not this time." I didn't want to run and I wasn't going anywhere.

He grabbed hold of my waist and pulled me against him, my front molding to him, his hands possessive as they slipped lower to caress my hips. Such a different sensation this time around. Such light to the darkness of Madam Muerte's tent.

It overwhelmed me.

Our lips touched, desperate. Starved for each other as we leaned into the embrace. I gasped as he deepened the kiss, his tongue threading through my lips as one hand took hold of my hair.

Heat and desire. More than desire. *Need.*

His other arm encircled my waist and I clung to him as though I would be absorbed into his body. The rush was even stronger this time, mixed also with surprise and a tidal wave of joy. This was our second kiss, and I wondered if I would ever get used to it. Ever get used to knowing Mike liked me the way I liked him, when I'd spent most of my life believing I was nothing but a freak.

A boy liked me.

A boy who was smart and good and funny. A *prince*, who could have any girl he wanted, in any world. But he was here with me. I sighed against him.

Mike was the one who broke it off this time. "Tavi, you are amazing," he said, swiping his tongue along his bottom lip and smiling.

I gave him a tremulous smile back. "You still think so?

Even though I just got accused of being some harbinger of disaster or whatever?"

He chuckled. "Madam Muerte is a crazy person trying to make money by telling dramatic fortunes. Forget about it. It had nothing to do with you personally."

But as he led me back into the lights and noise of the carnival, I wasn't so sure anymore.

18

The storms reached a peak in the coming days, the sky growing blacker with no end to the thunder. Lightning split the sky and sent even the bravest Fae deep into their homes to wait for a pause in the needle-like rain that seemed to deliberately drive into the skin.

The weather had gotten so bad the next two games were rescheduled. With classes out for break, I had a miraculous opportunity to take a chunk out of my back load of homework and maybe get caught up on reading some of the textbooks I was supposed to study for the coming semester.

"Get your head out of your rear, girl, and focus! You're not paying any attention to what you're doing."

Raelynn's voice ricocheted through me and the plate I held crashed to the floor and snapped into three clean pieces. I groaned, bending down to pick them up. "I'm so sorry."

She scoffed, one of her favorite forms of communication when it came to dealing with me. "What are you sorry about? This is easy magic. You should be sorry about the terrible job you're doing of kneading the sourdough bread."

"What do you mean, easy magic?" I clasped the plate pieces to my chest.

This time, in response, her eyes crossed, as though I'd told her a terrible joke. "Do you mean to tell me no one has ever taught you how to mend a broken piece of crockery?"

"I don't think anyone calls it crockery anymore," I said dryly.

"And if that's what you've chosen to focus on, then the answer must be *no*. My goodness, girl, what *do* they teach you at school? Clearly nothing practical, otherwise you wouldn't be near tears over a shattered plate. Well, go on!" Raelynn impatiently gestured for me to set the pieces down on the countertop. Then moved me into a standing position facing them. "It's very simple. One of the reasons why we don't sweat the small stuff when things break around here."

"Then why are you yelling at me every five minutes?"

"Because you have the skills of a dishrag and half the charisma," Raelynn snapped back, although I noticed a hint of a smile on her face. She grabbed my hands, holding them in the air above the plate. "The word is *raksash*. We connect with the element of earth when we fix or mend. The materials for the plates came from the earth, and it is that magic we access when we say the word. Understand? Try it."

It sounded like nothing but a hiss to me. Still, I did as she instructed, letting the spell loose and watching to see if the plate responded. Nothing.

"Don't worry. It takes a little bit of practice to get the right inflection," Raelynn instructed. "Not to mention the connection to the land. I'm not sure if it will come as easily to a transplant like yourself. Try the word again, and this time with more emphasis on the last syllable. Feel the magic deep in your gut."

It took me several more tries to get what she called the *right inflection* and the three pieces of the plate finally mended themselves back into a single unit. I stared at it for the longest time, unsure as to why something that to most was a small piece of magic seemed to me one of the most important things I'd ever accomplished.

"Holy crap. I did it!"

Raelynn swatted me on the back for a job well done. "Yeah, and about time, too. You're going to need a few more lessons on useful magic before you pass the Raelynn test. More important than any you'll face at your fancy school. Now get back to work. Your shift is almost up."

Although I still had to work, I had another big event to look forward to at the end of the week: the Solstice Ball. Plus having the games scheduled for this week pushed back? Awesome! If the weather weren't a factor, I'd say things were finally starting to turn in my favor.

It was too much to ask for and I knew it. Although I spent the rest of the week working and focusing on the upcoming ball, I waited for the other shoe to drop, so to speak. Waited to see what other bad things would fall straight on my head.

If I'd thought the Solstice Carnival a marvelous sight, including all the preparation leading up to the big night, it was nothing compared to what went into the Solstice Ball. There were servants crowding the hallways night and day.

Friday afternoon, I got off work earlier than expected and hurried to change before meeting Melia to go dress shopping. She knew a place in town, having explored at leisure—at least she had the time, I thought enviously—and assured me we would find something perfect for the occasion.

I wished she were coming with me to enjoy the festivities. Unfortunately, she hadn't received an invitation, telling me over the phone only the elite attended the party.

Was that who I was? One of the elites?

Nah, I thought hastily, hurrying my steps to keep ahead of the rain.

Although I'd grown up with money—well, my uncle's money—I'd never felt like wealth made me someone special. A little entitled, maybe, and a little spoiled because I could buy whatever I wanted, but there were more important things I lacked that money couldn't buy.

Such as *parents*.

The streets in the village were quiet; everyone had been driven inside by the constant rain. I grasped the umbrella handle tightly and hurried along toward the address Melia had given me.

It wasn't long before I saw her huddled next to the door with her arms wrapped around her chest. The moment she caught sight of my umbrella, her face lifted. "Tavi, come on! You're going to float away. This rain is a little insane, isn't it? I can't believe it! And people are saying it isn't natural."

I sloshed toward her and shuffled the umbrella to the other hand to give her a hug with my right arm.

"This weather is disgusting," Melia went on. She had her hair up in a messy bun but there were wild curls fluffing around her face from the rain. "Come inside. Here, they have a place for you to stash your umbrella."

I did as she asked, stowing away the umbrella before following her into the store.

"Meli, I'm sorry," I said, wanting to get the awkwardness out of the way quickly.

She blinked at me. "About what?"

"About going to the Solstice Ball with Mike. I hate that you aren't going too, but to be honest I never expected him to invite me. At most I figured I might be needed for extra help—"

"Girl, please." She waved my concerns away like batting gnats out of the air and pushed me further into the boutique. "I have to work, anyway. Although I will expect a full and detailed rundown of everything from clothes to food. Especially the food. Do you understand?"

I nodded seriously. "I won't fail you."

Melia walked to one of the racks and flipped through dresses without really looking. Ethereal fabrics fluttered beneath her fingers. When she glanced over at me, wondering why the hell I was standing so far away instead of right next to her, I hurried forward to join her. "So. Tell me about the games."

"You already know about the games." I didn't want to depress her, anyway. Shopping was supposed to be fun. "I'm sure you saw everything about my devastating defeat on television, since everything is for public consumption."

"I saw how the media painted things. I want you to tell me what *you* think. What you experienced. I mean, Tavi...it's not like you to fail at your tasks. You're one of the most determined people I know. Determined enough to—" Her voice dropped to a nearly inaudible level. "—to break into a warded room and steal a priceless historical object of power."

I cut a quick warning glance at her. There weren't many people in the boutique thanks to the weather but we didn't need anyone overhearing the conversation. "You keep those thoughts to yourself. And yeah, I know." Should I tell her about my suspicions? About the dogged reporter Selene and what we'd spoken about the other day? "It seems like no matter what I do, winning—or even doing well—is out of reach."

"Like I said. Not like you." She flipped through the rest of the gowns, shook her head, and moved on to the next rack.

I could finally relax. I followed her and let my own fingers trail over fabric that felt like silk but a thousand times softer. "You're right. It's not like me at all! The other students are getting ahead and I keep falling behind no matter how hard I try. Not to mention doing all this extra work in the kitchen. It's not a bad place, really, and most of the people who work there are nice."

"But?"

"Exactly. *But.*"

I told Melia about Raelynn and the other girls on staff. I told her about classes, about the headmaster, and how Magnus had magically transported us to different locations for each game.

"Whew. Sounds like some big magic going on at your school."

I scoffed gently. "You think?"

"So, you kinda feel like nothing you learned at the Fae Academy for Halflings has really prepared you for what to expect now."

I shook my head. "I'm not sure if it's lack of preparation or if someone is intentionally making things hard for me. I mean, I don't want to sound like I'm complaining, but—"

Melia placed her hand over mine and silenced me. If I didn't know any better, I'd say she looked worried. "Your complaints are justified, Tavi," she murmured. "Stop getting so down on yourself."

"Anyway," I said with a sigh, "I don't want to talk about it and drag you down. This is our fun time together!"

I pulled out a dress in a shade of green that reminded me instantly of Mike's eyes, then put it back on the rack, thinking it would be too on the nose. He'd know right away I'd picked it on purpose.

"It is our fun time, but it's also a chance for you to really air out your suspicions," Melia agreed quietly. "I mean, what do *you* think about the reporter and what she kinda planted in your head about being sabotaged in the games on purpose? Do you feel like there's any truth to the statement?"

"I don't know. Yes. No. I think I might be making a big deal out of it because I feel like I don't fit in."

"I mean, do you even *care* about the games?" she asked. She grabbed a dress from the rack and held it out to me, frowning when I shook my head. "You didn't want to do them in the first place. And who cares what other people think of you? You know who you are and you know what you can do."

"They *hate* me, Meli."

"They are a bunch of snobbish boors who think because they were born here it entitles them to act like assholes. Don't pay them any attention. You know who you are and you know what skills you bring to the table. Now." She lifted another dress from the rack and smiled wide, showing almost all of her teeth. "How about this one?"

She was such a devil! "It's a little short, don't you think?"

"Yeah, *duh*. We want it short! Don't you want to turn heads? Or rather, the head of someone in particular who may or may not have asked you to the ball?" Melia indulged in a squeal of delight. "You are going to a *ball* with a real honest to God *prince*! I mean, I'm so excited for you I could die right now."

"I still can't believe he asked me. I...I guess I should tell you something I've been keeping to myself."

Her hands stilled on the next hanger. "Something about Mike?"

"Something big about Mike." My stomach flipped just thinking about it, like the memories were somehow not mine anymore. "And how he may or may not have kissed me. *Twice*."

Melia's squeal could have shaken the rafters of the building. She slugged me on the shoulder and nearly pushed me into a rack of glittering gowns. "How could you wait to tell me until now? How long have you been sitting on this secret?"

"I'm sorry! I wasn't sure how to bring it up," I said with a wince, rubbing my shoulder. Even the dull throb of pain couldn't dim my pleasure at the look on her face. At the unadulterated excitement in Melia's eyes. "I wanted to wait for a good time."

"Who cares about waiting for a good time? *You kissed the prince!*" She squealed again. "I can't believe I wasn't there. Where was I when this happened?"

"Probably busy sleeping because it was at the carnival. Well, the second time was at the carnival. The first time was after the welcome home dinner."

Melia ran her hands through her hair. "What? You've been sitting on that one a *long* time, and I know we've gotten together since. You should have let me know. I hate you. It's official."

I smiled. "Please don't hate me."

"Promise me you will tell me everything. What was it like? What was he like?" She squealed again, much softer this time but no less excited.

I spent the next thirty minutes going over everything about our kisses. It felt good to share, and to have someone be as thrilled with the kisses as I was. At the end of my story, something in my face must have set her off because Melia suddenly lunged at me, wrapping me up in a hug. Hopping up and down like she'd just found out she won a free trip to the Bahamas.

"I *knew* he liked you! I knew it this *whole time*."

"I know you did," I said. Loving the way her arms tightened around me, and making no move to pry her off. "Now help me find the perfect dress so he doesn't regret those kisses."

Melia made a face and skipped toward the next rack. "He could *never* regret those kisses. I'll make sure of it." She laughed, as though making His Royal Highness suffer for love would be her life's greatest accomplishment.

After almost an hour of sorting, perusing, inspecting, trying on, rejecting, finally deciding, I purchased a dress I hoped would get Mike's attention. Melia and I walked out of the shop and down the road to eat at a tiny restaurant she assured me served up the best fried zucchini blossoms she'd ever tasted. A glutton for anything fried, I agreed without hesitation, riding high on a crest of excitement.

Except when we got there, someone was already waiting. He waved to us from a table in the corner. I would have ignored him had Melia not dipped her head in embarrassment. "Okay, I guess you weren't the only one keeping secrets. I should have told you this when we first got together but I didn't want you to run away."

Run away? Something inside of me hardened. "Meli, what's going on?"

"It's the, ah, half Fae, half shifter I told you about. You remember? Well, he's here to meet you."

19

I stared at the man for a moment longer and my heart shriveled in on itself. I turned to Melia and tried not to let my disappointment at the betrayal show. "You tricked me."

Crestfallen, she tried to wrap her arms around my shoulders and bring me close. "Oh my God, Tavi, please don't be mad at me. I knew you wouldn't call him and he can help you!" she exclaimed.

"I can't believe you did call him."

"Tavi, please. I'm sorry. I thought it would be good for you to talk to someone who has firsthand experience with the same kind of thing you're going through. Look, if you don't want to meet with him again after today, it's okay. But at least give him a chance to talk to you. To see what kind of things he has to say and decide from there. Plus dinner. Dinner!"

I couldn't stay mad at Melia and she knew it. Even when I gave serious consideration to walking out the door.

"Dinner," I repeated dully.

She took it as consent and smiled wide, drawing me toward the table and the white-haired man sitting there.

We slowly approached the guy, me clutching my shopping bag to my chest and Melia leading the way with a blinding smile I knew she used to put us both at ease. It wasn't working but I didn't want to tell her. My sneakers felt like they had lead for soles.

"Hey there, Onyx. Thanks for meeting us here," Melia said as we approached the table. "I hope you weren't waiting too long."

"It's no problem, Melia. No problem at all." He rose to greet us and held out a hand for me to shake. "You must be Tavi."

"I guess you must be Onyx." I repeated the name Melia had used.

I remained hesitant of him despite his scent. No one else in the restaurant recognized him for what he was. But I knew.

He smelled like pack.

He smelled like *wolf*.

Jaded eyes stared down an aquiline nose at me. Platinum-white hair, cut short at the sides and longer at the top, fell toward his ears, and a goatee and mustache of the same color followed the line of his jaw. Dark eyebrows emphasized the turquoise-blue of his eyes. Onyx had the looks of an alpha male but the bearing of a beta.

I still wasn't sure I could trust him. But for Melia's sake I wouldn't be rude. I took his hand.

His fingers closed around mine, drawing me. My nostrils flared as I analyzed his scent. Familiar yet foreign at the same time. A tight-lipped smile was the best I could do.

"Why don't we all sit and get started on some of those yummy zucchini blossoms?" Melia said. She grabbed the seat next to him, leaving the opposite open for me. The mediator, I thought, watching her. The mentor still looking out for me no matter what.

Good. I would rather face him head on so I could observe.

"Does anyone want to order? No? I've got this." Melia took the lead and turned her attention to getting one of the Fae waiters in our direction.

He and I stared at each other for the longest time. Both trying to take the other's measure. Finally, I couldn't take it anymore and said, "How long have you been in Faerie, Onyx?"

He shrugged casually. "Most of my life." His voice was rough, as though rusty and using it took effort. I wondered if he lived in isolation, in hiding, or if he had one of those voices more at home in the wild than in civilized company.

"How did you get here?" I continued.

"I escaped. Not like you. You earned your place. I had to carve mine out of nothing."

I knew what *escape* meant. "You were running from something."

Another shrug. "You could say that. I came from a very unfortunate set of circumstances."

I didn't have to know the details to read between the lines. His eyes bored into me and I had trouble offering up my next statement, though it was sincere. "I'm sorry for whatever you experienced."

Melia finally caught the attention of a pixie server and, amidst the fluttering of tiny wings, placed an order for the table. Whatever appetite I'd had before had quickly disappeared since meeting Onyx. My skin began to prickle the longer we stared at each other, trying to see who would come out the victor.

In the presence of another halfling, another person like me, I didn't want to hold back. I didn't want to have to staple my lips shut and worry about what I could and could not say in front of him. I wanted everything out on the table if we were going to do this.

"How old are you?" I asked him.

"I'm twenty-six."

"Not so much older than I am, then. Although you look distinctly uncomfortable here."

He shifted to cross his arms over his chest. "I don't get out much."

"Then how did you and Melia meet?"

"She tracked me down using some kind of spell of her own design. It penetrated right through the shields I had in place to keep me hidden. So much for trying to fly under the radar." He spared a look at Melia, happily waiting for her order to arrive and doing her best to ignore us.

Then she finally noticed his attention. "What?" she asked. "When I put my mind to something, I always follow through. I wanted to help my friend. I did what anyone would do."

"It's called *stalking*," I said, only half in jest.

I could tell Onyx wasn't used to talking about himself. At all. I understood his kind of reticence but if the whole point was for the two of us to come to an understanding, this was kind of an awkward start.

A moment of silence reigned. "Have you had to hide your entire life?" I finally asked.

His eyes darted back and forth. "Most of it, yes." He paused when the pixie brought over a platter of fried blossoms smelling delicious enough to have my mouth watering. The moment the pixie left, he continued. "Why don't you tell me everything about your situation, Tavi? From the beginning."

I glanced once at Melia, who nodded. An encouragement for me to be honest. I watched her fingers wave and at once the air around us thickened. Condensed in such a way

I knew no one else would hear what I said today. Good thing, too, although we couldn't be sure her spell was one hundred percent effective. I'd have to watch the details I gave out right now and hope we had an opportunity for absolute honesty in the near future.

"My parents died when I was six," I told him. "My father was a wolf, my mother Fae. Once they were gone, my uncle took care of me and raised me to be pack, since the mantle of alpha fell to him after my father's death. On my eighteenth birthday, Uncle Will disclosed an arranged marriage between me and my so-called fated mate. A terrible, awful beast of a man, and I knew the only way to escape him was to get as far away as possible. The Halfling Academy was a long shot but the best one by far. And with Melia's help, I made it here."

Onyx asked for details and I gave them to him sparingly. I would lay out the whole sordid tale later, in private. Still, he knew enough to get the basic idea of the situation, and when I finished speaking, he nodded.

"A similar thing happened to me. Not an arranged marriage, but I was raised pack and always expected to take over my father's pack when he retired. Although Lord knows the man will live forever through sheer spite. Lucky, he called me. Lucky because I would be handed this pack, this gift, when he'd had to fight for it. I never wanted the responsibility."

"I can understand."

"I'm a painter. All I ever wanted to do was paint."

Odd, the idea of the man in front of me painting seemed both foreign and perfect. "Do you have something of yours you can show me?"

He nodded again and took out a phone. Right then, despite the magic pulsing around us, we could have been any three friends in any world, hanging out with our tech gadgets.

"These are a few pieces I've been working on. Watercolors mostly. I find the depth of feeling you can evoke with the medium freeing." He scrolled through a gallery of paintings, and in the swirling colors I saw familiar sights. I saw mountains and forests and streams. I saw magic and barely controlled chaos.

My heart gave a twang of recognition. Somehow, Onyx had managed to capture the wildness and the freedom of a run through the woods on four legs.

"Thank you," I said when he was done. And for the first time since we stepped into the restaurant, I felt some of my walls come down.

"Those are really beautiful," Melia agreed. "You have a gift."

Onyx looked distinctly uncomfortable with the praise and quickly stored his phone back into his pocket.

"Do you know where your father is?" I asked him.

"No, thank goodness. Which is why I understand why you had to get away." His hands dropped to the table and maybe some of his walls fell, too. "I know the feeling of wanting to get as far away as you possibly can, wanting to carve out an entirely new life while keeping the integral pieces of yourself intact."

"Right now, I just want to get through the Elite Academy so I can find my own space. Begin my own life. Like Melia." I smiled at her then and she returned the smile.

"You should have no trouble accomplishing that goal."

I almost snorted. "Easier said than done."

He gave me a kindly smile. "You have great gifts, Tavi. The trick is learning how to harness them for use together, because together they make you strong. Taken one by one, in this place, they produce less than the desired result."

I gave him a long look. "How do you know what my gifts are?"

"Because I have the same gifts,"

That gave me pause. "And you really have the...the power to..." I twirled my fingers in the air and hoped he would pick up my train of thought.

"I do. It's a rare power but there are a few of us who have made it to this land with the magic. If you can trust me, Tavi, then I can help you control it," Onyx said.

By the time the meal was finished, I'd ended up agreeing to accept Onyx's help. Because I had to face the fact that I didn't really have a choice.

20

The Solstice Ball loomed large on Saturday. Although the bulk of the festivities took place at night, the castle was a hive of activity through most of the day as servants attended to last-minute details.

I stayed in my room for most of it but even the thick walls could not block out the noise or the excitement. It permeated every stone, every floorboard. I went down to the kitchen to sneak a little food for lunch only to have Raelynn scold me and guilt trip me into a few hours of work with the culinary delights they were preparing.

Yeah, I still wasn't any good with the baking, which only made her more determined to teach me. She didn't want to take my word on my hopelessness. Soon my fingers ached from all the pulling and kneading and rolling.

The moment I could manage it, I snuck out the door, knowing I'd need another shower thanks to the dusting of flour on every inch of my skin. I had no one to help me do my hair and makeup. Melia wanted to help, bless her, but with her own work, she didn't have a chance to get away. It didn't matter. I'd managed to get a few spells from her for just such an occasion.

My fresh, clean hair practically curled itself, arranged in intricate swirls on the top of my head though a few locks danced delicately across the back of my neck. The dress I'd chosen flowed like water around my ankles. Spaghetti straps left my arms and shoulders bare, the material a blend of sheer mesh and blue sparkling flowers. The neckline cut down in a deep V, the shape mimicked by a provocative slit across my midriff. It left enough to the imagination yet showed a bit of enticing skin. To me, the dress was a piece of magic. The material was woven in beautiful lines and contours, fitting me perfectly.

I wondered about the other girls Mike might have chosen to accompany him, and whether he was glad he'd picked me. His kisses told me I might have a leg up on the thousands of competitive females, but really who knew? The niggling sensation of self-doubt never completely went away.

Mike sent a text at eight o'clock saying he was on his way up to my room and hoping I was ready. *Gulp.* My stomach did flip-flops as I waited, crossing from the bed to the window and back again, trying to get my breath back.

I waited with my hands clenching and unclenching at my sides. Trying not to wrinkle the fabric of the dress. I'd done minimal eye makeup, choosing instead to accentuate my lips with a full-bodied red color. A perfect offset to the hues of my hair.

The knock on the door sounded and I scrambled to answer it, almost tripping over my own feet in the process. The heels were a little higher than I usually wore but I needed the height due to the length of the dress train.

I threw open the door on a whoosh of air. Then lost the rest of my breath entirely.

Mike stood staring at me, his hair bright and shimmering, an imposing, tall figure with moonlight from my open windows lighting him in shades of gilded silver. He positively *gleamed*.

Oh. My. My mouth went dry and stayed like that.

It was as if he'd cast off whatever plain humanity he'd worn throughout our friendship. Here stood the Fae male in his prime. The broad-shouldered golden child of the realm. The crown prince.

His Royal Highness in the flesh.

If you asked me to this day, I couldn't tell you what he wore. I couldn't tell you if his tie matched his pocket square or the color of his pants. I saw only those eyes. Bright green. Rounded with surprise as they took in the dress I'd bought.

For him.

He stunned me. The same way it seemed I stunned him.

No, I clearly didn't...right? Not me. I was too plain, too—

"You..." His voice trailed off, that single word sounding like something not entirely of this world. Or maybe it was as if I was hearing it for the first time. Or hearing what he *didn't* say, perhaps.

I suppressed a shudder. "You look wonderful, Mike," I said. Keenly aware of my every nerve ending. His every breath as he took a step closer.

My chest constricted painfully at his nearness. He was magic itself.

"Thanks. Um... You, ah, ready to go? To the ball? With me, I mean. Are you ready to go with me?" Mike hiked a thumb over his shoulder. Despite his devastating looks, he was still a rather shy boy when it came to some things. And that just endeared him to me more.

I nodded violently, a stray curl finding its way into my mouth and nearly choking me. Power swirled in his eyes, belying that earlier timidity, and I suddenly saw that there were two sides to Crown Prince Michael Thornwood. Here in Faerie, his nobility was tangible. Something he was born with and destined to manifest for the rest of his life. I couldn't help but hope that the shy boy I knew yet lingered there somewhere or if I'd imagined him.

He rocked back and forth on the balls of his feet for a moment longer before realizing he blocked the doorway. With an awkward laugh, he stepped aside and held his elbow out for me to take. "Okay, then. Let's go."

I realized then we hadn't really talked about last week's kiss. Or what was happening between us. *Was* there anything happening between us? I couldn't think.

"There's going to be dancing tonight," Mike warned me as we walked. The train of my gown glided across the floor in a *shush* of sound behind us. "I made sure to wear my shoes with the toughest leather. In case you felt the need to step on my feet again."

I playfully swatted his arm. "Don't blame me for stomping on you. I told you I didn't know the steps. You promised you would lead."

"I promised I would lead because I thought you were light on your feet. I've seen you run and leap and dive like an athlete. I figured you could handle a little dancing."

"You are attributing an awful lot to a few games of Capture the Scroll. That doesn't mean I am coordinated when it comes to other physical activities." Except I totally was. The wolf in me took care of those things with ease.

The stray thought reminded me of the huge secret between us, and the worry that we would never be able to make any kind of relationship work. It was nothing but a pipe dream.

Those thoughts took a back seat soon enough as we arrived at the grand ballroom.

I stepped into a real dream as Mike and I crossed the threshold into the ballroom. I remembered how it looked the first night, during our dinner to welcome Mike back to the realm. That memory of magic and perfection was shattered under this newest incarnation. The ballroom had been doubly enchanted for this evening, starting with a set of magnificent marble steps curving away from the entrance doors. I lost my breath for a moment just trying to take in all the splendor.

"Hold on," Mike whispered, keeping me in place. "We need to wait."

"For what?" I whispered back.

He nodded toward a man I hadn't seen, the black of his suit blending in with the shadows.

"Now announcing the arrival of His Royal Highness Prince Michael and his companion for the evening, Miss Tavi Alderidge."

Hearing our names together, in the fancy butler's magically enhanced voice, had my heart speeding up until it felt like a hummingbird beating against my ribs.

Mike began to ascend the stairs and I had no choice but to follow since he still held my arm. I just hoped I wouldn't trip over my own two feet and make a spectacle of myself. The ball attendees already present in the room applauded our arrival. I'd never felt more awkard in my life. Luckily Mike seemed to notice the way I tensed and kept a strong hold on me for support. He immediately led us toward a fountain in the nearest corner.

Champagne. It was a freakin' fountain of champagne.

He snapped his fingers and two flutes appeared. Filling both, Mike handed one off to me.

"For courage and stamina," he said, raising his glass to mine in a private toast. We both sipped, and I was almost transported by the sweet bubbly wine. "We must greet my parents first," he said softly, his gaze scanning the other guests. "It's customary."

I swallowed a nervous giggle that luckily did not end on a snort.

In all the noise and colors of the ballroom, I hadn't even thought about the queen. Or the king. I took another sip of my champagne—it should be called *ambrosia*; mere *champagne* didn't do it justice—then set aside my glass and followed close behind Mike. A raised dais had been set up near where we'd dined the first evening and two splendid oak thrones now perched there.

Mike bowed from the waist, keeping his gaze averted from his father. I did my best to curtsy. When I straightened, I saw King Tywin staring at me, his brows knitted together.

"Michael. You've decided to arrive at last. Fashionably late is still late, son," King Tywin said. Tonight, he'd drawn a royal robe in midnight-blue around his shoulders, the hems and collar adorned with white fur putting me in mind of Onyx's hair. The jewels of his magnificent crown glistened under the diamond-bright lights of the chandeliers overhead.

A magical fairy tale, indeed. Except I remembered what I'd read in the past. More times than not, fairy tales didn't have happy endings.

Mike inclined his head. "My apologies, Father."

"Hmph. I expect it from you at this point. And you, Miss Alderidge." I physically felt the weight of his attention when the king spoke to me, and a frisson rolled across my nerve endings. "I trust you're enjoying yourself in Faerie thus far?"

"Very much, Your Majesty. Thank you for the opportunity to be here," I hurried to add.

I fought to keep from blushing. No way did I want King Tywin ferreting out I'd been kissing his son. Would he be able to tell using his powers? Did he have some kind of parental sixth sense outside of the magic?

"And your studies?" he continued. When I glanced up,

he leaned forward, one hand stroking his beard lightly. "I'd hate to think I made a mistake in allowing you a place at the Elite Academy."

"No, sir." *Keep it short and simple*, I thought. "I am doing my best to maintain my grades."

He appeared satisfied with the answer, if the short hard jerk of his head gave me an inkling. Queen Laina sent her son and me a soft smile. "Well, enough small talk for now. Go enjoy yourselves, dears. Mingle and dance." She accompanied the directive with a wink for Mike.

I knew then I liked the queen. A lot. Her affection for her son cemented the feeling.

Still, we couldn't get away fast enough. Fingers clenched around Mike's arm, I followed as he led me toward the melee of dancers.

He gave my hand a pat where it rested on his sleeve. "I know. They get to me too," Mike said. His right hand then went to above my waist and just below my shoulder blade as he held out his left hand. "Don't worry about a thing."

I grabbed the train of my gown and draped it over my arm as I took his hand. My left hand went to his shoulder for support. "At least I know I'm not alone, but they are your parents. They shouldn't *get to you* at all."

Mike didn't appear concerned. If anything, he was resigned. "You're probably right."

"Don't you know me by now? I'm always right," I joked.

We danced and Mike spun me until my head wanted to fly off my body and float toward the ceiling. Laughing, I leaned back, safe in his embrace, vowing to stay in the moment even if it killed me. I etched the scene in my mind. These memories...I didn't want to forget them. I wanted to cherish them for the rest of my life.

"I think this is the first time since we came to Faerie I've seen you look this happy," Mike commented, drawing me closer.

My hand moved automatically up his shoulder toward his neck. "What do you mean? I've been happy before."

Not often, though, my subconscious reminded me.

He shook his head and his lips twisted in a small, heated smirk. "You had a good time at the carnival, I know, but whenever I look at you, there's this sort of underlying sadness. No matter how hard I try, I can't get it to lift."

I wanted to melt at his concern. "It's nice you're worried. And how you've been trying."

"Why wouldn't I want to see you happy? You have to know I care about you, Tavi."

I thought about our kiss at the carnival and blushed. I couldn't help myself. Anytime I thought about the man's lips, my body seemed to go up in flames. "I know you do," I murmured.

His right hand drifted lower, just past my waist, barely brushing my tailbone as if testing the waters before coming to rest at the small of my back. "What about you?"

"What *about* me?"

"Do you...care about me?"

I tightened my arm around his neck, trying desperately to keep the rhythm of the dance. I felt thrown off by the question. "What do you think?"

"I think it takes a strong kind of person to chance starting something with a crown prince. I even understand why you wouldn't want to, given the circumstances."

I relaxed a little. "I don't see a prince when I look at you," I said with a tiny shake of my head.

He paused for just a moment before resuming the dance. "Oh no? Everyone else does." Even though he tried to keep his voice light, I heard how it bothered him.

"As if you didn't know by now, I'm not like everyone

else. When I look at you, I see kindness and compassion. I see a guy who would stop on the side of the road in the middle of the night to help out a stranger in need. I see a good friend."

"You're so pretty. It wasn't a hardship," Mike joked.

I grinned, allowing him the deflecting jest. "You know what I mean. You took a chance on me the same way I did you. And even through a few rough patches, well, here we are."

"You want to know what I thought, that night on the road? When I pulled over to help you out?"

"I can guess. 'Look at the crazy person! I'd better be careful or she might murder me and stuff me into her already super heavy suitcase!'"

Mike laughed. "No. I thought 'There's someone worth helping. I wonder what it would be like to taste her.'"

My stomach curled and heat shot through me. Also, I forgot I had feet and I was supposed to instruct them on what to do. Mike quickly righted me, though. "Oh."

Real smart thing to say, but the ability for rational thought had flown the coop.

"It's true," Mike insisted. "Does that change your opinion of me?"

His confession gave me courage. I shook my head slowly and then took a chance and gave voice to my own admission for the first time. "To be honest, I thought you were the most handsome guy I'd ever seen in my life."

Mike raised his brows. At least he didn't look angry. Or flattered. He just looked...skeptical. "Oh, come on."

"It's true. Don't tease me for it. I lose my head whenever you smile at me."

I probably shouldn't have revealed so much. I should have played my cards closer to the chest. I should have done a lot of things differently, but stepping down a path ending in a relationship with Mike, His Royal Highness the Crown Prince of Faerie, wasn't one of them.

Because here I was, in his arms, slowly twirling to a haunting violin melody while courtesans and high officials stared at us. I could ignore them all because there was Mike, and he was looking at *me*.

And he was smiling. That devastating smile that drew the very breath from my lungs. "What about now?"

"Hmm?" My brain couldn't engage fast enough to follow.

"Have you lost your head?" Mike pressed, teasingly. "Am I still the most handsome guy you've ever met, when you've seen what Faerie has to offer?" He used his chin to indicate the ballroom. "There are many other eligible Fae gentlemen here tonight, many of whom are from good families. More than one has had their eye on you, you know."

Now and always, I wanted to say. Mike was now and would always be the most handsome guy to me. Instead, I forced myself to shrug and playfully said, "I don't know...I've had my eye on a few of them, too."

Mike drew me closer on a growl. I hid my secret smile by pressing my cheek to his shoulder.

We continued to dance, stopping only for another glass or two of champagne here and there. Soon the air around us grew hot and Mike's touch sent sparks of lightning through me. I could tell he felt the same. His eyes burned my skin, his fingers slipped lower and lower, skimming across the small of my back and my hips. Soon I couldn't breathe.

"Come on. It's getting hot in here. Let's get some air." Mike had released the first few buttons on his shirt, giving me an enticing view of his collarbone. This time he was the one to offer the excuse of an escape.

He took hold of my hand and laced our fingers together before tugging me toward the glass doors leading to the gardens.

"Won't we be missed?"

"No. They are too fixated on themselves to notice our exit," he replied.

I couldn't have argued if I wanted to. Which I didn't. We'd both had a little bit to drink and I knew the fresh air would do wonders to cool me down before I got so hot I did something bad. Like inviting Mike back to my room to see what those lips could really do.

Because once I opened that door, there would be no going back. At least not for me. I needed to tread very carefully.

I followed him down the stone steps into the garden. The light of the moon filtered down through the clouds— finally, a clear night—and the stars shone like glistening specks of diamonds in a velvet sky. Night flowers opened and turned their blooms toward the light, white moonflower and fragrant blooming jasmine.

Magical.

Beautiful.

Mike continued to pull me along through the maze of plants and beds until we came to an alcove of shrubbery. The flowers had been magicked into the shape of an arch. The perfect spot for a clandestine getaway.

I didn't want to run this time. I knew it with every fiber of my being.

And I didn't want to wait any longer to taste him.

Apparently neither did Mike.

His arms came around me and he pulled me close. He brought his lips to my ear and nipped. "You're driving me mad," he growled, and the sound trembled along my spine, up my neck, and even towards my belly until everything within me vibrated. "Do you know how hard it is for me to keep my hands to myself, especially in there?" he asked, bringing his face closer to mine until we were a breath apart. "Especially when there were too many eyes on you?"

"Why did you stop yourself?" I asked breathlessly. Then shuddered, closing my eyes as my body went taut at his answer.

"Because doing what I want to do to you in public would offend many, *many* people, Tavi."

He said my name like a plea, the syllables a caress, and his breath tickled my ear.

I arched toward him.

The moment I turned to face him he lunged passionately for me, his hands cupping my chin and raising my face higher. Our lips crashed together, our tongues dancing and teasing. His teeth nibbled my lips and my world narrowed to the feeling of him. To lips and teeth and tongue against my skin, to the grind of his hips against mine.

I shouldn't have, I knew. But I didn't care. I wasn't sure I would ever care again, no matter what came up between us. No matter the secrets I had to keep because it meant the difference between life and death.

There was only me and Mike and how we felt.

"No one comes out here," Mike managed to whisper between kisses. "It's a secret. A garden all to ourselves. Just us."

Just us.

I couldn't get enough of him, looping my arms around his neck to keep him in place and to keep him with me. His tongue slashed across my lips to get me to open again, his hands hard on my hips before drifting lower to caress my rear slowly and deliberately.

Oh, God.

The heat. The sparks. I couldn't take much more of this without combusting. Without exploding into a million pieces and flying up to the moon. His chest pressed into mine and I couldn't get enough of him. I wanted more.

I wanted everything in a way I'd never wanted in my life.

That, I think, scared me more than anything. How elated I felt in his presence. How I knew kissing Mike was not a smart idea. With the secrets I harbored, I was all wrong for the prince. What would happen if he discovered I wasn't exactly who he thought I was?

My heart hurt imagining it.

But I didn't stop kissing him. I didn't cut our moment short, because it might be our last. If I was smart, it would be. That didn't stop me from wanting him. His kisses became territorial. Heat pounded between us and his body ground against mine, pressing to every aching spot and drawing a low moan from me.

Mike echoed the sound, his fingers tangling in my hair. It was all I could do to keep standing instead of melting into a puddle.

He finally reared back, smiling in a wild way. "I needed to taste you," he said, his voice deepening to a purr rippling through me. Bringing things to life and lulling me into a fantasy. "It was driving me crazy."

The moonlight turned his eyes to the color of moss. I wanted more. I wanted all the hardness of his body crushed to mine. I wanted his mouth and tongue on every inch of my skin. Between my neck and my shoulders. On my breasts. Everywhere. I wanted everything and the need nearly drowned me.

"Tavi."

His nostrils flared as he drew in my scent, inherently knowing what I wanted, the need raging through me. The breath rushed from me in a whoosh. I was only vaguely aware of voices not our own. Part of me distantly registered and recoiled at the intrusion, disappointed at having this moment spoiled.

The interruption came in the form of two heated voices from somewhere nearby. A man and a woman having an argument.

"I said I'm not going!" That was definitely a female voice.

"Do you have a choice?" a male voice growled.

"If you knew what was good for you, you'd walk away," the woman replied. "Walk away and don't look back."

Mike gathered me closer, and he groaned, low and frustrated. "You hear something?"

"How can I not?" I whispered. "They're making it very hard to ignore."

The woman again, louder, more strident. "You think you can push me around? I have news for you. This is my show. You are nothing but the side act!"

"I don't recognize the voices," Mike whispered in my ear. "But a great many people come from all over to the ball. Someone must have stumbled upon our secret place."

My heart warmed at *our secret place*, but the feeling was short-lived. The couple continued to argue, their voices louder and louder, sounding like they were right next to us but hidden in the shrubbery.

I didn't like the way the argument made me feel. Huddling against Mike, I tried to get his attention. To get him to take us back to the castle, back to the ball. "Come on, Mike. Let's leave them to it."

"Wait here. I'm going to find a guard before their fight gets out of hand."

I blinked at him. "Are you sure that's wise?"

He kissed the top of my forehead. "Don't move. I'll be right back."

He strode off into the darkness, leaving me with nothing but my thoughts and a sudden chill.

"Get your hands off of me!" The anger in the woman's voice broke. I could hear the tears beneath the plea.

"Fucking *bitch*."

The woman began to sob, the man yelling to be heard above her. I couldn't take it anymore. I crept closer, wanting to see who they were in case they left before Mike and the guard could return. Venturing toward the edge of the shrubs, I peeked around, seeing the shadowy figures locked together.

"No. *No!* Don't—"

A flash of light exploded from the area. The woman screamed.

Then silence.

21

I froze, fear keeping me in place. Where was Mike? Where were the guards? What was taking them so long? Was there no security here at all?

A figure suddenly bolted past me and I stumbled, holding my arms out in front of me like a shield in case he stepped too close. It was too dark to see his face but I knew instinctively he was male and he was large with a powerful build.

I needed to move. To do something. Instinct had me fleeing away from where Mike had gone and toward the direction the figure came from. Toward the scream.

I ran toward the woman on the ground and pulled up short at the stench filling the air.

Death.

She was dead, and I knew the face. I recognized the curling hair and the red bandana. Madam Muerte, the crackpot soothsayer.

I bent to check her pulse automatically although clearly it was futile. The woman's eyes were wide open and her lungs had stopped working. Like the mystery man had sucked the life right out of her.

My fingers closed around her wrist anyway and I waited five seconds before releasing her.

I'd been standing right over there when it happened. How had I not gotten a good look at the man who did this? He ran right past me. It all happened so fast. I felt guilty that I hadn't tried to intervene.

"Who was that, Madam Muerte?" I asked, needing to say something to fill the silence.

Madam Muerte didn't answer. She wouldn't answer anyone ever again. What had she been doing this close to the castle? I figured she'd left when the rest of the carnival came down.

Unfortunately, this wasn't my first dead body. Hell, it wasn't even my second. Or third. I knew my way around the recently deceased, and just my bad luck, they kept popping up.

The chill night air bit deep into my exposed skin and I shivered. A few more minutes went by before Mike and one of the castle guards arrived.

"Tavi?" he called out.

I glanced up from where I was still kneeling near Madam Muerte. *Mike, you'll be interested to know that my penchant for finding dead bodies has apparently followed me into Faerie.* "I'm over here."

He followed the sound of my voice and rounded the corner seconds later with one of the castle guards behind him. Although Mike approached, the other man pulled up short, assessing the situation.

"Oh dear. I know this doesn't look good," I told the guard when I saw his posture change.

The guard looked from Mike to me to the corpse. Then back again. His face hardened. His hand went out in front of him and magic began to crackle between his fingers.

"Miss, move away from the body. I'm going to need you to come with me."

Mike stepped in front of him. "Now, hold on a minute. I told you she and I were out here together. I left to get you. There's no way Tavi had anything to do with this," he said. And it wasn't the voice of the boy I'd been kissing. This was the voice of the future monarch.

Unfortunately, it did look bad. I knew that, and I should have done something to prevent it. I should have stayed where I was without moving instead of giving in to the need to investigate.

The guard took another step toward me with his hands held out in front of him, ignoring Mike.

"Hey, I told you to stop," Mike commanded. "Don't even look at her."

"Miss—"

Mike grabbed the guard by the forearms to stop him from advancing and the two scrambled for the upper hand. The guard had a good few inches and about fifty pounds on Mike and soon had the crown prince pushed to the side to get to me.

My heart plummeted.

"I'm the authority here. I am in charge in this situation, Prince Michael," the guard said only half apologetically. "If you have an issue with the way I've handled this, then you will have to take it up with the king and queen." A snap of the guard's fingers had a pair of handcuffs manifesting, electric blue and pulsing with power. "Miss, you are going to have to come with me. This will go easier if you don't put up a fight."

My teeth began to chatter. Clearing my throat, I tried to back away, toward whatever escape I could find. "Where are you taking me?"

"You'll be confined and under surveillance until we can sort things out."

"She's not dangerous!" Mike insisted. "What are you doing?"

"I'm doing my job, Your Royal Highness."

The handcuffs slapped down on my wrists and I felt an immediate drain. My magic, as meager as it was here thanks to my halfling blood, had no chance against them. I didn't even have time to kick off my shoes before he'd dragged me away from Mike. My ankles twisted and I stumbled away from both the man I loved and the woman they now thought I'd killed.

The guard led me along a dark stone corridor, the ripe scents of mold, mildew, and decay assaulting my senses. Empty cells lined both sides where condemned thieves and murderers and enemies of the state awaited their trials. Wind ripped through the passage like an echo of the moans of the past tortured.

I stumbled over the same ground where others condemned had walked for hundreds of years. My chill didn't go away. If anything, it snaked higher, spearing through my abdomen and coiling beneath my heart.

"In you go, Miss."

When I hesitated, the guard practically tossed me into an open cell filled with dry straw. The scent of decay was even worse here. Each stone held an echo of neglect, of fear and panic, of blood and unwashed bodies. I saw chains attached to the wall.

"We'll come to retrieve you in the morning."

I barely heard the guard's voice over the sound of metal grating against metal. The door slammed closed behind me and he sealed it with a spell. Any desire to magic my way out of this slipped away, my thoughts weak and watery.

Utterly defeated, I covered my head to hide my tears. The rest of Faerie's elite danced beneath the stars, sampled the best the kingdom had to offer in terms of wine and food, and rubbed elbows with the monarchy.

The guard hadn't even given me a blanket before throwing me into the cell.

Shudders wracked my body, knees knocking as I curled up on the small bench set into the stone wall. I spent the sleepless night shivering in a dungeon built for criminals and enemies of the empire. I was neither a criminal nor an enemy but it didn't seem to matter.

There was no window, no light at all except a few lamps here and there for the guards. I could not tell the passage of time, had no idea morning had arrived until I was fetched.

Now I stood, still in my gown from the party albeit much the worse for wear, in front of a weary king while Madam Muerte's assistant testified about the last night I'd seen the deceased woman. When I looked up at King Tywin, I saw lines drawn into his face which hadn't been there before. Yet his eyes were bright spots of blue.

Then I noticed Mike standing to the side, a little behind the throne, his expression hard. I wondered if he had pled my case with his father. I felt sure he would have, but had his father listened? Impossible to know at this point. The assistant went on with his witness testimony.

"I was there, Your Majesty," the young man squawked, his voice like a parrot. "Madam Muerte spoke of a strange prophecy around this girl at the fair last weekend. The girl was there with your son the prince, having her fortune told."

"This man wasn't there!" I objected.

"I was indeed. I stay behind the scenes, naturally, as Madam's assistant. Afterwards, Your Majesty, Madam

Muerte wanted me to keep a close eye on this girl after her startling revelations. She didn't feel safe alone."

"That's not true." My muscles seized and I tried in vain to hide the reaction. "She said some terrible things, sure, but I never saw her afterwards. Mike and I left in the middle of the scene she was making. I didn't even know she was still in town until last night."

"Lies!"

Shards of panic drove into my skin. Somehow, my world had shifted on its axis until the impossible became reality. To be held captive in the dungeons, cut off from my magic, with false allegations dragging my name though the mud—was I going mad?

Mike had heard enough apparently and stepped forward to grab his father's attention. "Of course we were there. Most of the kingdom was standing in line waiting for the crazy seer to tell them something interesting. That doesn't mean Tavi had anything to do with the woman's death."

"You should have heard her, Your Majesty. Such dire predictions," the assistant countered.

King Tywin volleyed his attention back and forth between the two. "Tell me more," he said to the witness.

"Madam Muerte had a violent reaction to this girl's presence. She began to speak of storms and secrets. The coming of the end. She mentioned the Faerie Prophecy." The assistant swung his own attention to Tavi with a smirk while a collective gasp went up over the words *Faerie Prophecy*. "Odds are good the girl didn't like what the finest seer in the land had to say about her and decided to take her revenge."

Ice clenched my heart. Damn the consequences. *I have to get out of here.*

"Tavi was in the gardens with me," Mike argued forcefully. "There was a man there arguing with the seer. The two had gotten into a heated argument when I left to get help."

King Tywin listened to his son without interruption but I could tell from the way he looked at me he wasn't buying any of this. Though his face remained impassive, his gaze seared through me, judging me. Ferreting out what I tried to hide.

In this particular case, I had nothing to hide, so I met his gaze head on without blinking. Let him think what he wanted of me. I had plenty of secrets in my life, true, but I hadn't touched Madam Muerte no matter what kind of nonsense she'd screamed at me.

The king didn't trust me.

He was right not to.

Except this time, I hadn't done anything.

I also hadn't been given the opportunity to defend myself. I stood as still as possible with feet aching and hands cuffed together at my front. The beautiful dress Melia had helped me pick out had torn at the hem and now boasted stains I wondered if magic would be able to remove. Probably not.

"Tavi is *innocent*," Mike insisted. He kept his posture rigid and his eyes narrowed, unblinking. "We were together almost the whole time. And the vision of the future which Madam Muerte saw might have been about anyone. She was vague and hysterical, looking to make her money and give her audience a cheap thrill. Theatrics. Pure drama. Nothing more."

The room fell into silence as King Tywin continued to stare at me. "Guard, release the girl from those cuffs."

No one broke the staring match as the guard from last night slowly made his way toward me.

"You are free to go, Miss Alderidge," the king continued. He pinched the bridge of his nose once, the only indication of his exhaustion. Having gone from the Solstice Ball to an unexpected interrogation, I was betting he hadn't gotten much sleep last night, if any. "On the condition you keep your head down and stay out of trouble. Do I make myself clear?"

Tywin's eyes speared through me, the skin near his temples pulling taut against his skull.

I didn't trust myself to speak. Not when it was clear he wasn't convinced I didn't in fact kill the woman. I saw it plainly. But what reason would I have for murdering a woman I didn't know? The seer had given a vague prediction that might not have even been about me, if Mike's impassioned speech was to be believed.

"Do you understand me?" Tywin repeated with a snap of sound. Even Mike winced.

I nodded slowly, head bowing. "Yes, sir."

What else could I say?

Anything I might have aired to defend myself would not have been taken as I meant it. I stood rooted in place until the handcuffs dropped, then I made an attempt at a curtsy and gathered my dignity to walk out of the room, listening to the footsteps behind me and the door clanking shut.

Shivering, I barely noticed Mike coming up beside me, ready to escort me to the second floor. We both stopped when I paused to lean against the wall. Relief flooded me but suspicion accompanied the feeling, and I wondered why the king thought so little of me. And since he did, why he had let me go. With nothing but a warning.

"I'm so sorry about what happened," Mike said softly. "Are you okay?"

Um, no, I wasn't okay. "I spent the night in the dungeon," I replied dully. What kind of answer did he expect?

"I know, and I hate myself for letting them take you away. I tried everything I could to get them to release you, but with my father busy at the Solstice Ball, no one wanted to listen to me."

"Those dungeons are creepy, Mike. There are things in the walls skittering around, little claws on stone. There are leaks everywhere and straw growing mold. There are chains set into the walls with weird stains on them."

I shuddered at my own words. The experience had shaken me more than I liked to admit.

Mike raked a hand through his hair, mussing it back from his forehead. One day he would be king, I thought, looking at him. What did I think would happen to me on his journey? I had no place there. "I never want you going down there again," he insisted.

"You think *I* do?" The words rang hollow. The fire had gone out of me.

We came to a stop in front of my door and all I wanted to do was crawl into bed. After a nice long bath. Maybe a good cry too.

"Would you like to get together later? Hang out a little?"

I shook my head. "No. I think I want to have some alone time for right now. I'm sorry."

"Oh, okay," he said slowly. "I understand."

I left him there, crestfallen, and shut the door behind me.

22

Magnus Crackenbush and his team of torturers decided to go forward with the second week of games the following Monday, once the storms had abated for one day, and my heart sank at the announcement.

The third game was set for Tuesday, I found out during homeroom. I didn't want to play. I didn't want to be set up to look like a fool again.

I had no choice.

I walked down the hall with Mike, struggling to find something neutral to say. It was the first time we'd seen each other since he'd dropped me off at my room Sunday morning and I couldn't fight the odd bashful feeling in his presence. I also couldn't stop thinking about how we'd made out Saturday night, and how getting caught up in whatever subterfuge was happening with Madame Muerte felt like a horrific omen for our budding relationship.

"You're quiet today," he said, staring straight ahead.

"I'm worried about the game."

He glanced over at me and a lock of blond hair fell over his eyes. "Is that all you're worried about?"

"No," I answered honestly. "It's not."

Since school had let out for the two-week break, the castle's arena hosted the games. Mike led the way and grabbed us two seats with the rest of his friends. Lane looked up and offered me a quick smile, while Arlyss kept his attention on the stage, just like the rest of them. The place looked like a football stadium, set to the left of the castle toward the edge of the village. High stone walls blocked the area from general view; the large center area was completely clear of everything except grass.

The longer we sat, the sicker I felt, listening to the dull roar of voices raised in anticipation for the game.

It wasn't long before Magnus strode toward the center of the green space with his arms raised. The crowd roared at his appearance, the air crackling with energy and anticipation. Today his horns were polished to a sheen and he wore a suit jacket in a matching color.

"Students, welcome! *Welcome* to the start of the third game. Let me hear your excitement!" He waited for the cheering to settle down before continuing, his face replicated in a gigantic shimmering hologram in the air above him. Easier for those in the farther-out seats to see.

"Now, I have some news for you. Only those students who won the first two games will be allowed to compete in the second week of games. I don't make the rules...well, actually I do." Magnus offered up another dazzling smile. "It's the name of the game, guys and gals! Now. Where are my lucky fifty who plucked the relics from the clouds?"

Mike shot me an apologetic look. "Sorry. I have to go."

"No worries. You go do what you need to do."

He pushed past me and into the aisle to the sound of even more applause. Yeah, he definitely still had a fan club here.

Only having the top fifty students competing today, well,

it was awesome news for me. I got to sit in the stands and cheer for Mike instead of being scrutinized or squashed under Selene's reporter thumb. The snake.

Still, many of the left-out students booed about the announcement. They'd wanted to be involved.

I leaned back and watched Mike make his way down to the center green along with the other forty-nine students who would be competing today. *Better this way*, I told myself. Much better, and an unexpected silver lining to the recent shit situations.

I cupped my hands around my mouth and yelled, "Go Mike!"

He stood out among his peers, a spot of bright sunlight with his golden hair.

The same hologram that had broadcast Magnus's face to the crowd now showed something different entirely. Magic swelled and the green space disappeared. Large hedges grew in a labyrinth, morphing into twists and turns designed to obscure the players from physical view.

Magnus spoke about the rules of the game, how this game had been designed to test knowledge and response time. Thinking on the spot and adjusting course, he said to another round of cheers. Soon the students went to work. They were to traverse through the labyrinth, blindfolded, and use their powers to get past obstacles and find their way out.

With my luck I probably would have walked right into another pit of quicksand. It was a good thing I watched from a safe distance.

Okay, maybe the other shoe wouldn't drop after all. The thing with Madam Muerte had seemed like a huge setback but I clearly had nothing to do with it, so the king and his guards couldn't find evidence that didn't exist. And now not to have to participate in the Summer Games?

Silver lining for me!

The first few minutes ticked by, with tension thick enough to choke an elephant. Even the rest of the students left behind stopped booing long enough to hold their breath and watch the proceedings. Soon multiple images of thickened air popped up around the arena to give spectators an in-depth view of each participant.

Part of me didn't want to watch. I had a bad feeling in the pit of my stomach. I was no better than the rest of these vultures, leaning closer to see how their friends and fellow students would fare during the competition.

There were a few moments where I lost my breath and my heart stopped. A few students went down quickly under the obstacles. Crazy fairy creatures and bogs took them out one by one. They were blindfolded and *literally* fighting blind.

Yet when I took a step back from the labyrinth and tore my eyes away, I noticed the other side of things. I noticed the television crews and the cameras floating in the air above the maze. Magnus and his team of producers directed the show.

This whole thing was a game, I thought as I adjusted in my seat on the benches, but not the way I'd first thought. This was a game because of the puppetmasters pulling the strings. Everything that they'd done to us had been done for the sake of the watching crowd. It was nothing but a reality television show. A dangerous one, too, one designed to take full advantage of the chills and thrills.

A flood of anger had red tinting the edge of my vision. How could they do this? How could Magnus go to sleep at night knowing he'd purposely set up a series of games where kids were in actual danger?

As long as I lived, I'd probably never understand why

the Fae did certain things. And the way it was going, I'd have quite a long time to try to figure it out.

I held my breath when the camera turned to Mike. A red strip of fabric was looped over his eyes and tied at the back of his head. He felt his way along the edge of the hedge, turning a corner when he met another obstacle. He obliterated it with a whoosh of magically produced flame and the crowd went wild.

They didn't see what I saw.

They didn't notice the smoky shape slinking along the labyrinth toward the prince. I jolted to the edge of my seat.

The knowledge hit me fast and hard. I knew what it was *because* I could hardly make out the shape, *because* of the smoke and mirrors effect and how my eyes slid right off of it.

A muskie, in the proverbial flesh.

I also remembered Mike telling me about his genetic defect, the one that kept him from being able to smell the creature. The more he walked, the closer the muskie came to him, until I couldn't take it anymore. I pushed Coral aside —one of the only members of Mike's group to not make it into the third game—and bolted down the steps toward the patch with Mike's face on the airborne display above the game green.

If I didn't do something, Mike was going to die.

23

_____

I couldn't think. I couldn't do anything except react.

Mike was going to die and the crowd was living for the excitement.

Did they know about his genetic defect? Probably not. It wouldn't be something the monarchy wanted to get out.

"Mike! *Mike!*"

No one heard my screams above the roar of the crowd. Their eyes were glued on the screens, on the larger than life versions of the students competing. I glanced up at the nearest one and saw the distance between Mike and the muskie decrease.

Faster. I needed to go faster or I'd never make it in time.

Adrenaline surging, I raced away from the arena as fast as I could. Down the steps, out toward the village, and turning right toward the thick trees of the border forest. I waited until the trees hid me from view of the crowd before calling my magic in a rush of heat.

The best thing I could do to save him, or so I thought.

It had been a hot minute since I'd used my power of transfiguration, the rare power given at birth only to shifter children, and I held an image in my mind before sending a push to the rest of me. Feeling the image as real. As *me*. Seeing and feeling the details I would need to change my body into a new shape.

The last time I'd done this, I'd merged with the walls of the Halfling Academy castle, using the transformation to get into the locked and warded room housing the Augundae Imperium. Now I used the power to help Mike.

The image of the crow from my windowsill filled my head until my arms shrank, bones warping and feathers bursting through my skin. Pain ripped through me and I ignored it to focus on the crow. The animal was the first thing I thought of, and I knew crows had vicious little talons because I'd seen them clutching those damn notes I kept receiving.

No, I thought with my rapidly shrinking consciousness, I wouldn't run, no matter who knew I was here. I wouldn't run because Mike was in danger and he needed me.

It wasn't long before my human body fell away and a large black bird occupied the space. Though the wolf remained in my blood, I had access to the instincts of the crow as well, eyesight sharp and focused.

I launched myself into the air, soaring toward the labyrinth and looking desperately for Mike. Panic rose the longer I flew in search of him. Wind rustled my feathers, the keen eyes of the bird taking in the smallest details. My talons clenched for a fight.

Where was he?

Please don't let me be too late.

The human in me wanted to give in to the panic. What if I *was* too late? What if I'd wasted too much time during the transformation and something happened to him?

Mike could not die. I would never be able to survive it.

I swooped low over the shrubs of the labyrinth. Several

audience students looked up at my passing but didn't give me another thought.

Come on, Mike. Come on!

It took me a long time to locate him in the maze and when I did, I nearly went into a seizure. The muskie's smoky arms were wrapped around his neck, tightening by the second. And though Mike tried to fight the creature off, his face had turned purple, his fingers passing through nothing as he ran out of air.

I reacted. I dropped down and slashed at the muskie's eyes. Or where I thought its eyes should be. The crow took over, pushing part of me to the side, using its talons to gouge away at the monster. It was enough to have the muskie let go of Mike.

He dropped to his knees, drawing in a deep, rattling inhalation while I attacked. The crow's sharp beak proved to be a formidable weapon. I lunged, using my large bill to my advantage.

The muskie *did* smell. I detected it now, a decaying, putrid scent burning something inside of me like acid. Though the crow had good eyesight, I couldn't keep track of the thing. It moved like sentient mist.

"Watch out!"

His call came a moment later, and when I flew back toward the hedge, I saw Mike with his hands out in front of him, blindfold ripped to shreds on the maze ground. His fingers twisted, a blast of magic pulsing out from his palms. It hit the muskie and sent it scattering on the wind.

For a moment it seemed as though the whole arena went silent. I didn't know where the cameras were and if they were focused on us or not. I didn't care.

My gaze darted over Mike, watching him collapse to his knees, hunching over himself. It took close to a minute for him to rise to his full height, his shoulders slumped as he raised an unconscious hand to his neck, rubbing front and back.

He turned to the crow with a sigh. Then his nostrils widened and when he saw the bird, he sniffed. "Tavi?"

Oh *shit*.

He stared at me incredulously, eyes terror-wide.

I did the only thing I could: I flew away with a squawk. How did he know it was me? How had he sensed me?

No need to worry, I told myself on a loop. Except all I did was worry. Even after transforming back into my human body and hurrying to my seat in the stands, I worried.

How did he know?

Mike made it through the rest of the labyrinth and crossed the finish line with a weary high five to one of his competitors. I cheered for him from the stands, waiting happily for him to come back to me as though nothing had happened. With not a hair out of place.

The winners gathered with Magnus, who handed out small trophies along with an invitation to take part in Thursday's game.

I saw Lane and Arlyss circling around Mike, along with a few other people I recognized from classes. They remained huddled together for a moment after the officiant dismissed everyone.

Stupid game. And people found this amusing.

I waited until the stands emptied. Then I waited some more. The sun burned my skin and the longer I sat, the more agitated I became. Finally, Mike noticed the lone person waiting after the rest of the crowd had cleared out. He stalked toward me, not saying a word as he pulled me aside.

"What did you *do*?" he hissed.

I'd never seen him look at me with such fury.

His hands clutched my shoulders. "Dammit, Tavi. How could you?"

"You needed help! I saved your life," I replied, but Mike cursed violently. There was no sense in hiding what he'd seen or trying to make excuses.

He had to know...right? All of the politics and the games had stopped mattering the instant I saw his life was in danger. I refused to sit idly by while he got hurt.

"I know you did and I'm pissed about it," he said, his voice rising. Then glanced behind him to make sure there was no one around to hear our conversation. "What you did was cheating." He broke his hold on me long enough to drag the tiny golden statuette from his back pocket. "I don't even deserve this trophy, Tavi—"

"Hear me out," I said with a shaky smile. I lifted my hands to silence him before he could chastise me more. I already knew what he would say. "You were in *real danger*. I couldn't sit there and let you get killed. You mean too much to me." Before I knew it, I had raised my voice as well, hating feeling like a child having to defend myself.

"It's *exactly* what you should have done."

His eyes filled with a thousand emotions I could not name. But before he could say whatever else he wanted, before he could wring my neck, I grabbed the front of his shirt to get his attention and keep him next to me.

"No," I insisted. "I'm not going to stand by and watch something happen to you."

"No one was going to let the prince die," he insisted with a snarl. "Don't you understand? I had it handled."

Oh. He had a good point. I stuffed my hands into the pockets of my pants. How easy to forget Mike's status. "I...I panicked."

He scoffed. "Clearly."

My face became hot. The intensity of his gaze snatched away the rest of my words except for: "I'm sorry."

Mike sighed, staring off at the hedges behind me. Thawing even as I watched. "Tavi, you can't barge in on the games. Especially when it's not your place to do so."

"I'm sorry," I repeated. "I saw the muskie and... I thought you were in danger and I care about you too much to let you be hurt. So I reacted. It was instinct." My face burned hot enough to have sweat beading along my hairline.

Mike just stared at me, his face expressionless, eyes devoid of concern when they met mine. To the point where a chill went through me. I couldn't say I was surprised when he stomped off.

I swallowed my nausea and returned to the castle.

It made me sick thinking of Mike in danger, or how easily the thing he feared the most could strip him away from me. But hearing him talk about cheating... Some part of him was worried more about being called out than losing his life.

I should have sat in the audience and calmly thought about the situation before diving in. I should have realized he couldn't have been in any *real* danger. The games were for entertainment, and he was the crown prince, after all. Unfortunately, patience and logical thinking in a stressful moment definitely weren't my strong suits.

24

Friday after work, keeping away from the guards on my way out, I snuck out of the castle for my first training session with Onyx, the other half Fae, half shifter in Eahsea, and one I'd never expected to meet in the first place.

Talk about adding to an already packed plate. I wasn't in a position to turn down his help, especially after meeting him. But Mike could never find out. I'd make sure of it.

Onyx lived in the village. At least, that's what he'd told me before our dinner ended the other day. However, it wasn't safe for us to meet at his house, so he'd chosen a place in the forest where the magic was thin and no one would think to look for us.

The perfect place to talk, he'd assured me.

It had better be. Because I didn't want to think about what could happen if someone saw us together. Alarm bells rang in my head regardless.

The night breeze felt deliciously cool on my overheated skin. I didn't expect the village streets to look so empty, especially not on a beautiful night like tonight. Most of the village had taken advantage of the good weather and used the daylight hours to do their shopping and socializing. No one was out tonight. I wondered if it was some kind of an omen I should pay attention to, and maybe stay home instead of sneaking around as if I was doing something wrong.

I chalked those thoughts up to an overactive imagination and told the alarm bells to shut up.

Mike's disappointed expression dogged me through the streets and into the forest. It was burned into my memory, how he'd looked at me, emotionless. Like his father.

Ugh, I hated the comparison. It was the first time I'd purposely thought of the two of them as being related, no matter their titles, because Mike had never acted like the king before.

I still didn't think I'd done anything wrong by saving his life. I'd reacted, and although he was probably right about the whole no one would let the prince die thing, I couldn't take that risk. Not with him. Even if he didn't appreciate it.

He should have shown a little more gratitude.

"Those are some deep thoughts. I would hate to get in the way of whatever's going on in your mind."

I stopped when I heard Onyx's voice and turned around to see him crouched near a rock, staring at me.

I hadn't heard him approach. Now that I saw him, moonlight reflecting off of his hair and newly shaven goatee, I felt a shiver of anticipation. The first of the night. Was I actually excited?

"They're dangerous thoughts because they keep me distracted from potential enemies lurking around," I threw back.

He rose and balanced on the balls of his feet, standing almost a foot taller than me and imposing in his own right. I looked up and up until I met his gaze. Without fear. Or so I hoped.

He wore a dark blazer over a black t-shirt with pants of the same color, and if it weren't for the hair, I might have missed him in the shadows. "I almost didn't think you would show up," he grumbled.

"You'd rather I hadn't?"

He shrugged his left shoulder, lips pursed. "I'm saying I wasn't sure you were serious about this."

"About training to keep myself alive?" I questioned. "Believe me, I am very serious about staying alive."

Onyx turned his back to me, his arms going behind him on a stretch. "I saw what you did for the prince today."

Okay, surprising. "You knew it was me?"

"I had a feeling when I saw the crow dive at the muskie." My stomach flipped when he said it out loud. "I didn't know for certain until you confirmed it just now. An impressive but *stupid* use of your powers, Tavi."

"You're not telling me something I don't know. Why don't you save the lectures until we've gotten a little better acquainted?"

"Transfiguration can be highly dangerous if you're not properly trained." He motioned over his shoulder for me to follow him.

The two of us cut a path through the dark woods and I knew his eyesight to be as good as mine. Our wolves could see through the blackest nights.

"Well, who trained you?" I asked.

Onyx kept his gaze focused ahead. "I had a mentor when I first came here. She's part of the reason why I agreed to meet with you when your friend tracked me down. Kind of a paying it forward deal."

"How nice of you."

"There are more half-shifters here than you think. Oh, did you think you were the only one?"

What if I had? "I knew we existed but I wasn't sure of the

numbers. I mean, halflings of almost all species are bound to exist because the Fae aren't exactly good at monogamy."

Onyx stifled a laugh. "You're right there. Tell me, Tavi. What have you transformed into so far?"

"I have been a moth. A pen. A crow, as you saw today. And a wall." I listed them off on my fingers.

Onyx whistled, holding a branch aside for me and allowing me to step through. "You're doing pretty well for a newbie, for sure, but the wall thing wasn't a good idea."

For some reason I appreciated his gruff honesty. Weird? Probably. "I know. I thought I was going to die," I confessed.

"You probably should have."

A lead ball formed in the pit of my stomach at his agreement. Onyx continued to lead the way through the forest. A few hundred more feet and he stopped, turning to face me. We squared off against each other for a moment and I'm ashamed to say it took me a whole damn minute to realize what was different about this place.

I stared at the clearing, the tall trees bowing slightly in the wind and the stones cropping up between their trunks. I no longer felt the buzz of magic in the air. The oppressive static I'd noticed since coming through the portal.

"It's quiet," I said, my voice automatically dropping low. "It's...*normal.*"

And right now, normal felt pretty weird, considering how used to the constant swell of magic I'd become.

At least Onyx looked pleased, like I'd given him the right answer on a test. "Yes. This place is thinner than the rest of Faerie. As if the mortal world is slowly creeping through. Most Fae are unaware of the press of magic in the atmosphere because they are born to it. They are born *part of it.* They have a connection with the land and she is as much a part of them as they are of her. But our wolves are sensitive. That half of us was not born here and so we are aware of the constant flux more so than any other creature. It's why I brought you to this space. You can feel it."

I threw back my head and drew in a deep breath. It felt like some kind of weight had redistributed inside of me. I liked this place already no matter how strange it was to me.

And I liked Onyx better for showing it to me.

"Now, just because we are extra sensitive to the magic of this world doesn't mean we have to allow ourselves to be affected. There are a number of ways for us to harness the power, as shifters, and use it to our advantage."

I turned to him, seeing him tensed, poised for motion. "Elaborate. Please," I added.

"Let me tell you about my first impressions of Faerie, to help you a little bit before we get started." Onyx gestured for me to sit, and he folded his body to the ground in a cross-legged position though he never lost any of the tightly wound energy. "I already told you I was trying to outrun an overbearing father who wanted me to take over his pack," he said.

I nodded.

"I knew my mother was Fae, from one of the northern territories, and that's what helped me hone in on the magic I needed to get here. I found someone with a key and made them let me in. Keep in mind I had no formal training like the kind you receive from the Elite Academy. I learned about my magic on the fly. And the first moment I stepped through the portal, I threw up."

My eyes went round. "You seriously *threw up*?"

"Everything, gone. The faery I hitched a ride with took off and left me in the forest, dead midnight, no one else around. The pressure in my head could have knocked over a moose, my wolf went nuts, and the rest of me felt about as limp as a bowl of jelly. Took me days to get my bearings and even then I didn't dare venture close to any kind of town or city."

I found myself leaning closer, listening to the soothing lull of his voice.

"The force of the land itself can be overwhelming to anyone with shifter blood. I learned how to meditate. I learned how to do some breathing tricks to get in the right frame of mind and stay there. Not only does it help me deal with life here, but it helps me with my own powers and controlling them," Onyx said. He held his palms up and as I watched, each finger lengthened into a jet-black feather before returning to their normal form.

The control! He didn't look winded or strained in any way. He hadn't even *blinked*.

"I've never had a problem with my wolf," I told him. "She is always there when I need her." And I'd even stopped taking the potions Nurse Julie had taught me how to make in order to keep my shifter half hidden. The world here was so drenched in magic I simply tapped into it to manifest a constant shield of sorts at all times.

"It's not about her," Onyx patiently explained. "It's not about your Fae half. You have to stop thinking about the pieces as separate entities, one or the other to be squashed and the opposite given dominion. It's about them working together in harmony as a single cohesive unit. *You*."

"I'm not sure I understand." And I didn't, because honestly, I'd had to separate the two halves all my life.

Onyx clapped his hands on his knees. "Okay. When you were growing up, you were immersed in the pack. Yes?"

I nodded. "It was the only way for me to survive."

"Exactly." His voice dropped lower. "You tamped down your Fae gifts because it would have given you away to explore them. The opposite became true when you were accepted to the Fae Academy for Halflings. You took a potion to hide your shifter side."

"And almost died anyway," I said ruefully. "There were other shifters hidden at the school when there weren't supposed to be."

Onyx didn't look impressed. "It's not good for you to stay in either one of those extremes." His eyes flashed yellow for a moment.

"Aren't you worried?" I couldn't help but ask, then shivered. "About someone discovering who and what you are?"

"I am *me* no matter where I am. I'm here for a reason and no amount of prejudice is going to change my blood. From either community. The least I can do is help someone else get a better handle on themselves. Improve their quality of life."

I wasn't sure what to say. We sat for a moment longer before Onyx told me to get to my feet. "Okay," he said, "show me what you can do."

"Right here? Now?"

"Do you have someplace important to be? I need to gauge your level of expertise with a demonstration. Then I'll know where to start."

And of course, what happened? My mind completely blanked.

"What do you want to see?" I asked.

Onyx named off a shape he'd like me to take and I tried to do what he asked without complaint. Anything from a rock on the ground—not my favorite—to a mouse scurrying near the edge of the woods. It felt strange and different to cram my subconscious into these various forms under his watchful gaze.

What choice did I have? If I was to survive and thrive in Faerie, I needed to learn to control my powers.

After a few rounds of practice, I was out of breath and

struggling to keep my knees from wobbling. The jelly thing he'd mentioned before? I had it now.

"I've never been good with meditation," I said when he asked me to clear my mind. "My old nurse tried to show me a few tricks but I have a real problem keeping my attention focused."

"Everyone does," Onyx snapped, although I didn't think he was mad at me. More just gruff in general. "It's not something you can master overnight. It takes practice and diligence. Trust me. It will help you in the long run, not only with your transfiguration skills but with your studies."

I took him at his word as he walked me through the meditations he used, as well as breathing exercises to get in the right frame of mind. When I'd done enough to be considered satisfactory—for the time being, at least—he had me transform again.

Faster this time, I noticed right away. Faster and with less discomfort. The mouse no longer felt strange or unusual. Neither did the rock.

Back in my regular form, I smiled at him.

Much to my surprise, Onyx offered me a small smile in return. "Before you know it, you'll be able to become *anything* in the blink of an eye. But be careful. You're in the early stages of learning about transfiguration. If you stay in one form for too long, you'll have a difficult time turning back."

"What's too long?" I had to know.

"It depends on you personally. For some, a couple of hours might be too long if they aren't properly trained. For others it might be a day. For you right now, I wouldn't recommend anything longer than an hour. To be on the safe side."

I thought about when I'd turned into the crow. As much as I hated to admit it, I was pretty sure I'd ruined things with

Mike by interfering in the last game. My hesitance to move forward, along with this latest round of cheating to save his life...well, it didn't feel like we were moving in the right direction. More like we were at a stalemate.

Maybe I could spend more time with Onyx. I mean, sure, he was older, but he knew my secrets, all of them, because he was like me. He was kinda cute too. And smart.

I shook my head and the thoughts fell away with a small smile. I couldn't even imagine liking another guy. I'd been falling for Mike since the day we met.

"We're done for the night," Onyx said, pulling me out of my head. "We'll pick up another day."

"What works best for you?"

He shrugged. "I'll get in touch with you. I'm not big on making plans in advance."

"Too many important places to be?" I threw his earlier words back at him.

"Yes. The Wild Hunt is afoot."

The words stirred something in me, only I wasn't sure what. "The what now?"

Onyx rolled his eyes. "It is so easy to forget you literally know nothing."

"Hey, I know *some* things. I passed my History of Faerie class," I argued.

We walked through the woods side by side with enough space between us that I didn't feel closed in. It was more like a quiet camaraderie where we'd both found a neutral footing with each other. "Then you should know all about the Wild Hunt," Onyx said. "It takes place on the eve of the Summer Solstice and all Fae participate. *Willingly*. It's a celebration of the land. A celebration of fertility, of abundance, of renewal. Everyone dresses in a costume and mask, losing themselves in nature while their loves hunt them."

"Excuse me? Hunt...as in there are weapons?"

"Ha! No, no weapons. The females are pursued by their men. It's tradition. So when you asked if I have more important places to be? Yes. I do. There is a certain female I've had my eye on and I will be doing my best to claim her during the Hunt."

A tendril of heat began to climb higher from my core, and in my mind, I saw Mike's green eyes. "What...what happens when the males claim the females?"

I didn't need to turn to him to know that Onyx rolled his eyes again. "You do the math, Tavi. It's hot, it's hedonistic, and it's magic." This time I wasn't imagining the growl in his voice. "Figure it out."

When I returned to the castle, I knew sleep wouldn't come easily. I settled down on my bed with a piece of paper and pen. More personal, I decided, than a text.

Mike,

I'm sorry about what happened at the game. I saw the muskie grab you and I couldn't think. I never meant to cheat. I promise I won't step in again. I mean it.

The Wild Hunt is coming up in a few days. I'll be wearing—

I stopped, thinking about the Wild Hunt. What would I wear?

Once I finally figured it out, I finished my note, adding a line at the last minute and sending it off without thinking twice.

I hope you will claim me.

25

Saturday was the Wild Hunt.

The heat curling in my stomach, the anticipation, grew bigger and hotter as the days progressed until my skin itched with the excitement.

Literally, for the Hunt, Fae dressed up in costume and "hunted" each other and it was supposed to be a way to connect with each other and with nature and the wildness of full summer. It was the final celebration for the solstice sponsored by the palace.

The objective, as Raelynn so helpfully filled in missing details from Onyx's explanation, was to find your "partner" and consummate your love beneath the night sky.

I wasn't really clear on the *consummate* part but I hoped Mike would show up to be mine.

I hadn't heard anything from him since sending the note, which worried me. I'd expected a *little* something in reply. Even a text response to say he'd gotten it. I tried to tell myself it didn't matter one way or another, since I'd been wishy-washy with him as well.

He was probably still working through his feelings on

the *cheating*. I could understand a little hesitation on his part but it would have been nice to have some contact.

Raelynn didn't beat around the bush. "The bad mood has got to go!" she said, rapping me on the knuckles with a rolling pin. "I'll not stand for your brooding anymore, Teri."

"Ow!" I brought my hand to my chest. "What was that for?"

She shot me a warning look and held the rolling pin aloft in preparation for a second smack. With her butter-yellow hair sticking out at all angles and a maniacal glint in her oddly shaped eyes, I knew I was in for a world of hurt if I didn't do as she said.

"For daydreaming and bringing gloom into my kitchen when it isn't necessary. You're young and attractive. You should be panting in anticipation for the hunt. Whatever is going on in your head, kill it and get excited for the chase," she warned. "I mean it."

"Will you be participating?" I set my hands back down on the dough and winced at the ache where she'd smacked me.

I definitely didn't expect to turn around and see Raelynn fanning herself and looking ready to swoon.

"What are you doing?" I asked with a giggle.

She leaned against the counter with an exaggerated sigh. "My own charming prince will be hunting to claim me tomorrow. The thought of it gets me riled up." She slapped the rolling pin down again, unexpectedly, but this time I was ready and moved my hand at the last instant. "I need this dough proofed. I want to have enough time tonight to get in the mood."

I shook my head. "I don't want to know what you do to get in the mood."

But I understood.

It took me the rest of the day to get my thoughts

together, working with the kitchen girls for food preparation for the Wild Hunt, and most of Saturday to prepare for the evening ahead. The evening loomed and I still hadn't seen Mike at all.

No word, no sighting. He'd disappeared—and still I held out hope. A nebulous feeling inside of me grew brighter and stronger as the day went on. I yearned for him. I knew he was out there somewhere. If only we could connect.

As the golden light of afternoon shifted into peach-colored dusk, I found myself standing out in the gardens with the rest of the castle help and some of the villagers.

All women.

All dressed in different costumes and fidgeting with anticipation. I saw several women with bird masks to accompany the wings flowing out of the back of their dresses.

I'd gone the opposite route, dressed in a flowing midnight-blue skirt, with plenty of room for movement, and a skin-tight black top. I'd left my hair loose and curling around my shoulders. And I'd chosen to wear a wolf mask.

A pretty obvious, on-the-nose nod to my blood and one I couldn't resist. Tonight, as Onyx had said, the wolf and I were one. There was no boundary between the two of us, and despite feeling like I'd messed things up beyond repair with Mike, she and I both yearned for our mate. We craved him. With the sun beginning to set, our blood boiled, our skin shivered. We wanted. We *needed*.

Let the chase commence.

The very land pulsed with the magic of the day, like drum beats in the distance. The forest lay beyond the green meadow, deep in shadow. Something called to me like a lover's summons.

I stood with the rest of the women of the castle by the garden stairs, gazing out over the vast space as the sky washed the land in shades of red, gold, orange. Soon the bonfires would be lit and the hunt would begin. The scent of burning wood and smoke twined through the air.

The women began to titter among themselves, laughing about the festivities to come. I did not pay attention to them. Not with the beat calling me forward, growing louder. Although I had gotten used to the overwhelming feeling of magic, my limbs prickled with its rising tonight. Stronger than any other moment I'd sensed since stepping through the portal. Until my insides buzzed with it.

The castle loomed behind me but my soul drew me toward the shadows of the woods. The Wild Hunt. Yes, I understood it then. I respected the sacred holiday and everything it meant.

Like the land itself pulling me toward the forest. Commanding I take the first step down, then the next, because Mike would find me there.

"When do we go?" I managed to ask one of the ladies, anxious to begin.

They looked as eager as I felt. The closest one with iridescent wings like a dragonfly jerked her head toward the forest. "Once the sun touches down on the first leaves. Then...we run."

We run.

My heart began to beat a tempo echoing the wildness of the magic. I pictured Mike and those green eyes, not shadowed as they'd been the last time I saw him, but uplifted on a laugh. The wicked beat demanded I go to him. That I run and allow him to catch me, claim me.

By the time the sun set I could no longer keep my feet still. And the moment the first bonfire was lit, I ran.

Magic hung thick in the air along with smoke from the fires. I breathed it in and pushed my body to move faster. Faster.

Behind me I sensed the crowd, more numerous than just the women from the castle, with their features hidden beneath their costumes and masks. Where had they all come from? Was all of Faerie here tonight? Or did different towns hold their own celebratory Wild Hunts?

No matter. Mike would find me, regardless of the numbers. They became a blur of color, of life, pushing me toward those trees. It was a kind of magic in itself, so many of us moving in unison for the same purpose.

Swirling shadows disguised the border of the forest and I pushed through. Somewhere in the trees I lost sight and scent of the various Fae. We each ran in a different direction. Lured by the pull of love. I place my hand on a solitary oak, savoring the pulsing beat of magic until it resonated up from the soil, through my shoes, toward my head.

I watched some of the other girls being claimed immediately then following a path between the trees. I noted some high Fae moving as I did. On this one night, there was no class distinction, apparently. Everyone participated in this ritual, high and low. My excellent eyesight helped me distinguish where to run, as the smoke and the night veiled some of the others. The masks, however, made it difficult to search for Mike.

But I laughed. I laughed because of the feral need I sensed. Like a drug pumped into the air. This ritual came from wild roots in the land itself.

Still, the longer I rushed through the dark, the more I began to think Mike was not coming for me.

Suddenly an arm came around my midsection, grasping me from behind and lifting me into the air. Whirling me in a circle.

He had found me!

Exhilaration pulsed through me and I laughed. "You recognized my costume in the dark?" I'd honestly started to think he wouldn't come, that maybe he was still too mad at me or had decided I wasn't worth the effort.

The arm around my waist tightened.

"No, please! Don't hurt me," I protested with a giggle in the spirit of the hunt.

Snuggling back into his warmth, I marched with Mike farther into the woods. Past other couples lost in their embraces.

"You're really getting into this whole macho man thing. Does this mean you forgive me?"

He kept going into the woods, keeping me slightly in front of him, my back pressed to his front. I tried yanking my arm away so I could reach around and touch him. To see what kind of costume he wore tonight. But he kept going. And going.

Then I realized. It wasn't Mike behind me.

His free hand reached out to brush a lock of hair away from my face and I twisted, trying to get away from his touch. The man held firm. There were no Fae here, this deep in the woods, away from the bonfires. No one to come looking for me.

If I tried to cry for help it would do no good.

"Let go of me," I growled. Struggling to break an unbreakable hold. I yanked my arm with all my strength but his grip tightened until pain radiated through my ribs.

Finally, the man stopped, throwing me down. My knees knocked against the earth and I didn't have time to break my fall with my hands.

"What the hell are you doing?" My voice boomed out loud and angry. Especially given the way my insides shook.

The fires were gone now, and it looked as though the forest had gobbled up the last of the light from the moon overhead.

I bared my teeth at my attacker.

Until he ripped off the gold mask covering half of his face and I saw Kendrick Grimaldi smiling at me. In the flesh. In Faerie.

"It's been so long, baby," he crooned. "Don't you have a kiss for your betrothed?"

No words came out. I jerked back away from him when he bent to touch me, scrambling across the ground.

He hissed and it took me too long to realize he laughed, laughed at me desperately trying to get away from him.

"I knew it was you, Tavi. I know you by smell."

His arms and shoulders were larger than average and grossly muscled. Scars covered his hands and he'd exchanged the short shirt I'd seen him wear last time for a flowing tunic in black. It covered his tattoos and left nothing but the rippled skin on his hands visible.

Now I saw the earring in his right lobe, nearly covered by the dark wavy hair. I'd once described him as a bad boy wet dream.

He'd become the stuff of nightmares.

Taking a step forward, he said, "Aren't you going to say anything to me, sweetheart? Aren't you curious how I found you, Tavi?"

I could have swallowed my tongue. Carefully I rose from the ground, watching warily, hoping for a chance to escape.

"You see, this realm has a curious fascination with televised games. Most specifically the televised Solstice Games. I'm sure you're wondering how the mortal realm has access to the feed. A story for another time. You can imagine my surprise when I turned on the television and saw your beautiful, familiar face running through a jungle. It broke my heart, sweetie. Broke my damn heart."

He was done with the monologue. Taking a big step forward, he grabbed the arm I held up in defense in front of me, squeezing hard. My breath hiccupped as fire and pain erupted from the spot he held, flooding my body. I cried out and nearly crumpled to the ground again.

"You're my fated mate," he barked out, and any pretense of peace and calm disappeared, replaced by fury. "You ran away. You know I've been looking for you for almost a *fucking year*?"

Before I knew what was happening, the back of his free hand tore across my cheek and I saw stars.

Kendrick's eyes glowed, unnerving when he bent close to hiss at me. "How dare you bring disrespect down on the Alderidge pack? On *my* pack? There is going to be hell to pay when we get home, Tavi baby. I can promise you that."

His fist came down on my head and I let the blackness take me.

26

I woke up bound and with my head split open.

Not physically split open, no, but it sure felt like someone had taken an ax to my cranium and left it buried in the bone. Repeatedly. Trying to move, I lifted my arms and found them heavier than usual. My heartbeat echoed in the cut across my forehead and I wondered why it hadn't healed.

I found out soon enough.

Kendrick had taken me back to the mortal realm through whatever hole he'd managed to scurry through between the worlds. I recognized the inside of his garage although I'd never been there alone before.

It was located in my hometown in Virginia, and I'd been there once or twice with Uncle Will in the past although I'd always stayed far away, making sure not to cross through the front doors.

Home. Kendrick had brought me *home*.

My stomach plummeted and the floor seemed to dissolve beneath me. My mind blanked. Surely this was a dream. Chills crawled down my arms and when I glanced down, I saw the manacles attached to large iron loops of chains.

He'd shackled me to an engine block with *iron*. At least that was what it looked like. I tugged at the chains again and found them unrelenting. Most people, including shifters, believed iron weakened and poisoned faeries.

Which meant Kendrick knew.

He knew what I was, what secrets my blood hid, and he'd come for me anyway. What little I'd eaten that day threatened to come up and I ground my teeth together, swallowing hard. Vomiting wouldn't do me any good. At least, in this case, he'd believed what most people said about iron and Fae to be true. I'd believed the same until the woman from the school told me differently.

I could work this to my advantage. Hopefully.

The harder I fought against the manacles, the more they seemed to tighten on me. Although they didn't sap me of my energy, I knew without a doubt I couldn't perform magic this way. I wouldn't be able to shift my way out without loosening the bands of metal away from my skin.

"Help!" I called out, my voice echoing back through the emptiness of the garage. The scents of motor oil and engine fluids filled the air and stung my nose. Stupid mortal realm and its lack of magic. I'd appreciated the feeling of the thin spot in Faerie, thinking it reminded me of what I used to love about the mortal world. Now that world simply felt dull. Average and dull and a little itchy, to be honest. Stifling. "Is anyone there?"

After being in Faerie for so long, the mortal world definitely felt like someone had flung a blanket over my senses. The land no longer felt welcoming and abuzz with life. It felt dead. As though each breath had become saturated with the decay and slowly worked to do the same to me from the inside out.

"Someone, please!" I tried yelling again until the force bruised my throat. "*Help me.*"

I had a swollen spot as big as a goose egg where Kendrick had slammed his meaty fist into my head. I felt it pulsing with each breath.

It must have been late at night because only silence answered me and a glimpse out the dirty windows at the top of the cinder block walls showed blackness. I tried to stand, nearly dropping to my knees under the weight of those chains.

Holy damn, they were heavy. How had he even managed to lift them?

Also, how had Kendrick Grimaldi gotten into Faerie? Had he found a loophole somewhere, a rip he could exploit? And did it have anything to do with the wolves I'd seen in the crowd during the Fae Academy for Halflings graduation ceremony?

"Anyone! Are you there? Help me!" My voice cracked.

Without my normal strength, I had no way to move the engine block. The chains had been shortened to the point I could take no more than two steps in either direction without resistance.

A throat cleared and I whirled around to face Kendrick. He wore the same costume he'd donned during the Wild Hunt, only this time he'd left the mask off. Leaning against the doorway to a back office, he laughed ironically, surprised to see me standing up.

"You can scream if it makes you happy, baby," he said. "In fact, I like the sound. But you know as well as I do no one is going to come rescue you. This area belongs to the Grimaldi pack and they know better than to disturb me when I have company. They've been well trained."

I hated the way he said the word. *Company*. As though I actually wanted to be here with him.

He took a step closer and I plastered myself against the engine block to get away from him. I didn't want to look at his ridiculous face. Especially not when he stopped in front of me, holding something out for me to take.

Kendrick flexed his jaw. "It's water."

I tamped down the anger before he could see the hint of rebellion in my thoughts. Would it be better to fight or to give him what he wanted? He wanted me to drink. *A small display of agreement now*, my mind offered, *and we save our strength to make our escape later.*

"Tavi."

My name was a snap of sound. A barking demand leaving no room to say no.

"Thank you."

I made a show of taking the bottle, opening it slowly and drinking it, as though the manacles had slowed me down. Made me weak.

Kendrick sniffed, watching me swallow. "Don't you feel better now?" He glanced down at the manacles with a glare and a curl of his lip even though he'd been the one to place them on me.

"No," I answered honestly.

"Too bad. It really would have been better for you to be in top shape, although I have to say, the outfit looks great on you. Your figure is fuller than I remember. I spoke to the priest."

Fear hardened in my gut.

"He'll be along shortly to perform the service." Kendrick placed his hand on my waist knowing full well I couldn't get away from him. His fingers caressed me softly, proprietarily.

I belonged to him.

I turned away from him. "What service?"

"Aw, baby, don't play dumb." His fingers tightened. "It's

not a good look on you. We'll be getting married tonight. The priest is hurrying to get here."

I shook my head, feeling heavy. "I don't want to marry you." *Why do you think I tried so hard to run away?*

"Cold feet isn't a becoming look, either." He straightened with a groan, finally dropping his hand from me and stretching his arms overhead. I tried to ignore the strength I saw in him, those muscles not just for show but for brutal force. "Don't worry about a thing. I've got you now. You won't be returning to Faerie."

I wanted to fight him. To claw out his eyes and hear him scream in pain, but for some reason even swallowing another sip of water became difficult. Woozy, I swayed against the engine block, listing to the side.

Kendrick grinned at me. "There you go, beautiful. Good. You sleep. I'll wake you up when the priest arrives."

He'd drugged me. The asshole had—

I ran through the forest during the Wild Hunt, except this time I wore my dress from the Solstice Ball. No longer covered in grime, the blue flowers hugged my curves, my bare feet flying over the ground with magic in my wake. Black crow wings sprouted from my back and I took off above the treetops looking for Madam Muerte.

To see who she'd argued with, figure out what it would mean for me. To listen to her recite the rest of the Faerie Prophecy, the one I'd been too scared to hear the first time and one I hadn't been able to find in any book since.

I knew it was a dream when I took off flying toward the moon, with my stomach flipping and feeling like I would be struck with vertigo at any moment. That's when I tried deliberately to wake up.

Drifting in and out of consciousness, I saw people passing through the garage, beyond the open door to the room where Kendrick held me. Some kind of office, yes. The Grimaldi wolves looked at me in hunger, leered, licked their lips and congratulated Kendrick on his conquest. On his acquisition and the young, pretty thing he'd soon marry.

No matter what I did to free myself, I could not move. My head spun again.

Between glimpses of the garage and the office, I saw the woods outside of the castle again, with couples leaning against dark trees, giggling and breathing heavily in the night. I scented the bonfires, the motor oil, the moss and dirt and fuel burning.

Nonsensical things. Reality versus memory.

The Wild Hunt still continued?

Until finally I sat in the library of the Fae Academy for Halflings. I recognized the stacks of books I'd used to peruse and the long table Mike and I had claimed as our own during our late-night study sessions. I sat in my usual seat with Mike across the table from me.

Oh, Mike.

I hadn't seen him in a week and this vision of him hit me in the gut like a ton of bricks. He looked rough, worried, with dark circles under his eyes and his hair sticking out at all angles. In my dream, he raised his head to face me. And jumped, his hand slapping against his heart.

"Tavi, Jesus! I've been looking everywhere for you. The hunt ended and you were nowhere to be found. But I had your note, saying you'd be there."

There but at the same time feeling disconnected, I watched him lean closer, wondering why my dreams would want to torture me this way.

"I was there," I told him, my voice disjointed from the

rest of me. Still floaty and dreamlike. I think I shrugged, though I felt nothing. "I waited for you. I hoped for you to find me, Mike. But someone else c-claimed me." My vision went blurry and the rest of me felt untethered, insubstantial.

Mike snapped his fingers in my face. "Tavi, hey, wake the hell up and focus! This isn't a dream. I'm astral-projecting to try and find you. Where are you? You have to tell me."

His second snap finally got my attention. At once the seat beneath me felt real, the scents of the library rushing over me, and I anchored. The details of the room sharpened and instead of floating, I centered. I grounded and tethered myself to *him*.

"Mike, what are you doing? This is third-year magic," I said in surprise.

He laughed at me but the sound rang hollow. "Yeah, I know. Which is why I am not going to be able to hold this connection for long. It's taking a lot out of me as it is. Tell me where you are. I'm coming to get you."

I didn't know how he'd managed to home in on me or how he'd gotten the connection between us in the first place. I reached out to take his hand and our palms passed through each other. "I'm in trouble. Someone from my past managed to get into Faerie and find me. He took me." But I couldn't bring myself to speak the truth even in this dream state.

I couldn't stand it if Mike saw me differently. If he saw the truth of what I'd fought so hard to hide.

Besides, this really might still be a dream, after all. My brain was grasping at straws.

"Where. Are. You?" Mike repeated through gritted teeth. Sweat broke out along his brow.

"I'm in the mortal realm," I struggled to say. "I'm—"

Before I could finish my sentence or Mike could speak again, I jolted awake to the sound of vehicle doors slamming outside of the garage. And I heard Kendrick Grimaldi greet the priest by name.

"Father McGregor, it's nice to see you again."

I was out of time.

27

The good news?

The drug Grimaldi had given me wore off by the time I woke up, for real this time. My soul burst awake inside my body and the rest of me came alive, still a bit woozy but nothing I couldn't handle.

The bad news?

I had seconds at best before Kendrick walked through the door to fetch me.

Struggling against the manacles, I fought for freedom before realizing the drug had given me a clarity Kendrick hadn't bargained for. I didn't need the iron off to work magic. Because I had something no other Fae did.

I had the power of transfiguration. I didn't need brute strength to break free. I needed wits.

God, I was so *stupid*. Stupid enough to let myself get caught by a madman, and stupider still for believing he'd had me trapped.

Hope restored and turning my thoughts inward, I focused on the image I wanted, holding it in my mind and believing it to the point my body began to shift. My arms shrank, black feathers bursting through my skin, fingernails disappearing and toes shifting into razor-tipped talons.

The crow had been on my mind lately. It made sense for me to transform into one again tonight.

The moment I completed the transformation I slid my wings right out of the manacles and took off. Freedom. The bird relished the feeling, flapping overhead and zooming through the garage. Right over Kendrick's head as he led Father McGregor inside. The drug remained in my system and I couldn't fly straight, dipping low enough I nearly hit the priest in the eye with my wing.

"What the—" Kendrick batted at the air, ready to smack me down. "Fucking bird!"

I didn't stay to get a good look at the priest. I winged it out of there and took off into the open sky before Kendrick realized his mistake in letting me out. A warm night breeze filtered through my feathers and I flapped hard to put as much distance between myself and the garage as physically possible.

Holy shit, I'd made it out. Relief felt fickle and ready to break at any moment, like I would somehow blink and find out this was all a dream.

Where did I go from here?

I'd gotten into the mortal realm through Grimaldi's trickery. And although he'd left me in my clothes from the hunt, I hadn't made it a habit of carrying my key to Faerie around while actually *in* Faerie. I had no way back home. No cell phone to call Melia for help, and definitely no power left to try whatever third-year trick Mike had worked to find me in the first place.

Where do I go?

From this vantage, I saw the city glistening beneath me like dull gems in need of polish. The atmosphere was heavy with pollutants. Somewhere below sat my old neighborhood, my old house. My uncle was probably wondering what had happened to me. Surely Kendrick hadn't contacted Will to tell him I'd been dragged home?

The thought brought sadness and I refused to slow or stop. Not when I needed to escape.

What options were left?

I could go to the Fae Academy for Halflings. A far flight by any standards, but...

I had to hope there was someone there who could help me.

~

The flight took hours, and somewhere near New Jersey I took a rest in the branches of a tree lining the highway. Tired, too tired to keep flying. But I couldn't stay there for too long. I was sure Kendrick knew about the academy, but I took a chance he wouldn't think I'd return there, considering the wolves I'd spotted at the school. I'd deal with them when the time came, if necessary.

I had no idea what exactly *was* televised in the mortal realm. About the games, about me—

What if the reporters had spoken about the halfling student who hailed from this school? If they had, then not even the academy was safe for me.

I pushed myself to the brink of exhaustion, watching the night sky begin to lighten to shades of gray. Dawn wasn't too far off. It neared morning when I finally reached the familiar grounds of the castle, relying on instinct and scent to guide my way.

I landed on the back lawn and tried to turn back into my human self.

The bird body remained no matter how hard I pushed.

Panic interceded and I squawked, flailing around the lawn in a swirl of feathers.

Come on!

Nothing I did mattered, because my magic didn't work.

I was trapped in crow form.

28

Onyx had warned me.

I could trap myself if I stayed in my transfigured shape too long. Even remembering his words didn't stop the terror and desperation in my veins as the bird body continued to jerk, fighting against itself.

I tried desperately to shift back, in vain. Nothing worked! And the harder I tried to push this body, the more it fought back, the more it refused to yield to me. I held the image of myself and ended up squawking and cawing, jumping up and down on the grass like I'd lost my mind.

If someone saw me like this then they'd know I was a shifter. Mike had, after all. I had to hope the one person in this school who understood my secret would not only be awake but would know a way to help me.

Pushing myself off the ground, I flapped up and around the windows, searching for Nurse Julie's office. Another halfling like me, she'd gone to great lengths to keep her bloodline a secret, working for the school instead of moving to Faerie permanently.

Julie had once told me she lived at the academy year-round. Although school had let out for summer months, she *had* to be here. She was the only person I trusted to help me.

The crow darted around the windows, growing more frantic as time passed. Eventually I made my way around to the front of the school and found an open window near the divination classroom. Cracked enough for me to squeeze inside. I darted through the corridors toward the nurse's office. And when I finally found the right room, it was empty.

Damn!

I had no idea where in the castle Julie's living quarters were. I couldn't risk flying around inside any more than I already had, on the off chance I'd run into someone who could see me or, God forbid, try to hurt me.

If I saw Headmaster Leaves, would he know it was me?

Landing on the floor, I hopped around the room, looking for a way to draw Julie here, although it was unlikely she spent any time in the office during the summer off-season.

She might be able to hear me if I broke something. Or would it be a waste of time? I wracked my brain but all the crow knew was panic.

The castle was large enough no one would hear a trapped bird.

Then I saw the fire sprinkler on the ceiling. Yes! It took a lot of pecking and grasping and yanking but I finally managed to set the thing off. A burst of water sprayed from the small nozzle, nearly knocking me out of the air. Still, I'd managed to accomplish something.

I hid underneath Julie's desk next to a file cabinet to avoid the stream of water as the sirens began to wail. The sound hurt my ears, especially knowing I had to stay close, but I didn't have a choice.

I had to wait it out.

The sirens ceased outside the school about ten minutes later. Time passed and eventually even the sprinkler stopped running altogether.

Standing there, beak clicking, I shifted from foot to foot, already tired of the wait. The dizziness from the drug had long since worn off only to be replaced by a crippling fatigue from the hours of flying. I wanted to rest. I wanted to tuck my bill beneath my wing and close my eyes.

The more time passed, the weaker I became. Clearly no one was coming.

I must have drifted off at some point because I almost missed the sound of footsteps entering the room, followed by that of a ladder unfolding. Soon a fireman's boots appeared and he climbed up the ladder, his partner holding the rungs steady.

"Yup, it was this one," the man climbing the ladder said. His boots slipped on the rungs but he held tight. "Looks like someone did a bit of damage. This wasn't set off naturally."

"What do you think it was?" the second man asked.

"Not sure. Something with enough strength to bend the sprinkler head. We've got to go tell Leaves what we found."

At least someone managed to come. Just the wrong pair of *someones*. After the two men left, I dozed again. Unsure how long I'd slept before the door opened and a stream of light from the hallway flashed across the floor.

A feminine sigh rushed through the room and white tennis shoes squeaked across the floor.

I knew those shoes.

"This is going to take me forever to clean. Why is it no one is ever willing to help out with the aftermath?"

Elation had me on my feet, lunging out from under the desk. Or at least that's what I tried to do. I was so weak I managed a single hop before keeling over on the still wet floor with a pathetic cry.

Julie gasped. "What do we have here? Oh my, you poor baby. How did you get inside?" Her sweet voice rolled over me.

She bent at the knees and picked bird-me up, cradling my body in her hands. I opened my eyes long enough to see her face coming into focus. Another species of Fae, one with gangly limbs, pointed ears, and shiny wings protruding from her shoulder blades in blue a shade lighter than her skin. She didn't wear her habitual nurse's uniform now, but a pair of black checkered pajama pants and a matching shirt.

Julie gasped again. "Wait. Tavi...is that you?"

I snapped my beak once in affirmation. Thank goodness. She knew.

She placed me down on the examination table, her movements steady and efficient. "Hold on one minute. We're going to get you out of there."

A tiny piece of magic had my limbs lengthening, feathers shrinking, and teeth growing through my jaw until I sat before her in all my human glory, my clothes from the hunt ripped nearly to shreds.

I slumped forward as Julie stepped in to catch me. Her arms moved around my shoulders.

Happiness cut through me and, relieved, I burst into tears.

"Oh, honey. No. No crying, now," she soothed. "Everything is going to be all right."

Julie held me while I sobbed, the tears unstoppable. It took me too long to compose myself and stop sniffling, to release my hold on her and realize I'd wrinkled and dampened her shirt.

When I finally managed to calm down, Julie pushed me back to search my face, her nimble fingers moving the hair out of my eyes. There was something comforting in her presence. In the way she held me, her gaze filled with concern.

"Are you going to tell me what's going on? Or must I guess?" she asked. "After all, you aren't supposed to be here. You certainly aren't supposed to be trapped as a bird and pecking away at the fire sprinkler."

"I'm happy to see you," I managed to get out.

Her fingers laced through mine and she squeezed briefly. "And you know I'm happy to see you. Happy, confused, and a little peeved you made such a mess."

Keeping her hand in mine, I took her through everything from the moment I walked into Faerie until I escaped Grimaldi's garage, watching her face grow more horrified by the moment.

Her wings fluttered once before going still. "How you've been treated, how hard things have been for you..." She trailed off, shaking her head. "Worse yet, how did a full-blooded shifter somehow find his way into Faerie? He kidnapped you. Did you ever find out how he did it?"

"No. I didn't even think to ask. I was focused on getting out of there, and I didn't realize he'd drugged me until it was too late." I wanted to slap myself for real this time but found my limbs unresponsive. Maybe Julie would do it for me? "I shouldn't have drunk the water he offered."

"Either way, it's a good thing you managed to get out. Stop beating yourself up about how long it took you. You did it. And you did it in time before the wedding could be performed. Or the marriage consummated."

But I could tell from the way she no longer met my eye, Grimaldi worried her more than she wanted to let on. The fact he'd managed to find a way through into another world, without a portal, without a key... I wanted to know how he'd done it just as badly.

"You are going to need something much stronger to

protect you from him," Julie said decisively. "Something to ensure he will never find you no matter how hard he looks."

"Don't you think I would have found a way by now?"

"No, child, I don't. I think you've been distracted enough trying to *survive* and praying the natural barriers between the worlds would be enough to protect you. Now we know he has a way in, we have to find something with more power. Some kind of magic. I've got one in mind, but it's not going to be easy for you."

"Tell me."

Julie moved to her desk and pulled out a piece of paper and a pen, writing down a potion recipe. A glamour, she explained, one similar to the potion I'd had to use when I was in school to hide my shifter side. The same potion Julie still took in order to blend in at the academy.

"Some of the ingredients are hard to find," she warned, still writing. "I only know about this spell because I'd done my research before making my own escape. I considered using it, but once I found a place at the academy it seemed like overkill, and I knew it would be nearly impossible to get a few of the ingredients for the potion. You are going to need to make this glamour and wear it every single day. Think of it like birth control."

The words made me blush.

Julie didn't care. "You miss a dose and it's no longer effective. The spell will work only if taken on the regular, reinforced like clockwork. It will keep this Grimaldi goon from being able to see you, if you concoct the blend specifically with him in mind."

She handed off the paper and I glanced down at the ingredients. Some of them I'd never heard of before. I was tired enough to have trouble reading the lines.

"Thank you for this," I said, tucking the paper into my shirt.

"Tavi, you know I would do anything to keep you safe." Julie stared at me and I did not miss the way she worried her lower lip. "But you have to help. You can't keep putting yourself in dangerous situations and expecting everything to work out."

"What good will the potion do if I can't get back to Faerie?" I asked.

"Oh, child. I forget. You act like you know everything sometimes. Let's try a little less talking and a little more listening from here on out, Tavi. Okay? The lips stay shut and I'll do the same for you." Her smile lessened the scold.

I locked my lips with an imaginary key as Julie dug into her pocket with a smile and brandished her own key to Faerie. Which she apparently kept on her person, unlike me.

"Now. Let's get you home."

29

I kept the image of my bedroom in the castle in mind as Julie used the key to open up a portal. Not like the one the headmaster and the council used to transport us during the graduation ceremony, and much smaller than the one in the castle that Mike and I used to get to school.

This one looked more like a door to an apartment, or, I noticed with a start, the door to the nurse's office. It was as though Julie's key manifested an opening in the shape of what she found most comforting.

Early morning sun streamed in through a familiar window and Julie walked both of us through the portal, keeping her hold on me to maintain contact. Otherwise I wasn't sure what would have happened to me.

"Hmm, nice place you have here," she commented offhandedly. "It's very pretty."

I wanted to fall into my bed and not get up again. "Thank you."

She looked even more beautiful in this place, I thought. Like the light somehow accentuated everything good about her and turned it up a notch. I hated knowing she'd leave.

"Feel free to come visit me anytime you like," she

offered, finally dropping my hand. "And remember: Take your potion. Stay safe. You know where to get the ingredients?"

I shrugged. "I'll do the best I can."

"Good."

We hugged and said our goodbyes, then I was alone, heart aching. The portal closed behind Julie and I flipped on the light by my bedside table. Only then noticing the crow nestled among the pillows near the headboard.

Even surprised, I didn't have the energy to jump. "Dammit, not again."

I hurried to close the door to the room and sighed, the both of us staring at each other.

"What have you got for me now?" I asked the bird. "Some poison, maybe? Because you trying to give me a heart attack didn't work."

Instead of dropping a note on the bed and leaving, a corona of magic swallowed the crow's body and when it shifted, I saw a girl my age.

"Hi, Tavi," she said softly, casting her eyes down. "It's been a long time, hasn't it? I'm sorry our reunion had to be like this."

Her identity didn't sink in for the longest time, because hey, here sat the sender of the cryptic notes in a human form I didn't expect. And I *knew* her. At least I thought I did.

I took in the girl's round face, the splash of freckles across her nose and cheeks, the slight curl of pine-trunk colored hair. She had been part of the Alderidge pack, a girl I'd grown up with who disappeared when we were kids.

"Bronwen Minuti?" The name came to me in a flash. "You're *half Fae?*"

Bronwen pushed herself up from the bed and walked toward me, several inches shorter. She wore a short linen tunic laced up the front, dark blue jeans, and sandals.

"I am," she agreed with a shy smile. "The bird is my favorite form and one I use often because it's inconspicuous."

So, it seemed the rare power I'd worried myself sick over at the academy showed up pretty frequently, as did half Fae, half shifter children.

Despite my desire to flop on the bed and not wake up for an entire day, I drew her forward in a hug. We'd been friends once. Although Bronwen had disappeared a few years after my parents died.

"What happened to you?" I asked, my voice muffled against her hair.

Bronwen tightened her hold on me for a moment longer before breaking away.

"I mean," I continued, "why didn't you tell me who you were?"

We leaned back to stare at each other.

"I didn't know if I could trust you. You could have been any kind of person! Tavi, we were eight, and you yourself did such a great job of hiding your Fae heritage. My family and I moved here to Faerie around the same time the Grimaldi family came into power years ago."

I shuddered at the name.

"My parents saw how things were going to go bad and they got us the heck out of there. A lot of half-shifters did," she continued. "Although it took work to cross through to Faerie."

"Wait a minute. There are *more*?"

Bronwen nodded excitedly. "The Fae and the wolves may hate each other but children between the two are more common than you think. The elders on both sides like to keep it under wraps. Still, it happens. I mean, Kendrick Grimaldi's own son came to Faerie to escape him."

The floor dropped out from under me and because I was

so tired, I struggled to put the pieces together that were right in front of me. "Kendrick Grimaldi's...son?"

I'd had no idea he had a son. I knew he was a bit older than me but even looking at him last night, he didn't seem old enough to have a child. And it never occurred to me anyone would want to be with him in a sexual way involving reproduction. *Voluntarily.*

"Hold on, hold on." I held up a hand to stop Bronwen from continuing her truth bombs. "Kendrick Grimaldi's son is half Fae?"

"Yeah, he is. He sure is. He lives down in the village. Maybe you've already heard of him? His name is Onyx."

Oh. Oh, God. My mentor.

I had to sit down; my knees were wobbling. Onyx was Grimaldi's son, and he'd never said a word. I couldn't think, my mouth opening and closing on its own. Bronwen didn't seem to understand: I'd lost my capacity for rational thought under the weight of these revelations.

"I'm sorry about the cryptic notes, too," Bronwen said. "I didn't want you to worry but you had to know. There's a snitch among our kind."

"What do you mean, our kind?" I asked through numb lips.

"A half-shifter who sends information back to the mortal realm. No one knows who it is, but the word on the street came immediately. They knew you were here. Do you still have it? Do you have the wolf amulet I gave you?"

Kendrick had a son. Kendrick's son was here. I knew him. I'd trained with him.

Kendrick had found a way to grab me, which meant he had a path to travel between worlds.

Faerie crawled with half-shifters and one of them, someone I didn't even know, had sent information to Kendrick on me.

269

"Tavi? The wolf amulet?"

"Yeah, I have it hidden," I replied dully.

"You need to wear it. It will protect you."

I started to tell Bronwen I didn't need protecting because I had a spell in my pocket to keep Kendrick from finding me again. But I figured I had nothing left to lose, and if a piece of jewelry could be an added level of protection, then why not?

"Sure," I agreed. "I'll wear it."

"You have to make sure no one sees it on you. The symbol might not be recognizable to anyone on the street, but there are those among us who have a keener eye and a sharper brain and more magic than you and I combined. Those are the ones we need to watch out for." She paused, smiling up at me again with her moon-round face. "I'm really glad to see you."

I wanted to agree, to tell her it was good to see her too, but I was so tired. Tired enough to have my shoulders drooping and my muscles barely able to keep me standing. I wanted to go to bed but, like Bronwen said, I needed to protect myself.

She looked like she wanted to talk more, and we both knew there were too many questions between us in need of answers. We'd talk later, she assured me.

The girl returned to her crow form and zipped out the open window. I didn't want to think about the things I'd said to her when I thought her nothing but a bird. Or the chips I'd practically shoved down her throat. What would Melia say when I told her?

She'd probably throw a fit and give me the same lecture on safety that Nurse Julie had.

At least I knew what I had to do now. Despite my desire to sleep for an eternity, I needed to get the potion made and fast. By now Kendrick knew I was gone. He'd have his wolves scouting the area and trying to follow my scent. When nothing turned up, he'd come to Faerie. I couldn't take the risk of falling asleep without my layer of protection.

Glancing at the piece of paper with the recipe, my new necklace in place and hidden beneath my clothes, I headed down toward the kitchen, prepared to use my special privileges to gather the ingredients for the glamour against Grimaldi.

Anything it took, I'd once told myself. I'd do anything to escape him. Seeing him again was a reminder of why I'd wanted to get out. Why I'd had to.

Like Julie said, some of the ingredients were archaic and hard to find. Lucky for me, I was a wage slave with access to the largest ingredient storehouse in the realm, and no qualms about using anything I could find there.

I crept down the hallways, eerie in their silence. Even the guards at the front entrance to the castle leaned heavily on their staffs and looked ready to pass out at any moment.

Everyone still felt the effects of the Wild Hunt.

Most had probably not sought their beds until a few hours ago, and not alone.

There were only two women in the kitchen and neither one of them glanced up from their stations at my arrival. I fought to walk with purposeful and easy strides. I opened the pantry door, struck again with the vastness of the space and the sheer number of ingredients housed there. Then locked myself inside and withdrew the bag from my back pocket.

Time to pillage, I thought. Except I was too tired to appreciate my own joke.

It took me almost twenty minutes to find everything I needed, returning back to my room with no one the wiser, thank goodness. If the king knew what I'd done, in direct violation of his staying out of trouble mandate, then I'd be thrown back into the dungeons—or worse.

Nope. I should remember. There was nothing worse than being Kendrick's wife. Having him torment me, push me around, abuse me emotionally, mentally, *physically*…

I followed Julie's instructions to the letter once I was sure no one had followed me, whipping up the glamour potion and bottling it into thirty tiny bottles I still had from my last batch of potion making.

I'd carry one on my person at all times. Unfortunately, I knew it was back to having to avoid garlic and mirrors and moonlight.

I stared at the bottles. A small price to pay to escape Kendrick's notice and keep the glamour in place. At least by this point, I'd become pretty damn good at toeing the line between life and death.

30

I slept through the day, getting out of bed only to use the bathroom before falling asleep again. It took until Monday morning for me to feel halfway normal again. Luckily, with the last few games approaching, we had a few more days before school began again, leaving me with a buffer of time.

I was grateful.

Rolling out of bed, I knew I had to look for Mike. If my dreams had been correct, then he'd been searching for me, using magic he shouldn't have been able to access.

First, a shower. Running my hands through my hair, I caught on the bump from Kendrick's fist, and used a small healing spell to get the swelling to go down. Even with my natural healing abilities, the man managed to mark me and have it stick.

I didn't want Mike to see.

Dressed, I had one thing on my mind as I searched the castle. And finally found Mike alone in the dining hall. He sat hunched over a bowl of fruit and yogurt, with his spoon twisting listlessly between his fingers.

I called out his name and he jerked out of his seat, startled to see me there whole and alive.

"Tavi..."

He rushed toward me and grabbed me up. My arms moved automatically around his neck. Breathing him in, I felt a knot inside of me begin to relax, more so when he tightened his hold.

We stayed that way for a long time.

"I'm so sorry I didn't claim you in time during the Wild Hunt," he murmured into my hair. "I was too late."

His voice brought tears to my eyes and I swallowed to keep them in check.

"No, you weren't," I told him. "You weren't too late."

I'd been naïve enough to let my guard down. It wasn't his fault.

"What happened to you? Where did you go? In the dream you said someone from your past took you."

I swallowed. "I went to the mortal realm. But don't worry. I found my way back to you."

I couldn't tell him everything. Not without revealing all the secrets I'd kept from him.

"It was a guy from my past, someone kind of obsessed with me in my old school," I said. "My mortal school."

"Who?" Mike pushed, his voice hard. "Tell me. Some mortal shouldn't be able to access Faerie." When he leaned away from me, long enough for our gazes to lock, I saw something cold and unyielding in his face.

I fought to shrug and remain calm even as little explosions popped everywhere he touched me. "I think someone let him in, maybe." I remembered what Bronwen said about a mole, another shifter passing word back and forth between the worlds. Could the two be related? "I managed to get away from him. Found my way back."

I left Julie out of my story because she could get in trouble for using her key to get me back.

Mike's brows drew down in a scowl, his tongue darting out to lick dry lips. I knew without him having to say anything he thought I wasn't telling him the whole story.

Good instincts.

I wanted to crawl under the table and suddenly couldn't stand how we were this close to each other. The step I took in the opposite direction spoke clearly.

"I have to talk to my father," Mike said as he eyed me up and down. "Try to smooth things over with him."

"What do you mean?"

"Well, you disappeared during the Wild Hunt. You left the realm."

"Not by choice," I insisted.

"He doesn't know that. He only knows you left the realm after narrowly avoiding a murder charge."

Murder.

Reality sank down heavily on my shoulders. Too much else had happened since then; I'd almost forgotten about the night of the ball. *Almost.* My mouth went dry. "Has Madam Muerte's real murderer been found?"

Mike reached down and took my hand. "No. There are no leads, Tavi." He stared at me for a moment longer, and I felt the brush of his thumb against my skin. "Come on. I know where my father is."

"You want to talk to him right *now*?" I asked as Mike pulled me along.

"The sooner the better. He has people out there looking for you. It's best we don't keep him waiting."

Damn, *no.*

I didn't think it was possible to be more terrified than I was when I discovered Kendrick Grimaldi had found me.

But standing in the throne room, meeting King Tywin's cold gaze, I felt my bones fill with permafrost.

"Miss Alderidge. You do have a habit of disappearing and then showing back up. And to think we were worried for your safety." He shifted forward, royal-blue robes pooling around his feet. The queen did not sit at his side. The Elder Council and a few of the courtesans I remembered from the ball lingered around the thrones. Carrion scavengers waiting for a free moment to tear the carcass apart. "Care to enlighten me as to your whereabouts this weekend?" King Tywin continued.

Since dying on the spot wasn't an option, I repeated the same story I'd told Mike, that someone from my past had found help getting into Faerie and captured me during the Wild Hunt.

The king believed me the same way people believed the moon to be made of cheese.

"Miss Alderidge, if I understand you correctly, one of my people helped a mortal man track you down and kidnap you from Faerie?" He tapped his fingers on the elaborately carved arm of his throne.

I swallowed hard. "Yes, sir."

Sparing a glance to Mike, I saw him watching me.

"Honestly?"

I wasn't sure what to say to him, or what he *wanted* me to say. Clearly, he didn't believe my story, and from the way Mike stared at me, neither did he. Not deep down. Although I believed he wanted to.

What else could I do in this situation?

Squaring my shoulders, I vowed to let the king's confrontation roll past me.

"If you refuse to tell me the truth, I must assume you ran away of your own accord," said the king.

"I did not run away." But that's as much as I would say

for now. I didn't even add "sir" or "Your Majesty" because at that moment I would offer no subservience.

Tywin tapped on his knees. "What do we do with you now, Miss Alderidge? It's clear we cannot count on you to stay where you belong. I don't understand why you ran away. Yet something must be done."

I'd done nothing wrong. "I came back of my own accord," I protested.

But the king didn't trust me.

"Even if that part is true, it is apparent that certain measures will need to be taken with you. Safety precautions, if you will." A surge of magic filled the room, and for a moment the king's eyes blazed from within. I ducked my head to avoid the explosion of light surrounding him and when I looked up, he had something in his hand.

Something I definitely didn't want to come within ten feet of, let alone touch.

"Come closer."

I didn't have a choice. Stepping forward, I moved to the edge of the dais and kneeled in front of the throne. Not that I wanted to kneel. I was simply relieved when I didn't have to maintain eye contact with him anymore.

"I call this the Faerie version of house arrest. This device will monitor your whereabouts at all times. It will track your every movement and every spell." If I wasn't mistaken, the king sounded almost gleeful. "Anywhere you go, any piece of magic you work will be reported back to me."

As I opened my mouth to protest, the air deadened. The device disappeared from his hand, wrapping around my ankle and biting into my skin until only a line of tattoo-like ink remained. A faint buzz radiated from the area.

"It's for your safety."

I barely heard the murmured agreements of the council members around him. I turned to Mike, desperate for...

what? I couldn't think. The tattoo was out of place and strange. And totally unnecessary.

Mike did nothing, standing with his arms at his sides and his focus on the king.

I was on my own here.

"You're free to go," Tywin stated and waved a hand casually.

Again, I had no choice but to follow his instructions. That was that. I backed away from him, feeling the constant tug of energy around my ankle.

Anywhere you go, any piece of magic you work will be reported back to me.

Mike didn't hurry after me, as I'd thought he would. I wanted to talk to him so I waited outside the throne room for a good five minutes before he finally strode out.

"Hey," I said, immediately pushing away from the wall.

He closed the doors behind him and stood for a long tense moment with his fingers on the handles and his back to me.

"Your story doesn't make sense, Tavi. Well, parts of it."

I had a gut feeling that even if I filled in the missing pieces for him, the story still wouldn't make sense. He wouldn't understand the soul-deep need to escape the mortal realm, to get out of a situation with all the potential to kill me. "I'm sorry, Mike. I don't know what else to tell you."

Neither of us made a move toward the other. Not until Mike turned around to face me, a veil drawn over his face. "A Fae helping a human cross…" He trailed off. "I'm not sure I can believe it."

"Well," I replied, my mouth gone dry, "you can believe what you want. I'm telling you the truth." Bits and pieces, at least, but no outright lies.

His gaze darted down to my ankle and the telltale tattoo

there. "At least now it will be easy to find you. In case something else goes wrong." He tried for a smile. "This might be a blessing. You know you'll be protected."

My eyes wanted to bug out. Maybe for him it was a safety measure, and although I appreciated how he looked for the silver lining, I didn't quite see it yet. To have my every move tracked was one thing. To have my every magic spell monitored? That was something else entirely. Good thing I'd made up a thirty-day supply of the glamour potion. As long as I maintained it and never let it break, I should be safe. For a few weeks, at least.

Then what?

The walls of my prison grew tighter. Closer.

I needed Mike in my corner now more than ever.

So I plastered on a smile as if everything was normal. "Do you want to go finish breakfast?" I asked him. "I'm starving!"

He nodded, and we walked toward the dining room together. Mike's steps were slow. As though he looked for another place to be and couldn't quite find one.

31

School resumed for the summer months, back in session until Yule, and the games had completed with one standout winner. *Arlyss.* Unfortunately, his outstanding performance in the last game had him strutting through the corridors like a peacock but without the plumage.

Or maybe he had the plumage hidden. I didn't know a thing about his heritage and I didn't want to know.

Still, the first week of school passed easier than the last two. It felt like I finally found a rhythm, and maybe that was because I had almost watched everything in my life fall apart at the hands of the evil shifter I'd done so much to avoid. Who wouldn't be grateful for this respite?

Kendrick's kidnapping definitely gave me a better appreciation for my place at the Elite Academy. I dove into schoolwork with everything I had and left little time for anything else. Including thought.

Things were somewhat back to normal between me and Mike friendship-wise, although I couldn't shake the tension between us when we were alone. Or help wondering why he'd grown a little quieter than usual. Why he never really wanted to hang out more than necessary to study for our shared classes.

He also didn't make any further moves to brush my hand or put an arm around me the way he did before.

I might have ruined everything with him for good this time. And walking down the halls with books in hand, I thought maybe it was for the best.

A relationship could not be built on lies.

It didn't make my heart hurt any less.

I'd gotten a notification to meet Onyx at his apartment for a talk once night fell. With the tracker monitoring my every move now, I didn't wish to endanger him. So even though the games were over and the television crews had slunk back to the caves they'd crawled from, it was still not safe for us to meet in the village.

But I needed to talk to him, so I hoped one last foray into the woods would be safe enough. At least for tonight.

I hastily scribbled off a response to be sent back to him via Bronwen—who didn't stay long but snapped at the offered chip before winging away in crow form.

It would be better not to practice any magic tonight. Which of course I'd have to explain to Onyx before we went further with training. The tracking device would send notification of my spell work to the king, along with any kind of transformation I might try to do. That wasn't a risk I was willing to take, at least not so soon.

Still, there were things to say to Onyx. Answers I needed. Deserved.

Making my way around the outskirts of the village and into the woods to our former meeting place took much longer than I'd anticipated. My nerves were on edge, of course, with the threat of discovery hanging over me at any moment. This would have to be quick, since my only defense if caught was to say I'd merely taken a stroll in the night air. No way could any hint of a meeting with Onyx Grimaldi be whispered.

Even hearing the name in my thoughts brought a scowl to my face which remained there until I reached the rendezvous point and found him already waiting for me.

"You look rough," he said right off the bat.

Peachy. Tell me what you really think.

"You can thank your father for that."

"Excuse me?"

"Kendrick Grimaldi. Your father."

His entire body visibly clenched at the mention. "How did you find out about my father?" Onyx said at last.

At least there were no halfhearted attempts to lie to me or twist the story around.

I knew Onyx had nothing to do with Kendrick finding me. First, because I knew the kind of man Kendrick Grimaldi was and I believed Onyx when he said he'd fled from his father. Second, Kendrick had specifically said he saw me on the televised Solstice Games. Still, there were things I needed to know.

"You answer my questions first and then we can have an honest conversation about that," I demanded, pointing a finger at him. "You should have told me the name of your pack."

Onyx cringed and then sighed. "Would it have changed how you felt about working with me?"

"Yes." My answer came immediately. "It would have."

"I don't identify as that person anymore. Grimaldi is no more my father than King Tywin is, because I chose to walk away."

"Well, you didn't manage to cut the cords entirely because he found a way here. Into Faerie." I pounded a fist against my chest. "He found a way to get to *me*."

Onyx's eyes widened and then narrowed. His brow furrowed. "You know my father?"

Guess it was time to put all the cards on the table. Especially considering the flash of fear I saw in Onyx's eyes at the mention of his father. "He's my fated mate," I admitted slowly.

And the look of revulsion on the other man's face...it was almost more than I could take.

"No. No, it's not possible."

"It also turns out he's much older than I thought." Energy filled me and I couldn't stay still. I couldn't stand watching parts of Onyx crumple in on themselves, because otherwise I'd be back in the garage. I'd be chained to the engine block again with Kendrick's hand on me and the bruises formed there. "My uncle led me to believe Grimaldi was only a few years older than me, in his twenties or early thirties maybe. Not exactly the case since you're his son."

"My father doesn't age the way other wolves do. He's much older than you think he is. I'm not sure what kind of spells he uses. It's not exactly a glamour, but along those lines."

"And he's been married before," I said.

Onyx shook his head. "Not married, no. He takes what he wants whenever he wants it. Just as he took my mother. Just as he took the Grimaldi pack for his own despite having no claim to the alpha title. You know him as the bloody Grimaldi alpha. I know him as a butcher, a destroyer. Whatever war he has to wage to get what he wants, he will get it, with a smile on his face. And it looks like he has his sights set on your people now, too."

When I looked down, I saw his hands shaking. I hid my own behind my back because I shared his fear.

"Why didn't he just take me, then? Instead of fooling the Alpha Council into giving him my hand?" I wanted to know.

But Onyx didn't have an answer for me. "All I can say is there must be something going on for him to go to such extremes. You said he's your fated mate. That's a rare match. It must mean something…"

He felt sorry for me, I saw immediately. Sorry and terrified, a combination I hated, one I never wanted to see on his face. On anyone's face.

"He's *not* my fated mate," I argued immediately. Then I stopped and groaned as I ran my hands through my hair. "The council is only saying he is to use as a bargaining chip. There's no way I'm tied to a man like him. *No way*."

"Look." Onyx came closer to face me. "I'm on your side, Tavi. Okay? If anyone knows how horrible Kendrick Grimaldi is, it's me, and I will do everything in my power to help you navigate this world. And help you keep far, far away from my father."

32

Friday evening, Mike led the way into the arena for the End of Games ceremony. A big to-do by kitchen standards, and one I had to be grateful for because it meant I got out of kitchen duty to attend.

Raelynn hated it. I couldn't hide my smirk on the way out, wearing a nice dress and sandals rather than my traditional apron. Luckily nothing had been said about my nighttime foray the other evening, and I'd confined my movements to the academy and the castle since then. Hopefully they'd tire of monitoring the same boring routine day after day.

I noticed Mike did not reach for my hand as we walked up the risers to claim a good seat, though he'd asked me to join him tonight. Heat pressed down on us like a heavy blanket only exacerbated by the sheer number of bodies packed into the space.

"Are you all right up here?"

I nodded to Mike, pushing past a row of other students to the spot he indicated. At least the magical holographic screens were floating in the air above the stage area so it didn't matter where we sat. We always had a view.

Since Arlyss had come out on top as the clear winner, the press would be having a field day over him. I hated him that much more. He hadn't been able to stop talking about his prowess and magical abilities since school began again. It took everything inside of me to block out the needling tone of his voice, especially when he appeared to be such an integral part of Mike's friend group at the Elite Academy.

Speaking of the devil…

Arlyss stood in the center of the arena practically crowing, his shoulders thrown back and a smug smile lighting his features.

"Good for him," Mike said as we sat.

"Seriously?"

"I'm serious. He's not such a bad guy once you get to know him. And the win really means a lot to him. I've known him for a long time."

I tried to disguise my sneer but failed miserably. "If you say so." I still didn't understand how the Mike I knew could stand to be friends with the ring of jerks who flocked to him. Jerks led by Arlyss.

Settling next to Mike, I watched the rest of the stadium seats fill before Magnus called for attention. His face appeared on the screens, and tonight he'd lined his eyes in black apparently to bring out the color of his horns.

"Hello, everyone!" Magnus began. "Welcome to the End of Games ceremony. Let's hear a big round of applause for our winner supreme, Arlyss Coldwater!"

The crowd erupted at the mention of his name and for Mike's sake I clapped along politely.

"Not only did he demonstrate exceptional abilities in all categories, but he proved himself to be a fair and honest opponent." Magnus drew a gold trophy from his robes and made a show of handing it off to Arlyss. "Congratulations. Your win is well deserved."

The ceremony continued with an announcement of the second and third place winners, along with an honorable mention for the top ten, in which Mike's name came up. I squirmed in my seat when the focus turned to him, my own face blushing next to his on the large screens.

"And now for the moment you've all been waiting for. Our royal oracle's yearly pronouncement."

I turned to Mike for an explanation but he had his attention focused on the woman striding out toward the center of the field.

"What is this?" I asked to get his attention.

"She's Orelle, the royal oracle. She reads the energies of the land every year and pronounces her findings at the end of the games."

He didn't look at me as he spoke, and I understood why. Orelle glowed brighter than a star captured and bound to earth. Her white hair matched the hue of her skin with only the barest touch of peachy blush at her cheeks. Black eyes swept across the crowd and live butterflies fluttered from within the yards of her hair.

She began without waiting for Magnus to say another word, which, I saw on his face, didn't sit well with him.

"Friends!"

And in the magical lilt of her voice, I thought of foreign lands. Farther away than Faerie and not nearly as accessible. A wave of power rushed over me and I found myself reaching over to clutch at Mike. To moor myself to someone stable when those black eyes pushed me out of my comfort zone.

"The energies of the land have spoken and the time of the Faerie Prophecy is at hand," Orelle continued.

The butterflies among her braids took flight. It felt like a few of them took up residence in my stomach.

Oh God, no, not again. I'd heard enough about the

prophecy from Madam Muerte. And don't think I missed the way Mike's hand tightened over mine.

He knew.

A hush fell over the entire arena as Orelle began to speak the prophecy. Goosebumps burst over my skin. I didn't want to hear it.

At 'croaching light of black moon morn,
A shifter child shall be born.
An innocent and pure of heart.
Born to rip the Fae apart.
Born to rip the Fae apart.
A wicked end, downfall's start."
And falling into endless night
Shall bathe the blood with sweet delight.
And as the light of day is done—

I couldn't stay there anymore. I couldn't sit there and let her talk about how wicked and terrible shifters were, and how one of them would mean the end of the Fae. Breaking Mike's hold, I walked down the risers. I was right back where I'd been a few weeks ago when the storms were battering the land. Guilt weighed me down. Guilt over the Augundae Imperium, guilt over Kendrick finding a way into Faerie...

There were too many things to list. Too many dark and terrible things I'd done.

With a hand pressed to my chest and anxiety making it hard to breathe, I rushed down the aisle and out of the stadium.

I was prophesied to bring the end of the world to Faerie.

What should I do now?

"Tavi Alderidge, a word!"

I heard my name called and turned around to see Selene strutting toward me.

"Not now," I practically groaned. *Please, not now.* I couldn't take much more at this point.

But something had me pausing to wait for her to catch up. "I'd like to interview you to wrap up the story of the games," she began with a smile.

I rolled my eyes. "Can it wait?"

Selene motioned for me to follow her and we strode toward a quieter quarter, a pergola covered in blossoms blocking most of the late evening sun. I listened to the click of her heels on stone and felt the anchor in my chest dropping lower, lodging in the pit of my stomach.

She stopped next to a bench, both of us sitting and facing the other. "Tell me about the last game," she began without hesitation.

"There isn't much to tell. Since I didn't pass the first two, I was not eligible to participate in the last round," I said dully. I focused on my feet, on the sandals I'd felt cute wearing hours ago.

A shifter child shall be born. Born to rip the Fae apart.

"What were your thoughts on the labyrinth?"

I turned to her suspiciously, wondering at her angle. Although props to her for finding me at my weakest. Reporters must have the same sixth sense most boys did. They always went in for the kill when they sensed you were down.

Boys, reporters, and wild animals. "I thought the maze was well crafted."

The rest of her questions were all very innocuous and boring, especially considering I didn't participate in the last two rounds. When Selene reached the last of her questions, she waved her cameraman away, setting her notebook aside.

"Off the record?"

I didn't know what to think and slowly nodded. And here she was, going in for the kill.

Making sure we were well and truly alone, Selene reached beneath her blouse and drew out an amulet. Silver and round, the size of a quarter. And identical to the wolf pendant I currently wore underneath my shirt.

Selene waited for me to get my bearings as I stared at her. Shocked. Then she tucked her necklace away again.

What was happening right now?

Where did she get the pendant?

"We're a small close-knit community," she whispered, "and we look out for one another. You're safe with me. Okay?"

Bronwen must have said something to Selene. Maybe I had more allies here than I originally thought.

How many shifters are there?

"I'm not sure what to say."

Selene shrugged. "There isn't much to say. Simply know you are not alone. Since you didn't want to take my advice and run, then it's better for you to understand who your allies are." She stood and brushed off the bottom of her dress. As she turned to go, she stopped and paused, grinning over her shoulder at me. "By the way, you should know. Consider the Solstice Games your warm-up. You have until winter to prepare for the Faerie Trials—which are mandatory for all second-year students. And they're not a bunch of fun, celebratory games like the Solstice Games. The trials will determine your fate in Faerie, and whether you live or die."

She winked and left me alone on the bench.

Mike came up to me moments later, bumping me to get my attention. "Hey, I'm starving. Are you hungry? Where did you go?"

But I couldn't think about food. Eyes unfocused, I nodded, stood up, and proceeded to join him in the dining hall.

Inside, I was screaming.

What the hell else was this world going to throw at me? And how was I going to make it through? My luck had all but run out.

THE END

Continue the Fae Academy for Halflings novels with *Faerie Trials*

ABOUT THE AUTHOR

BREA VIRAGH is a USA Today bestselling romance author based in the Blue Ridge Mountains. She is a proud Gryffindor, a graduate of Brakebills, and a member of Fairy Tail. When she isn't writing and daydreaming about her newest project, her hobbies include binge-watching HGTV, scouring thrift shops for goodies, and maintaining her alpha status among her puppy and three cats.

Read More from BREA VIRAGH
www.breaviragh.com

Printed in Great Britain
by Amazon